"That's not my baby," Quinn said.

Rachel jiggled the child in her arms, her gaze steady on his. Her eyes, those wide, expressive eyes that used to follow Quinn with naked adoration when he and Rachel were in high school, now held a mixture of accusation and disappointment.

"I swear it's not—"

"Right." She picked up one of the bottles she'd found in the bag. "Excuse me, but she needs to be fed."

"Rachel, I don't know how that kid got here, but I'm telling you, I had nothing to do with it."

"Your responsibility or lack of it isn't important right now. This child is hungry. Now, are you going to feed her, or do you want me to?"

"I don't know how—"

"Fine. I will."

It was a good thing Rachel had come by when she had…and that her love of children hadn't changed. But everything else about her sure had…

Dear Reader,

It's summertime. The mercury's rising, and so is the excitement level here at Silhouette Intimate Moments. Whatever you're looking for—a family story, suspense and intrigue, or love with a ranchin' man—we've got it for you in our lineup this month.

Beverly Barton starts things off with another installment in her fabulous miniseries THE PROTECTORS. *Keeping Annie Safe* will *not* cool you off, I'm afraid! Merline Lovelace is back with *A Man of His Word,* part of her MEN OF THE BAR H miniseries, while award winner Ingrid Weaver checks in with *What the Baby Knew.* If it's edge-of-your-seat suspense you're looking for, pick up the latest from Sally Tyler Hayes, *Spies, Lies and Lovers.* *The Rancher's Surrender* is the latest from fresh new talent Jill Shalvis, while Shelley Cooper makes her second appearance with *Guardian Groom.*

You won't want to miss a single one of these fabulous novels, or any of the books we'll be bringing you in months to come. For guaranteed great reading, come to Silhouette Intimate Moments, where passion and excitement go hand in hand.

Enjoy!

Yours,

Leslie J. Wainger

Leslie J. Wainger
Executive Senior Editor

Please address questions and book requests to:
Silhouette Reader Service
U.S.: 3010 Walden Ave., P.O. Box 1325, Buffalo, NY 14269
Canadian: P.O. Box 609, Fort Erie, Ont. L2A 5X3

WHAT THE BABY KNEW

INGRID WEAVER

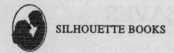

SILHOUETTE BOOKS

ISBN 0-373-07939-7

WHAT THE BABY KNEW

Books by Ingrid Weaver

Silhouette Intimate Moments

True Blue #570
True Lies #660
On the Way to a Wedding... #761
Engaging Sam #875
What the Baby Knew #939

Silhouette Special Edition

The Wolf and the Woman's Touch #1056

INGRID WEAVER

admits to being a compulsive reader who loves a book that can make her cry. A former teacher, now a homemaker and mother, she delights in creating stories that reflect the wonder and adventure of falling in love. When she isn't writing or reading, she enjoys old *Star Trek* reruns, going on sweater-knitting binges, taking long walks with her husband, and waking up early to canoe after camera-shy loons.

Ingrid is the recipient of the Romance Writers of America's RITA Award, Best Romantic Suspense Novel, for her book *On the Way to a Wedding....*

To Mark...again,
and always.

Chapter 1

An ordinary man wouldn't have heard the noise. Not over the drone of the ceiling fan or the splash of tepid water that trickled into the sink. No, the sound was too low, too subtle to attract attention, like a whispered sigh or a stealthy footstep in the grass.

But Quinn Keelor wasn't an ordinary man.

With a flick of his wrist Quinn shut off the water, then straightened up and turned around more quickly than he should have. Pain knifed through his back at the sudden movement, but he ignored it as he'd been trained to do, holding himself motionless while he concentrated on his surroundings. He was a long way from the jungle, or the ocean, but Quinn reacted reflexively, scanning the garage, his senses alert for anything out of place, for whatever unknown intruder had triggered this adrenaline rush.

Stainless steel tools and discarded engine parts gleamed in the harsh glow from the bare bulbs overhead. The car he'd towed in this morning was in the center of the floor, its hood propped open, the crumpled fender he'd pried off still beside the wall where he'd left it. Beyond that was his father's red tool cabinet, the crate with the new radiator and the bench with the discarded wrappings from the burger he'd eaten an hour ago.

The air was thick with July humidity, stirred up by the gently thumping blades of the fan, bringing with it the smells of metal and grease and damp cement. Beyond the gaping blackness of the open door, a scattering of stars silhouetted the oak at the side of the lane. Red smudges of taillights from a passing car winked through the fence that separated the yard from the street. In the distance a dog barked and a train whistle whined into silence.

Nothing out of place, nothing threatening. Only the ordinary evening sounds he'd grown up with.

What the hell was the matter with him? Quinn thought, blowing out the breath he'd been holding. This was good old Maple Ridge, Ohio, not some nameless dot on a map or another high-security mission base. How much longer was it going to take for that fact to sink in?

A sudden movement overhead caught his gaze. In a blur of white, a moth fluttered around the lightbulb. Fragile wings beat against glass in a subtle, stealthy whisper...like a footstep in the grass.

Quinn shook his head as he reached for his cane, disgusted with himself. Not only was he jumping at shadows, he was letting an insect send him into full alert. Time to call it a day before he did something even more stupid. He finished cleaning up and shrugged on his shirt, then walked over to the switch he'd installed last month and hit the button to lower the door. Creaking and shuddering, the heavy panel slid down the track and locked into place. After a quick check around the garage, Quinn pulled his keys from the pocket of his jeans and headed for the office. He turned off the interior lights, switched on the outside flood, then pulled open the back door and stepped out.

If it hadn't been for the training he'd been doing his best

to forget, he would have stumbled over the objects on the doorstep. Instead, out of the corner of his eye, he caught sight of the shadow just in time to shift his weight to the side.

"What the hell—" It looked as if someone had dumped their old clothes in front of the door. Next to a blanket-covered bundle, there was a large canvas bag that bulged with uneven lumps. Quinn scowled, shielding his eyes to peer past the glare of the floodlight on the pole in the center of the yard, but he could see no sign of whoever had left this here. He prodded the side of the bag with the tip of his cane and heard a faint gurgle of liquid from within.

Maple Ridge didn't have the big city problems of bag people or the chronically homeless. From time to time drifters passed through, sometimes taking shelter in one of the junkers beside the garage, but Quinn hadn't seen anyone hanging around lately. Could this stuff belong to someone like that? His scowl deepening, he leaned down for a closer look.

The bag was packed so full that the zipper hadn't been completely closed. He reached out to open it, then paused, his hand inches from the zipper's tab. Up until a year ago, he would have been more cautious about touching anything that was unfamiliar like this. It could have been rigged with explosives, or it could have been meant as bait to set him up for a sniper's bullet. One tug on the zipper could activate a timer. A minute's unguarded curiosity could expose him to—

"That was then, Keelor," he muttered to himself. "This is now. You're spooking at another damn moth." He completed his motion, grasping the tab and tugging the zipper open.

Released from the pressure that was holding the sides of the bag together, the contents sprang upward. Scraps of fabric, pale bits of terry cloth and cotton spilled into his hands. He dropped them on the ground and reached into the bag, pushing his hand through more fabric scraps until he touched a hard plastic object. Curling his fingers around it, he pulled it out and tilted it toward the light.

About seven inches long and two inches in diameter, the

clear plastic bottle was filled with white liquid that had the consistency of…milk.

"What the hell is this?"

But Quinn knew. He'd never had any reason to get this close to one. Still, he had no trouble recognizing what he held. With those volume markings on the side and that brown plastic nipple on the top, it was absolutely unmistakable.

Since when did derelict drifters start carrying around a baby bottle full of milk?

Shifting the bottle to his other hand, Quinn picked up one of the bits of fabric he'd dropped. A row of lace formed a cuff on the top edge, and an impossibly tiny curve shaped the bottom into a—it was a miniature sock.

Hell, this bag wasn't full of fabric scraps, it was full of baby clothes.

And just as Quinn was trying to figure out why someone would dump a bag full of baby supplies on his doorstep, the bundle of blankets beside his foot let out an impatient wail.

The rear bumper of her old Renault rattled alarmingly as Rachel Healey turned past the fence and started up the lane. Tightening her grip on the steering wheel, she eased back on the accelerator yet again. When that van had rear-ended her outside Springfield, the damage had seemed minor. She didn't think there was any need to delay her return just to get her car repaired, but with every mile since then, the noise from the back end had gotten worse. She suspected some of the clamps on the muffler had been knocked loose as well as the bumper. At least she'd made it this far without having to pick pieces of her car off the road, but what the highway hadn't done, the potholes in the lane to Keelor's Garage threatened to finish.

"Terrific," Rachel muttered.

The floodlight in front of the garage glared through her windshield as she passed the trees at the edge of the yard. The big door was shut tight, the interior dark. Wonderful. Keelor's Garage was evidently closed for the night.

Rachel paused, letting the engine idle as she considered her options. She had assumed Doug Keelor would still be here and would be willing to give her a ride home. She could try to drive there herself, but from the sound of it, her car might not make it that far. The only other choice was to leave the car here and walk.

Swallowing a yawn, Rachel steered toward the graveled parking area in the side yard. She turned off the ignition, then closed her eyes and did a few slow neck rolls to ease the tightness in her shoulders. The trip was finally starting to catch up with her, but she knew it wasn't only the long hours behind the wheel that caused this tension. This happened every time she visited her mother.

But Ann Healey was happy, she reminded herself. She was in good health, was surrounded by friends and had just been promoted to chief accountant at the insurance company where she worked. She was content, just like her daughter.

The visit had gone smoothly, as it always did. They never argued because they agreed about everything from their taste in music to their politics. Her mother was a wonderful role model. She was proud of Rachel's career and her accomplishments, and she approved of every decision Rachel had made with respect to how she handled her life. Furthermore, Ann was staunchly independent, just as she encouraged her daughter to be, so there wasn't any guilt or recrimination or possessive demands when it was time for Rachel to leave.

Then why did each visit leave Rachel more and more drained? Why was she restless and vaguely dissatisfied each time she returned home?

Shaking her head, Rachel reached for her purse. She was tired, that was all. It had been a long drive, and she still had a long walk ahead of her. Once she got home and got a good night's sleep, everything would look better in the morning. She took an envelope from her purse, scribbled a quick note of explanation on it for Doug, then sealed the keys inside. She'd slip this under the office door and call him tomorrow.

She got out of the car, taking a deep breath of the muggy air. Crickets and a train whistle. Another warm July night in Maple Ridge. The walk wouldn't be that bad, and she could use the exercise, considering the way she'd been sitting behind the wheel most of the day—

"You! What the hell do you think you're doing?"

The voice was deep and rough, vibrating with anger. Rachel whirled around in time to see a tall figure move toward her from the other side of the garage. One glance and she knew it wasn't Doug. No, this man had no comfortable paunch, no silver hair, no ready, generous smile. She drew in her breath. For an instant, a bubble of fear closed her throat as she realized how isolated she was here, alone in the dark.

But the fear swiftly dissolved into a confused jerk of recognition. This man wasn't Doug, but he wasn't a stranger, either. His straight blond hair, the tilt of his head, the set of his broad shoulders...it all stirred an echo of an old image that was buried somewhere deep, too deep, in a place she didn't want to remember....

"Oh, my God," she breathed. "Quinn?"

No, this couldn't be Quinn Keelor. This man was older. Harder. And he walked with a cane....

Realization burst over her. It *was* Quinn. She'd heard he'd come back to Maple Ridge at the beginning of the summer. She'd also heard he'd been in some kind of accident. Fifteen years had passed since she'd last seen him, but she would know him anywhere. His face and body were etched into her memory as indelibly as a childhood scar. She'd thought that particular memory had grown over, that it had healed with time, but all it took was one glimpse and she knew she'd been wrong.

"I should call the cops," he said, striding toward her. He closed the distance between them with surprising speed, despite his uneven gait. He'd always had a certain animal grace, whether he was running for a touchdown or leaning over to look under a car hood. His entire body would move in harmony, as if he had perfect control over every muscle and joint. But the control he exerted now looked strained, as if he commanded not through natural ease but through sheer force of will.

Her pulse thudding, her knees suddenly weak, she somehow managed to hold her ground. She was a grown woman, she reminded herself. And he was a grown man. Oh *God,* was he ever. Her gaze traveled from the damp hair that brushed the top of his collar to the bare skin of his chest. Lean, washboard ripples of muscle showed between the edges of his unbuttoned shirt. His jeans rode low on his slim hips, his belt buckle skimming just below the shadow of his navel.

She swallowed hard. She should have known this would happen. Considering the size of Maple Ridge, she should have known she would run into him eventually. But she couldn't possibly have anticipated the impact he would have, not after all these years. He belonged to a chapter of her life that was finished. It was carefully closed and locked away. So why was she reacting to him like this?

It must be surprise, or maybe the fatigue from the trip and the stress of visiting her mother. Her defenses were down, that was all. He was just a man, like any other. He was no longer the town's golden-boy football hero she had loved with all her adolescent heart.

Oh, God, how she had adored him. Fully and completely, with the all the painful intensity of a devoted puppy. She'd watched all his games, she'd saved every article from the paper that mentioned his name. She'd clipped his picture from her high school yearbook to keep in a locket around her neck. Her teenage years had revolved around devising opportunities to be near him.

Of course, he'd never known. No one had known. She'd kept her pathetic secret to herself. She'd been too easy a target for the teasing of her classmates. She'd already endured too

much of the cruelty that was passed off as humor. Even now
she didn't want to picture the humiliation she would have suffered if her secret had ever been discovered, if anyone had
found out that a girl like Rachel Healey was in love with
Quinn Keelor.

"Lady, you've got some serious explaining to do," Quinn
snapped.

She squared her shoulders. "You don't need to shout. I
thought the garage was closed when I got here. I didn't think
anyone would mind if I just left it here overnight—"

"I *should* call the cops. I can't believe anybody would do
that." Quinn stopped in front of her, his free hand curling into
a fist at his side. "Of all the stupid, irresponsible stunts."

Why was he so angry? The Quinn of her childhood had had
a ready smile for everyone, just like his father. But there was
no glimmer of friendship in those sky-blue eyes, no trace of
a smile at the corners of his tightly compressed lips. In the
glare from the floodlight his face was all harsh planes and
angles, distant and unforgiving.

The envelope with her car keys crackled beneath her fingers
as she held it up. "I'm not abandoning it. I was going to call
in the morning to explain."

He swore under his breath, his eyebrows shooting upward
in an expression of incredulity. "And in the meantime, you
were just going to leave it there?"

"Well, yes. You have the space. I thought you could get to
it whenever you had the time."

"I can't believe this," he repeated, reaching out to grab her
arm. He tugged her forward as he turned back the way he'd
come. "What kind of mother are you, anyway?"

Rachel's sandals skidded on the gravel as she tried to dig
in her heels. "Mother? Quinn, what on earth are you talking
about?"

"Whatever sick game you're playing, I'm not going along
with it, so you can just take your kid and—"

"My *what?*" She jerked her arm from his grasp and stopped moving. "What did you say?"

Quinn swore again, but he kept on going. "That's it, I'm calling the cops."

For a moment Rachel remained where she was, staring at his back as he strode away. His injuries from that accident must have been serious if he still needed a cane, but she hadn't heard any rumors about brain damage. Poor Quinn. What a tragedy if his keen mind was impaired.

Over the sound of Quinn's retreating footsteps, Rachel heard an infant's muffled wail. She glanced around the yard. Aside from a shiny red tow truck and a rusty cube van on the other side of her compact, there were no other cars in sight. And aside from her and Quinn, there were no other people, either. The Keelors' garage was set back from the road, separated from the closest neighbors by an overgrown privet hedge. Considering the lack of wind and the humidity, it was possible for sound to carry that far, but...

The wail rose in volume to a high-pitched, angry squeal. Quinn increased his pace and disappeared around the corner of the building.

That cry hadn't come from the neighbor's, Rachel thought. From the sound of it, that cry had come from the back of the garage.

Without hesitating further, she shoved the envelope with her keys into her purse and sprinted in the direction Quinn had taken.

The back door of the office stood ajar. Rachel got as far as the threshold before she skidded to a stop. An old metal-shaded goosenecked lamp threw a cone of light over the desk in the corner. And in the center of the desk, dressed in a one-piece pale pink flannelette sleeper and snugly nested amid a heap of rumpled blankets was...

"That's a baby," she breathed.

The child was only an infant, probably not more than twelve pounds, or older than two months. And judging by her pink clothing and the pink blankets she was lying on, she was probably a girl. An adorable, angelic little girl. With her plump cheeks, fine blond hair and tiny, delicate features, she looked as sweet and innocent as a cherub.

Why on earth was there a cherub in the office of Keelor's Garage? It couldn't possibly be Quinn's...or could it? He had been gone a long time. And apart from the major events like his ill-fated marriage and his decision to join the Navy, the details of his life were a mystery to her. What did she know about the man he was now?

While Rachel's brain was struggling to come to terms with what her eyes were seeing, the adorable little angel let out another wail. With her mouth wide-open, her eyes screwed shut, the infant arched her back and waved her tiny fists in the air. Chin quivering with each gasping sob, she screamed her anger with a force that left Rachel's ears ringing.

Quinn was fumbling in a bag that was on the chair behind the desk. "Hang on, kid," he muttered. He turned toward the baby, then glanced up. As soon as he caught sight of Rachel, he waved her over impatiently.

She rounded the desk, her mind churning with questions, but before she could ask the first one, Quinn straightened up and stepped back.

"Can you make it stop?" he shouted at her over the baby's crying.

"What?"

"Is it sick or something?" he shouted back. "Is that why you left it?"

"Why I—" She shook her head. "Why *I* left it? Left what?"

He gestured impatiently. "The kid."

She couldn't make any sense of his words, not with the din created by this baby's crying. But whatever Quinn's mental problem was, it could wait. The baby was obviously in distress. She dropped her purse on the floor and quickly scooped the child up in her arms.

The change of position momentarily surprised the baby enough to break the rhythm of her cries. Rachel shifted the baby to her shoulder, pressing her to the warmth of her body as she rubbed her back. "All right, sweetie," she crooned. "You'll be all right now. You'll be fine. No one's going to hurt you. Just calm down." She kept up her murmured assurances, not really listening to what she was saying as she swayed from side to side in an attempt to comfort the baby.

Quinn retreated to stand beside a filing cabinet, then crossed his arms and glared at Rachel. "Okay, what's the story?" he asked.

"Story?" Rachel frowned at him over the child's head, but she did her best to keep her voice steady. "How dare you treat a child like this? I don't know what your problem is, but—"

"My problem? You're the one who should be reported to the cops."

She stepped past Quinn to gain more room to move as she paced the floor with the baby. "I would think you'd be more concerned with the welfare of this child than with me leaving my car in your yard overnight. I told you, I was going to call and explain in the morning."

"What the hell does your car have to do with this?"

"Quit shouting," she said, jiggling the baby up and down as she paced. "You're scaring her."

He muttered something that was mercifully inaudible, watching her while she made several circuits of the small office. Two endless minutes later, the baby's cries tapered off to snuffling whimpers. When Quinn spoke again, his voice was low and tightly controlled. "If you didn't want the kid to be scared, then maybe you should have thought of that before you came here."

Against her breast, Rachel felt the baby quiver with a gasping hiccup. The whimpers gradually subsided into restless shudders. She pressed her cheek to the top of the tiny head. "Shh, sweetie. You'll be okay." She glanced around the cluttered office. This was no place for a baby. Except for the crumpled blankets on the desk, there wasn't anywhere to put her down. The canvas bag Quinn had been fumbling with appeared to be full of baby supplies, but apart from that, it didn't look as if he had made any attempt to accommodate this child.

No wonder the baby had been crying, Rachel thought. She felt a sudden surge of anger at his blatant neglect of her. "When was her last feeding?"

"How the hell should I know?"

Still rubbing the baby's back in soothing circles, Rachel walked to stand directly in front of Quinn. Tilting back her head, she glared into his eyes.

Fifteen years ago she used to dissolve into a tongue-tied puddle when she'd been this close to him. Echoes of her old feelings still swirled through her brain, but she was no longer the same girl. She'd come too far, she'd worked too hard to make sure she *wasn't* the same girl. "Look, Quinn. I don't care what kind of personal problems you have, but you have a responsibility to care for your child properly. You owe her a decent—"

"*My* child?" He narrowed his eyes and leaned closer. There was plenty of anger in his steady blue gaze, but no trace of madness. A muscle twitched in his cheek as he clenched his jaw and spoke through his teeth. "That's not my child and you know it."

"How would I possibly know that?"

"Honey, your sex habits are your own business, but I don't make a practice out of forgetting the women I've slept with."

"*What?*"

His gaze roamed boldly down her body before he focused once more on her face. "Believe me, I would have remembered the experience if I'd slept with you."

Her mouth dropped open in shock. "But, Quinn—"

"I don't know how you know my name, but as much as I'd like to have had the pleasure, I've never met you before in my life."

"But—"

"And you've got a hell of a lot of nerve lecturing me about responsibility," he went on. "What the hell were you thinking when you left your kid on my doorstep like a bundle of old newspapers? What if I had gone home earlier? What if it had started to rain? What if a stray dog had wandered by? Dammit, lady, you should be locked up for putting a kid into danger like that."

The baby released a snuffling sigh, her tiny body finally relaxing as she snuggled her head trustingly into the curve of Rachel's shoulder.

It took a moment for Quinn's words to sink in. When they finally did, Rachel felt the shadowed office spin around her, then settle into a different reality as everything he had said slowly began to click into place.

She glanced at the darkness beyond the office door, then twisted around to look at the desk. The blankets that the baby had been lying on were hastily bunched into lumps that formed a makeshift barrier to prevent the baby from rolling onto the floor. On the chair beside the desk, the canvas bag overflowed with tiny socks and terry cloth sleepers. At least two bottles full of milk gleamed from inside, as well as a folded stack of what had to be diapers.

"This is unbelievable," she murmured. "Do you mean to tell me that someone abandoned—" She swallowed hard, feeling the baby's body quiver with the aftermath of its frantic sobs. "Someone *abandoned* this innocent child? Here?"

"Damn right. Why did you do it?"

"Me?" Rachel turned around to face him once more. "Quinn, this isn't my child. I would never do something so cruel." She shook her head. "No wonder you reacted the way you did when you saw me. You thought I was the one who left her."

Some of the anger faded from his gaze. "Well, didn't you? From what you said—"

"I came here tonight to drop off my car," she continued, more pieces of their earlier conversation clicking into place.

"I assumed the garage was closed. I was going to slip my keys under the office door and call your father in the morning."

He rubbed his eyes, then raked his fingers through his hair and muttered an oath. "When I saw your car pull in, I'd assumed you were coming back for the kid."

"Yes, I realize that now."

He looked at the child in her arms. "That's not your baby?"

"No."

"Damn."

"And you were mistaken about something else, too."

"What?"

"We have met before, Quinn."

His gaze moved to her face. His brow furrowed, but there was no trace of recognition in his expression.

It was understandable, Rachel thought. It had been a long time, and she'd changed. Many people who'd known her back then had trouble recognizing her now. "I'm Rachel Healey. We were in high school together."

"Rachel Healey?"

Of course he wouldn't remember her. Why should he? "It's been fifteen years," she said quickly.

He looked at her features one by one, scrutinizing her in a way that brought warmth tingling to her cheeks. When he reached her eyes, he paused, the lines on his forehead smoothing out. "Rachel...*Healey?*"

Oh, God. Maybe she should have left well enough alone. She'd seen this reaction before. She knew what was coming next, some comment about how much she'd changed, how much better she looked now that she'd lost all that weight, how he never would have guessed she was the same girl....

And just like that the old insecurities flooded through her on a familiar wave of humiliation.

Blimp. Lardo. Beluga.

She'd heard them all. No doubt Quinn had, too. That's why her real name hadn't rung a bell. Sure, he'd never taken part in the teasing, probably because most of the time she'd been beneath his notice. Yet because he hadn't been cruel, in her blind devotion she'd built him up in her memory into an impossible ideal. He'd been popular, athletic and physically perfect. He'd been everything she wasn't. Now he was going to make some insensitive remark that would prove once and for all what an incredible fool she'd been to spend her adolescence worshiping him....

"You were in my English class in our senior year," Quinn said, his gaze intent, as if he were looking right through her to the past she didn't want to remember. "You tutored me in Shakespeare, right?"

She nodded. To her, it had been more than tutoring; it had been bittersweet torture. All those hours of secret yearning, all those lonely nights replaying the sound of Quinn's deep voice as he'd spoken of love and fate....

But that meant nothing to her now. She had changed far more than her appearance. "It was a long time ago, Quinn."

"Yeah, but you haven't changed at all."

She hesitated. "What?"

He gestured toward the baby. "You were always good with kids."

"Oh."

"You used to baby-sit for my cousin, right?"

"Yes, I did." She watched him warily, waiting for the inevitable comment about her weight.

"Thought so. You used to work in the nursery at the church, too, didn't you?"

"I'm surprised that you would have remembered something like that."

"Sorry about yelling at you earlier."

She nodded, still wary. So far there wasn't any hint of repulsion or pity in his gaze. But it was only a matter of time....

"And I apologize for that crack I made about your sex life," he went on.

"You were angry. So was I. And it was completely understandable that you'd jump to the wrong conclusion when you saw me, considering the circumstances." She stroked the back of the baby's head, her fingers lingering on the short, silky blond tufts. "I can't believe someone would deliberately leave their child like this."

"Damn, I really thought you were the kid's mother."

"And I thought you were her father."

"Well, I'm not."

The sincerity in his voice made her want to believe him. "And you have no idea who left her here? Or why?"

"No."

"Didn't you find anything in the bag?"

"I didn't get a chance to look. I had just brought the kid inside and unwrapped her from all these blankets when I saw the headlights from your car." He strode to the door of the office and looked outside, then swung the door shut and moved purposefully toward the desk. Picking up the telephone, he started to punch in a number.

"What are you doing?" Rachel asked.

"What I should have done in the first place. I'm calling the police."

"No, wait!"

He paused. "Why?"

Rachel felt the baby stir against her and tightened her hold protectively. "If you call them, this baby will end up with some social worker and—"

"It would be better off than with its mother."

"We don't know that. We don't know the mother left her. Maybe it was the father. And maybe we're jumping to the wrong conclusion about this, too. What if it's nothing but a simple misunderstanding?"

"Seems clear enough to me. The kid's mother chose a doorstep at random and left her kid. Probably ended up here because it's one of the last lanes before the edge of town."

"But why would she leave her baby at a garage instead of a house? It doesn't make sense."

"None of it does. The sooner I can get the kid someplace she belongs, the better."

The baby bumped her face restlessly against Rachel's shoulder, her body tensing before she let out a sudden wail.

Quinn looked alarmed. "What's wrong now?"

"She's probably hungry," Rachel said. Shifting the baby to her other shoulder, she squeezed past him and picked up the canvas bag from the chair. She tipped the bag over in the center of the desk. Diapers, a large can of powdered formula and two bottles rolled out. "I just can't believe anyone would deliberately abandon this innocent baby," she persisted.

"Like I said, the situation seems clear enough to me," Quinn muttered, completing the number.

With her free hand, Rachel was reaching for one of the bottles when a flash of white paper caught her eye. She pushed aside a diaper and grasped the edge of an envelope. "Wait a minute. I found something."

"What is it?" Quinn asked, covering the receiver's mouthpiece.

Tilting the envelope toward the lamp, Rachel read the scrawling handwriting across the front.

Disappointment stabbed through her, but she told herself the feeling was totally misplaced. Her memory of Quinn had been nothing but an impossible ideal, so it shouldn't matter to her in the least if his denials of paternity had been too hasty. She knew by painful experience that plenty of men didn't want to take responsibility for their children. After all, her own father had chosen to abandon her.

She swallowed hard. Seeing Quinn again…finding an abandoned child…this really was a night for opening up old scars, wasn't it?

"You might want to hold off on that call," she said.

"What?"

"I don't think this baby ended up on your doorstep at random." She held the note out to Quinn. "Here. This is addressed to you."

Chapter 2

The kid was starting to cry in earnest again. Quinn scowled and rubbed his face, trying to force aside the aches in his body and the buzz of exhaustion in his mind. He needed to concentrate, to assess the facts and approach this logically, but the situation was barreling out of control.

"I know what this looks like," he said. "But that's not my baby."

Rachel jiggled the child in her arms, her gaze steady on his. Her eyes, those wide, expressive hazel eyes that used to follow him with naked adoration fifteen years ago, now held a mixture of accusation and disappointment. "So you said."

"I swear it's not—"

"Right." She shoved the note into his hand and picked up one of the bottles she'd found in the bag. "Excuse me, but she needs to be fed."

"Rachel, I don't know how that kid got here, but I'm telling you, I had nothing to do with it."

"Your responsibility or lack of it isn't important right now.

This child is hungry. Now are you going to do it, or do you want me to?''

"What?"

"Feed her."

He looked at the red-faced infant in her arms and took a step back, holding up his palms. "I don't know how—"

"Fine. I'll do it." She brushed past him, giving the office a quick survey. "The milk needs to be warmed. Where can I get some hot water?"

"There's a sink on the wall of the workshop."

"All right." She headed for the darkened doorway. He barely had time to hit the light switch for her before she stepped into the workshop, weaving her way past the car and the tools to the sink on the far wall. Still holding the baby against her shoulder, with her free hand she opened the hot water faucet and held the bottle under the stream.

Quinn followed, gritting his teeth at the noise as the baby's wails echoed around the cavernous room. "Rachel," he began.

She spared him no more than a glance over her shoulder as she rotated the bottle beneath the hot water.

She still bore that disappointed, accusatory expression on her face. He couldn't really blame her for jumping to the wrong conclusion—he'd already done that himself when he'd seen her drive up tonight. Quinn opened his mouth to protest once more, but decided it wasn't much use until she got the kid quieted down again.

Damn, the entire situation was so unbelievable, it was almost laughable, except there was nothing amusing about the reckless way the baby had been abandoned. It was a good thing Rachel had decided to drop off her car when she had…and that her love of children hadn't changed. Quinn's cousin had always been singing her praises when she'd babysat that pair of hell-raising twins. While most kids Rachel's age would have been out doing some hell-raising of their own, she'd been solemnly playing mother to half the town's children.

No, her ease with kids hadn't changed. But everything else about her sure had.

Now that her attention was focused on the baby, Quinn allowed himself to study this new Rachel more thoroughly. His perusal started at her small feet and daintily curved ankles, then followed the sweep of her long, tanned legs. White shorts clung to her round hips and pert bottom, riding just below her waist, revealing a strip of taut, bare skin where she'd knotted the tail of her blouse at her midriff. Thick chestnut-colored hair tumbled in loose curls over her shoulders, grazing the upper curves of her generous breasts. He'd already noticed those breasts. How could he have helped noticing, when they were jiggling each time she jiggled that baby?

He never would have recognized her if she hadn't told him her name. She used to be so painfully shy, she wouldn't have dared to argue with anyone. Yet tonight she hadn't even blinked when he'd lost his temper. He'd been rude and downright insulting, but instead of ducking her head and pretending she didn't hear, she'd lifted her chin and had given it right back to him.

The Rachel Healey of his high school years wouldn't have done that. She'd never had the courage to stick up for herself when the other kids had teased her. God, he'd felt so sorry for her. He'd done what he could, and more than one of her tormentors had ended up with a black eye, but she'd been such an easy target it was impossible to stop it all. He probably should have tried harder, but that crush she'd had on him had made him uncomfortable. He'd been a kid himself, too wrapped up in his own life to pay much attention to the awkward, painfully overweight girl who'd always seemed to be hanging around.

But looking at her now, it wasn't pity that she inspired. A flash of awareness jabbed through him, tightening his muscles and stirring a response that took him off guard. No, it sure wasn't pity he felt. But considering the situation, he shouldn't be feeling anything at all. He couldn't let himself get distracted by Rachel's body, not if he wanted to sort out this mess.

Shaking his head, he forced his thoughts back on track as he looked at the envelope he still held in his hand.

"To Quinn Keelor."

That was clear enough. But he wasn't this kid's father. He knew that for a fact. Why anyone would choose to leave their baby with him was just another crazy element in this insane evening. Slipping his finger under the sealed flap, Quinn ripped open the envelope, then drew out a sheet of folded paper.

The note was written in a loopy scrawl on plain white stationery. Quinn's gaze immediately went to the bottom, but it was unsigned. That was no surprise. Anyone who would dump a kid on his doorstep like that in the first place wouldn't be decent enough to identify themselves. He frowned, his gaze going back to the top of the paper.

Quinn:
I'm in real trouble and you're the only person I can trust to keep my daughter safe. Her name is Charli, and she's six weeks old. It kills me to leave her, but now that her father's gone, I have no choice. Please, Quinn, take care of Charli until I can come back for her. You always helped the team. Don't let me down now.

Quinn turned the paper over, then checked the inside of the envelope in case he had missed anything, but this was all there was. Swearing under his breath, he reread the short note.

"I'm in real trouble..." No hint of what it was, no indication of how serious. He'd had more than his fill of trouble, and he sure as hell wasn't going to take on any more. Maybe it was a prank. But who would involve an innocent child in a prank like this? And why?

"Keep my daughter safe." So the kid's mother wrote the note. But keep her safe? Why safe? Just how bad was this trouble, if it even existed? And what kind of trouble was there in Maple Ridge? It was a sleepy college town, surrounded by nothing but farms and train tracks. It was about as exciting as flat beer, and that's one of the main reasons he'd chosen to come back here in the first place. Was this a plea from some unwed teenager whose parents had kicked her out of the house? Or maybe this was some kind of custody thing, and the baby was caught between two fighting parents. In either case, he really didn't want to get mixed up in anything like that.

"You always helped the team." The team. Was that why the mother had tracked him down here? Was she connected to his old high school football team? That was so long ago, he'd lost touch with most of his former teammates. The ones he did correspond with had moved away from town years ago. Besides, what did playing football have to do with keeping a baby safe? This didn't make any sense.

"Her father's gone." That could mean anything from out of the country to out of the picture to just plain dead. Quinn uttered a short, pungent oath. Obviously the mother knew damn well *he* hadn't fathered her kid. She must be nuts if she thought he was going to take on the responsibility of another man's child. He wasn't responsible for anyone, and he hadn't been for more than a year. He'd done everything he could just to ensure he *wouldn't* be responsible for anyone. There was no way he was going to do this. Why anyone in their right mind would think that he'd willingly—

"Excuse me, I need someplace to sit down."

Quinn lowered the note. Rachel was standing in front of him, the baby still crying on her shoulder. He raised his voice so she could hear him. "Use the chair in the office," he said, stepping aside so she could go by. "It's the only comfortable one."

Nodding curtly, she brushed past him.

He folded the note and slipped it into the pocket of his shirt, then raked his hands through his hair and turned around. Leaning his shoulder against the doorjamb, he watched Rachel settle herself in the large chair behind his father's desk. She shifted the baby to the crook of her arm, propped her elbow against the chair arm and brushed the nipple of the bottle against the baby's cheek. With a snuffling whimper, the child latched on to the nipple and began to suck.

The sudden quiet was almost as deafening as the noise had been. Rachel kept her attention on the baby, her gaze traveling over each of her features. And while she studied the baby, Quinn studied her.

Fifteen years ago her eyes had been her best feature. Long-lashed and expressive, the changeable hazel color had reflected her feelings with an awkward honesty, yet instead of the openness of youth, her eyes now held the wariness of a mature woman.

Her other features had changed, too. No longer cloaked by extra pounds, her face was a feminine oval defined by a delicate jaw and a smooth forehead. He'd already seen how her chin could look stubborn when she angled it upward, and how her lips could thin with anger, but as the baby continued to feed, Rachel's mouth slowly relaxed. Her lips weren't thin at all. They were rosy and sweetly curved with a fullness that was as lushly tempting as those breasts that pushed against the front of her blouse.

Damn, he had to stop letting himself get distracted by those breasts.

"Well, have you figured it out yet?" she asked, her voice breaking the silence.

He shifted his stance. "Figured out what?"

"Who this child's mother is."

"I don't know. The note wasn't signed."

Her lips pressed back into the straight line that signaled her returning anger.

"I'm not her father," he said. Again.

"I thought you claimed that you remembered every woman you've slept with."

"Look, I really am sorry for that crack I made earlier. I was wrong and I was way out of line. But that's not my kid."

"The baby is blond and blue-eyed like you. And why else would she be left in a place where you alone would find her with a note addressed to you?"

He hesitated. His first impulse was to keep the note confidential. He didn't owe an explanation to anyone, and it shouldn't matter what Rachel thought of him. Aside from their childhood connection, he didn't really know her. He couldn't be sure how much he could trust her, so it would be best to keep her involvement in this operation to a minimum—

Hell, old habits died hard. He was thinking of everything in terms of a mission, with its intrinsic need for secrecy.

Yet Rachel was already involved, wasn't she? And she was a lot more familiar with their hometown these days than he was, so she might be able to help figure this out. "The kid's mother knows I'm not the father," he said, moving toward the desk. He took the note from his pocket and held it out for her to read. "She said as much in the note."

Rachel read it through quickly, then studied it in silence for a while. When she finally raised her gaze, the accusation in her eyes had faded to puzzlement. "This doesn't make sense."

"None of it does."

"If you're not the father—"

"I'm not," he gritted.

"It's so…melodramatic, it almost sounds like a joke. Maybe you'd better call the police after all."

He looked at the baby. She was still sucking happily, patting the bottle with one chubby fist. "Yeah," he muttered. "I don't understand why the mother decided I'm the person to take care of her kid. She has to be crazy."

"She sounds frightened. What kind of trouble do you think she's in?"

"Whatever it is, it's not any business of mine."

"There must be some reason she came to you. What team is she talking about?"

"Like you said, it doesn't make sense." He glanced at the note again, then tucked it back in his pocket. *Keep my daughter safe. You always helped the team.*

Even if this kid was somehow connected with his old football team, why would the mother choose him as the one to help her? That was fifteen years ago. He might have thrown the passes that had helped take Maple Ridge High to the state championship, but his skill on the field had nothing to do with the skills needed to keep anyone safe.

No, the skills needed to deal with danger had been learned somewhere else entirely, in the oceans and swamps that existed now only in his memory, on his missions with another kind of team.

All at once, the significance of that phrase in the note struck him with renewed force, like a ricochet from an unexpected direction. *Keep my daughter safe. You always helped the team.* His pulse thudded hard in his ears, drowning out the soft sucking sounds of the baby and the bubbling of the milk in the bottle. In his mind he heard the voices of his team over the crackle of a shortwave radio, the smooth click of a bullet sliding into the chamber, the distant, rhythmic thump of the chopper—

With hands that were suddenly damp, he tightened his grasp on his cane. What if these weren't the words of some sick prankster or some small-town girl caught in a fight with her parents or a custody dispute? What if this had nothing to do with where he was living now or who he'd been fifteen years ago? What if the trouble the mother referred to was deep enough and dangerous enough to need the specialized kind of help he'd been trained for?

But he didn't want to remember those particular skills. He didn't want to remember that team.

Setting his jaw, Quinn leaned over the desk and picked up the canvas bag that had been left with the baby. He should have thought to check it earlier. The note had been inside. What else did it hold?

He upended the bag to empty it completely. There were terry cloth sleepers with snaps on the legs, sleeveless vests with tiny bows on the front, a rattle, a container of baby powder and more diapers. One at a time, he inspected every sock, sleeper, undershirt and diaper, methodically setting each item to one side until he had worked through the pile. He checked each of the blankets that had wrapped the baby, shaking out the folds, running his fingers along the bindings, looking for anything that might indicate whether this cold feeling in his gut was justified.

Maybe he was jumping at the sound of a moth again. Maybe he'd had one too many nightmares and was seeing shadows where there weren't any, reading a significance into the words of a scribbled note that wasn't there.

Or maybe it was simply fatigue and the muggy heat of the July night. It was crazy to think that trouble could have followed him here. This was home. Sanctuary. And except for him, the team was all dead. He couldn't help them anymore.

On the verge of giving up, Quinn picked up the empty bag and tilted the lamp on the desk to shine inside it. That's when he saw the small, zippered pocket that was sewn into one side. Quickly, he opened the zipper and thrust his hand into the pocket. His fingers touched a small, round object and he pulled it out.

When he saw what rested on his palm, he knew his suspicions weren't crazy after all.

It was a ring, fashioned from heavy silver, with an engraved design of intertwining letters. There were seven letters, just as there had been seven rings. He had one of them, but it was locked in the strongbox at the back of his closet along with his wedding band. The other six belonged to dead men.

He closed his hand over the ring, feeling the metal press painfully into his palm. It belonged to the life he'd left behind. He'd come to Maple Ridge to get away from it, to forget.

Rachel put the half-finished bottle to one side and transferred the baby to her shoulder. "What did you find?" she asked, the springs in the old swivel chair creaking as she leaned closer.

He didn't answer her. He couldn't. His throat closed with echoes of emotions he'd thought had died a year ago. They were all dead—his team, his feelings, the life he'd led.

And this ring was like a whispered demand from the grave.

Without moving his head, he glanced down at Rachel, where she still sat behind the desk. Her beautiful face was turned toward him, her eyes gleaming in the light from the goosenecked lamp. Her hand moved in slow circles over the baby's back, gently rubbing and patting. Quinn focused on the slow, sure motions of her fingers for a moment before he finally moved his gaze to the child.

The baby was bumping her head against Rachel's shoulder, her wispy blond hair brushing against Rachel's dark curls. Quinn tightened his grip on the ring. He knew none of his men could have fathered this child. He still didn't know what kind of trouble the mother was in, but he was holding the proof in his hand that somehow she had a connection to his team…and to the bond seven men had forged in blood.

The mother wanted him to protect her child. He hadn't been able to protect his team when the explosion had ripped through that warehouse a year ago. The six men who had been closer to him than brothers had been blown apart so viciously, so thoroughly, that there hadn't been enough parts left to fill the body bags.

Rachel lifted her hand from the baby's back to touch his wrist. "Quinn, what's wrong?"

At her gentle touch, the memory wavered. He clenched his jaw, breathing in deeply through his nose until the nightmare image faded. Opening his fist, he stared at the ring.

"Was that ring in the bag?" Rachel asked. "Do you recognize it?"

"It belonged to one of my men."

"Your men? What do you mean?"

The silver ring glinted like a silent promise, absorbing the warmth of his skin. Quinn picked it up and slid it onto his finger. "The men on my SEAL team."

"Your…" She leaned closer. "Did you say SEALs? You're a Navy SEAL?"

"Not anymore."

Past. It was all in the past, and there was nothing he could do to help them now.

No, he couldn't help his men, but at the very least, he owed his protection to the present owner of this ring. Whoever it was. He had no choice. He had to help, and he would do everything in his power to ensure he didn't fail this time.

Maybe it would help him atone for the way he'd failed before.

Chapter 3

The seat belt pulled tightly across Rachel's right breast as the truck hit another pothole. She grimaced and braced her legs against the floor.

"Sorry," Quinn muttered, changing gears as they turned onto the road. "I've been meaning to get that lane repaved since I got home."

"It's okay."

"How's the kid?"

"Fine," she answered. "She's still sleeping."

"Good."

She held Charli against her shoulder as steadily as she could. They shouldn't be transporting the child like this without a proper infant seat, but as Quinn had already pointed out, there was no way to obtain one at this hour with all the stores closed for the night. He hadn't asked for her help. As a matter of fact, he appeared unwilling to let her get further involved at all, but she couldn't very well leave him to manage driving alone with the baby.

Turning her head, she looked at the way Quinn's large

hands held the wheel. Even in the dim illumination from the dashboard lights, she could see that his knuckles were pale with the force of his grip as he steered along the quiet streets. His muscular forearms, bared by his short-sleeved shirt, were taut with tension. He'd been this way since they'd left the garage.

No, it had happened before that. From the moment he'd slipped that ring onto his finger, his entire manner had undergone a transformation.

Her gaze focused on the ring. He'd told her little about it, other than the fact that it had to have belonged to a member of his former SEAL team. That had come as a surprise to her, although it shouldn't have. Quinn had always striven to be the best, and it would be just like him to gravitate toward an elite unit like the SEALs when he joined the Navy. He claimed to have resigned from the service, but that didn't seem to make any difference as far as his sense of duty was concerned.

Quinn still insisted he wasn't the child's father—and from what Rachel had read in that brief, cryptic note, it appeared possible that he was right—yet he was determined to assume the responsibility of caring for this baby. Evidently the link that ring represented was enough to justify his complete co-operation.

The baby let out a tiny burp, then sighed softly against the side of her neck. Rachel splayed her fingers protectively over her back. The situation was getting more bizarre by the minute. An abandoned infant, a mysterious note, a piece of jewelry that was some kind of sign... It was unbelievable. How had a minor fender bender in Springfield led to this? She should have been home by now, soaking away her tension in a warm bath. Instead, she was holding a strange baby, braced in the front seat of a shiny red tow truck that was being driven by the embodiment of her teenage fantasies.

Her gaze slid to Quinn's face. It still jarred her to look at him. The years had honed his features from clean-cut boyish handsomeness to hard masculinity, yet there were enough traces of the old Quinn to evoke remnants of the same old response. It annoyed her. She should have been past that. She didn't want to be reminded of her old weakness. Besides, she was a grown woman, not the shy and awkward child who had been infatuated with a beautiful young man. She'd stopped fantasizing about Quinn years ago. More than twelve years ago to be exact, the day he'd married Louisa Gunnerson.

No one had been surprised when Quinn and Louisa had married. They had dated on and off all through high school. They'd been a perfect match, the star quarterback and the head cheerleader. Popular, athletic, gorgeous, lovable Louisa. Everyone had loved Louisa, especially Quinn.

Rachel hadn't deliberately sought out news of Quinn after he and Louisa had left Maple Ridge. As a matter of fact, she had avoided listening whenever the topic had turned to him. Because of her lingering embarrassment over her teenage crush, she had maintained a self-protective ignorance when it came to the details of his life.

Yet she had known when Louisa had died. Most of the population of Maple Ridge, including Rachel, had responded to the Gunnerson family's futile search for a bone marrow donor. Everyone was affected when Louisa eventually had succumbed to her leukemia. It had been a tragedy for the Gunnersons, and it had been a sobering loss for Louisa's former friends and classmates. What kind of effect had it had on Quinn? He must have been devastated.

Was that what had made Quinn hard? Was it grief? Well over a year had passed, yet was he still mourning his wife? Rachel's heart stirred with sympathy. So much had happened to Quinn since their high school years. Perhaps the boy she used to know was still there, buried inside this scowling stranger. Maybe all he needed was some patience and understanding....

Pressing her lips together, she returned her gaze to the road. This was ridiculous. If she wasn't careful, the fantasies were going to start all over again. She didn't need that. She was happy, successful, independent and in control of her life, just like her mother. She had no intention of getting involved with any man.

Relaxed in sleep, Charli's solid little body curved trustingly into Rachel's embrace. Her hold tightened as she returned her thoughts to the baby. How could any mother abandon her child in such an irresponsible manner? Whatever trouble the woman believed she was in, nothing could excuse such disregard for her baby's welfare. Quinn was right. What if he'd gone home early? What if it had started to rain, or a dog had come by, or...

Rachel rubbed her cheek along the top of Charli's head, inhaling the warm, soft baby scent. The child was safe now. And right or wrong, Quinn seemed determined to follow the mother's wishes. Regardless of the manner in which the baby had arrived, and whatever the real story of the mother's trouble, one thing was for certain. No harm would come to Charli as long as Quinn was responsible for her. Somehow Rachel was sure of it.

That was why she had agreed not to notify the authorities. For now, anyway. She had faith in Quinn's sense of duty. He would probably devote himself to his new obligation with the same intensity he directed to everything else. The baby would probably get better attention being cared for by Quinn than by the impersonal Child Services system.

The truck pulled to a stop. At the slam of the driver's door, Rachel blinked and looked around her. They were in the driveway in front of a large, two-story, redbrick house. She recognized the place immediately, although the last time she'd been inside had been in her senior year, when her heart had practically burst from longing as she'd sat across the kitchen table from Quinn and helped him cram for their English final.

She really had been pathetic.

The Keelor family home hadn't changed much since those days, except that the long front veranda sheltered what appeared to be new white wicker chairs, and the shutters that framed the windows had been painted green. The oak in the front yard was much more massive than she remembered, but there was still a tire swing dangling from one of the branches. It would be for Leona's children—Quinn's younger sister had taken over the house years ago when their father had moved out. Leona was younger than Rachel, yet her youngest son would be starting kindergarten in another year.

Rachel had been seeing more and more familiar faces on parents' nights at school lately—most women her age were comfortably settled into marriage and motherhood. But Rachel wanted neither of those things. She was happy with her career and with the decisions she'd made in her life.

And why was she even thinking about all of that now? It must be the lingering tension of the visit with her mother, and the pleasure of holding Charli, and the bittersweet memories stirred up by seeing Quinn again....

Frowning, she unbuckled her seat belt.

Quinn rounded the hood and opened her door. "Wait a minute," he said. His arm brushed her leg as he stretched past her to grasp the bag beside her feet. After dropping it behind him, he reached back for her.

"Thanks." She swung her legs so that she faced him, assuming he was going to lift Charli from her arms so that she could climb out. But he didn't make a move to touch the baby. Instead, he fastened his hands at Rachel's waist and smoothly lifted her to the ground.

Surprise at his action kept her immobile for a heartbeat. His palms seemed to burn the strip of bare skin where her blouse rode above the waistband of her shorts. The strength in his fingers sent a sudden flash of awareness through her body. It had been a long time since she'd felt a man's touch there. And she'd never before felt Quinn's. She'd longed for it, dreamed about it, woven fantasies around it as a way to escape the misery of her youth....

Setting her jaw, she took a step back, and Quinn's hands fell to his sides. A fantasy. That's what he had been to her;

naturally she would have some reaction to his touch. It didn't mean anything.

He picked up the bag he had dropped, slinging the strap over his shoulder so that he could grasp his cane. "Thanks for helping me get the kid here," he said, starting toward the house.

She followed, doing her best to forget the sensation of his hands at her waist. The sooner they got Charli settled, the sooner she'd be able to leave. "You'll have to get a car seat somehow before you go out again."

"There's probably one around here someplace. Leona's youngest boy is four, but my sister never throws anything out. If she still has one, I don't think she'll mind if I use it in the truck for a while."

Rachel nodded. "That would make things easier." She glanced at the dark windows of the house. "Your sister and her family must be asleep already. Maybe you should have called to warn her about Charli."

"They're not here," he said, pausing on the porch to unlock the door. "Leona's on sabbatical in France. She and my brother-in-law left with the kids a few weeks ago."

"Oh. I didn't know."

"I'm keeping an eye on the place while they're gone." He swung open the door and flipped a light switch, then stepped back for her to enter. "I don't want to leave the kid alone while I drive you home, so I'll call you a cab."

"That's really not necessary, Quinn. My apartment isn't that far."

"Is there someone you can call for a ride?"

"No, I'll be fine. I was planning to walk home from the garage, anyway." She carried Charli through the short entrance hall, then glanced around at the shadowed living room.

The changes to the interior of the house were more extensive than the ones to the exterior. The first thing Rachel noticed were the new floor-to-ceiling bookshelves, which was understandable, since Leona was a college professor. There was a glass-topped coffee table, two deep burgundy-colored armchairs and a matching couch piled with cushions. A stone fireplace was nestled between two long, narrow windows on the side wall. Everything had a neat and faintly deserted air. There were no discarded books or magazines on the coffee table and not one cushion out of place on the couch.

And there obviously wasn't a crib.

Rachel paused. "Where will Charli stay?"

"Here with me," Quinn said, turning on a lamp as he walked past her. He dropped the canvas bag of baby supplies on the couch.

"No, I mean where will she sleep?"

He hesitated, raking his fingers through his hair in a mannerism that was rapidly becoming familiar to her. "I'll think of something."

Charli heaved a restless sigh. Rachel swayed from side to side and gently stroked her back until the baby's breathing resumed the steady rhythm of sleep. She nodded toward the bag on the couch. "There seems to be a good supply of diapers and spare clothes in that bag," she said. "That should be enough for the night, anyway."

His eyebrows rose. "For the night? It looks like there's enough for a week."

She smiled, assuming he was joking. "I changed her before we left the garage, but she'll need to be changed at least once every time she has a bottle."

He wedged his hands into the back pockets of his jeans. "Do you think she'll be wanting another bottle before her breakfast?"

Rachel's eyes widened. *Breakfast?* "Quinn, do you know anything at all about taking care of a baby?"

"I watched how you did it. I'm sure I can manage."

She took a step toward him. "When you told me you were bringing Charli home with you, I had thought your sister and her family were here. I thought they would be able to help you, but—"

"This baby is my responsibility," he said. "I'll take care of her."

"How?"

Hesitating, he glanced behind him, then walked over to one of the bookshelves that lined the walls. "There's bound to be some information on child care around here somewhere," he muttered, his gaze moving slowly along the spines of the books. "Leona and Pete didn't know anything about kids before they had some of their own."

"But—"

"Psychology of the Child," he read. *"Nonallergenic Muffin Recipes."* He bent down to study the titles on a lower shelf. "Ah, here we go. *The Better Homes and Gardens Baby Book,"* he said, pulling out a tattered paperback. He straightened up and opened it, running his finger down the table of contents.

She stared at him in disbelief. "It's admirable of you that you're this determined to help out whoever sent you that ring but—"

"I have a duty to my team," he said.

"Yes, but I wouldn't want to think you're letting your pride interfere with Charli's welfare."

"Believe me, the welfare of this baby is my number-one priority."

"Caring for an infant is a difficult task in the best of circumstances, but if you don't have any experience—"

"I'll learn," he said firmly. He put the book on the coffee table, propped his cane against a chair and limped over to stand in front of her. "Show me how to hold her."

Her first instinct was to refuse. The baby felt so good in her arms, so natural, that Rachel wanted to keep holding her, if only for a few more minutes.

"Rachel?"

Carefully she transferred the sleeping infant to his arms.

He held Charli awkwardly in the crook of his elbow, his

expression filled with the wariness of a man who believed he was transporting a bomb.

Rachel sighed. "She won't break. Relax and hold her closer to your chest," she said, pushing lightly against his forearm. She could feel his muscles tense beneath her fingers and hurriedly dropped her hand. "That's it."

"Like this?" he asked.

"Yes, that's better."

"Thanks," he said.

As Rachel coached Quinn on how to hold Charli, she was struck by the contrast between his lean strength and the baby's soft helplessness. It was a touching picture, seeing this tall, tough man with the peacefully sleeping child. Rather than detracting from Quinn's masculinity, the way he held the baby only emphasized it.

And all of a sudden, her arms felt terribly empty.

Wiping her palms on her shorts, she glanced toward the bag on the couch. "There's plenty of powdered formula in that bag. And you should put those extra bottles in the refrigerator until she needs them. And don't forget to warm up the bottle before you give it to her."

"Fine."

"And she drinks fast, so you'll need to stop to burp her a few times."

"I remember how you did that."

"Do you want me to stay for a few hours, at least until you get her settled?"

The instant the words left her mouth, Rachel couldn't believe she had said them. What was she doing? What on earth was she thinking? It was bad enough that she had gotten mixed up in his business in the first place, but how could she volunteer to spend even more time with him?

There was an obvious answer to that one. Charli. The innocent child whose warmth Rachel could still feel in her arms. The baby whose father was gone and whose mother couldn't take care of her. The little girl who had been abandoned just like Rachel....

Lifting her chin, she straightened her spine and crossed her empty arms. How many scars was she going to scratch open tonight? This was nuts. She must be exhausted. She needed to go home and relax and remind herself how happy she really was.

Quinn stepped closer and lifted his hand to brush her arm. "You've already helped me more than I could have expected, Rachel. Thanks for the offer, but I'm sure I can manage. If I run into trouble, I'll call my cousin, okay?"

Quinn tossed his head, trying to escape the heat, but he could feel his skin burning. Caught with nightmare paralysis, he couldn't move away, couldn't even lift his arm to bat at the flames that crept toward his legs. The smell of smoke and fuel was all around him, choking his lungs, searing his eyes, but it still wasn't strong enough to disguise that other smell, that oily, spicy, stomach-turning stench of burning flesh.

"Larson, Norlander. Report," he mumbled. "Simms, Petrosky, Hoffman, Ferrone." He said the names like a litany, repeating them over and over, as if by saying them he could somehow—this time—gain the power to save them.

The second explosion came as it always did. No matter how many times he relived it, there was no escape. The fireball curled its deadly mushroom into the sky, raining twisted shards of metal and the other, softer, terrifying fragments that no longer could be identified as human.

"No." The word was a tortured groan, rising from his chest as he gasped for air. "No."

The shock wave picked him up as it always did, tossing his body like a smoldering rag on the wind. The screams of his men were swallowed by the force of the rushing air and the crackle of debris. And then Quinn was falling...falling...

His breath caught on a sudden sob. His eyes flew open and he saw...an open window with lacy curtains fluttering lightly on the breeze. The roar of death gave way to the chirping of robins. The flames became morning sunlight filtering past the trees in the backyard to warm his face.

Concentrating on his surroundings, Quinn forced himself to take deep, even breaths until his pulse slowed to normal. Gradually, mercifully, the helpless horror of the nightmare faded. Dropping his head against the back of the rocking chair, he curled his fingers over the arms and swore quietly.

How long would this keep up? How many times would he have to watch his friends die? Would he ever be able to sleep, just sleep? When would he stop dreading the night and his body's all-too-human need for rest? When would his memories leave him in peace?

He rolled his head along the back of the chair in a slow negative. He'd come home for peace, but he'd begun to wonder whether he deserved any. Maybe he should consider these nightmares his penance.

The investigation that had followed the accident had officially cleared him of any responsibility, but he knew he was to blame. During the months he'd spent flat on his back in that hospital bed, he'd had plenty of time to wish he could go back and change the way things had happened. In the first place, he never should have gone on that so-called training mission. He should have taken more time off after Louisa's funeral, but he had promised her he would go on. If he had done a better job of keeping his mind focused, if he hadn't let his emotions distract him, if he hadn't let his personal feelings interfere with the mission…

Emotions made a man weak. They eroded his defenses and sapped his resilience. Quinn hadn't given his last mission his complete attention. He'd been so wrapped up in his grief over the death of his wife, he hadn't concentrated on the safety of the living. No matter what the official ruling was, he knew he had failed his men because his judgment had been impaired by his emotions.

And Quinn accepted the guilt, just as he accepted the fact that he'd never be able to bring them back.

Yet now…now he'd been given an opportunity to come to terms with his conscience. Out of the blue, he'd been given a chance to earn the peace that was eluding him.

Lifting his hands from the chair arms, Quinn rotated the ring on his finger as his gaze moved to the rumpled bed across the room. The baby was sleeping soundly in the center of the mattress, the top of her head snuggled up against one of the rolled blankets he'd placed around her.

He wouldn't fail Charli the way he'd failed his men.

But if he was going to keep her safe, he'd have to do more than simply take care of her until her mother returned. Somehow he'd have to learn who the mother was and what kind of trouble she was in.

The ring wasn't much to go on, but it was a starting point. His team had always removed any jewelry before embarking on a mission—the gleam of silver or gold could have betrayed their positions. So the rings hadn't been lost in the swamp with the remains of his men; they would have been passed on to the next of kin, along with all their other personal possessions. If he could find out who had owned the one that he wore on his finger, he'd be able to trace Charli's mother. The first step, then, would be contacting the men's families to learn what had happened to the other rings.

In the year since the accident, Quinn hadn't kept track of the families of his team. He hadn't been able to attend the memorial service—he'd been so pumped full of painkillers that he hadn't even known it was taking place. And afterward, when he had finally understood what had happened, he had been too full of guilt to want to face them again.

But if he wanted to help Charli and her mother, he had no other choice.

Charli. She was much more than a helpless, innocent six-week-old baby. She was his chance at redemption.

She was also as effective a deterrent to sleep as the nightmares.

Wearily, he rubbed his face, listening to his palms rasp along his unshaved jaw. The baby had been sleeping so peacefully when Rachel had left, Quinn had assumed that would be it until morning. He'd brought her upstairs and put her here in his niece's room, then had gone across the hall to the spare bedroom he was using, intending to skim through the book on child care. He'd barely finished the first chapter when he'd been interrupted by the wails.

Looking at her now, it was hard to believe that such a tiny, helpless infant could make so much noise. Damn, he'd heard air horns and warning sirens that weren't that loud.

Rachel had made it look so easy. Back in the garage, she'd managed to calm the kid down in a matter of minutes, then had handled her with such ease that he'd been deceived into thinking that anyone could do it. After all, he knew how to handle everything from an Apache to a Zodiac. He could take apart, clean and reassemble every weapon known to the military. He could make his way from a drop point to a rendezvous undetected in complete darkness and silence. So how much of a challenge could there be in handling an eleven-pound baby girl?

Yeah, right.

Turning his head, he surveyed the shambles of what had once been a perfectly tidy room. The floor was littered with the diapers he'd had to discard before he'd gotten the hang of those tiny plastic tapes at the sides. A white trail of baby powder led from the table where he'd emptied Charli's bag to the top of the dresser. His niece's pink, eyelet-edged bedspread was draped over the closet door to dry, and he didn't even want to think about what he'd stuffed into the plastic bag at the foot of the bed.

The baby had fallen asleep just after sunrise. Hopefully that meant Quinn would have time to grab a shower and fix himself some coffee before he had to fix her another bottle. Slowly,

careful not to let the runners of the rocking chair squeak on
the floor, he levered himself to his feet. He was halfway across
the room when he heard a quiet knocking from downstairs.

Charli snuffled, pulling her knees beneath her. Quinn bit
back a curse and remained motionless until her breathing
steadied with sleep. As quietly as possible, he made it the rest
of the way across the room. He had just eased the door closed
behind him, when the sound of another knock drifted up the
stairwell. Heedless of the stiffness in his leg, he hurried down
the stairs and flung open the front door.

"Oh, my God. What happened?"

He raised his hand to shield his eyes from the sunshine and
squinted at the dark-haired woman on the porch. "Rachel?"

She looked at him in silence for a moment, her forehead
wrinkling with concern. "What happened?" she repeated. "Is
Charli all right?"

Bracing one hand against the door frame, he glanced down
at himself. He was still wearing the same shirt and jeans he'd
had on the night before, but there were blotches of dried formula on his shoulders and a dark stain that he didn't want to
identify across his thigh. "Yeah, she's fine," he answered.

"Oh, good."

He cocked his head, certain he had heard a noise from inside
the house. Damn, the kid was up again, all right. He knew
what was coming next. This was only a warm-up.

He could forget about coffee and a shower. He could forget
about starting to track down the owner of that ring, too. At
this rate he'd be spending all his time and energy tending to
the baby instead of getting to the bottom of her mother's problem.

"I was on my way to the corner store and I noticed that
your truck was still here. I just thought I'd check on how
you're managing," Rachel said, stepping back. "But as long
as everything's fine…"

Part of Quinn's training had included assessing situations
quickly in order to make split-second decisions. That's what

he did now as he reached out and clamped his fingers around Rachel's wrist to keep her from retreating farther. "Wait."

"Quinn, what—"

"You said you were going to the store. Do you have any plans after that?"

"It depends on whether your father can get my car fixed."

"Dad's gone to a stock-car rally. I can't promise that I'll get to your Renault today."

The baby let out a quavering wail. It lasted longer, climbed higher and was loud enough to get Rachel's attention. She glanced past him. "Is that Charli?"

"Yeah."

Her gaze returned to his face. "Are you having trouble?"

"You could say that."

"Maybe you could call your cousin for help," she suggested.

"I did. At about two-thirty this morning. She's at her sister-in-law's cottage for the month." He braced himself, knowing it was only a matter of moments before the next wail. "I'm taking you up on your offer."

"My offer?"

"Last night you said you'd stay and help me get the kid settled."

"I know I said that, but…"

Quinn could see she was hesitating. She had been so co-operative last night, and she was such a natural when it came to handling kids, he couldn't understand why she was unwilling to help now. Why didn't she want to stay?

He tightened his grip on her wrist. What Rachel wanted was immaterial. For the baby's sake, he needed her help. "Come on, Rachel. I—" His words cut off when the telephone in the hall shrilled suddenly. There was a second of silence, then an angry shriek came from upstairs.

Rachel's gaze darted past him once more. She appeared about to say something, but then she bit her lip.

Quinn thought fast. "Look, with my father out of town,

you're stuck without a car until I can fix it, and unless I find someone to help me with the kid, there's no way that's going to happen.''

"Yes, but—"

"I'll make you a deal."

"My car for my help?"

"Right."

She chewed her lip for another few seconds, then finally, she sighed and nodded her head. "Okay."

Quinn tugged her into the house and walked toward the telephone, feeling more comfortable now that he was in control of the situation once more. "I'll get the phone, you get the kid."

Chapter 4

Only until he could fix her car, Rachel told herself once again, cradling Charli against her shoulder. That was the deal. Then she would leave, and Quinn would simply have to find some way to manage on his own. It wasn't any business of hers if he looked like a wreck, was it? And there was no reason for her to dwell on the fact that he was at this moment less than six feet away from her and stark naked.

Pulling her gaze away from the bathroom door, Rachel paced the length of the upstairs hall. Unlike Quinn, she'd had a good night's sleep. She was once more fully in control of her feelings, and all those memories that had been stirred up last night had been securely locked away once more. She'd come here to check up on the baby, that's all. Anyone with an ounce of compassion would have done the same.

And if her compassion had spilled over onto Quinn, well that was only natural. Anyone would have been alarmed by his appearance when he'd answered the door. His clothes had been stained and wrinkled, his hair had been a tangled mess, his jaw had bristled with unshaved stubble, and shadows of exhaustion had darkened the skin beneath his eyes. The urge she'd had to reach out and give him a comforting hug had been a natural reaction to another human being's misery. It didn't mean anything. Nor did her agreement to watch Charli while Quinn took a shower. Again, it was the only decent thing to do.

Charli drew up her knees, snuffling. Rachel rubbed her back gently to calm her down. The baby was restless after what had undoubtedly been a miserable night, and was probably sensitive enough to pick up the tension in Rachel's body. Yet another reason not to dwell on her reaction to Quinn.

Rachel pivoted and retraced her steps down the hall. Movement seemed to soothe Charli. The poor child must be worn out considering the events of the past day—even a six-week-old infant would be aware enough to realize that her mother had left her. How could any woman, no matter how desperate, abandon her baby that way? Surely there had been somewhere Charli's mother could have turned, relatives or some agency she could have gone to for help instead of choosing to leave the child on Quinn's doorstep in such an irresponsible, cowardly manner.

Charli lifted her head and let out a weary sob.

"Sorry, sweetheart," Rachel whispered, deliberately trying to relax. It wasn't easy, considering the situation, but for Charli's sake she had to maintain her calm.

Regardless of the manner in which Charli had been left, the mother could have done worse with her choice of guardian. Despite his obvious inexperience, Quinn had done his best to take care of the baby through the night. Like him, the bedroom he'd used for her had been a disaster, but at least the baby was clean and fed. And his determination to accept the responsibility for her welfare hadn't dimmed, despite the problems he was having.

Yes, Charli's mother must have had a glimmer of rational thought when she'd chosen Quinn. Still, now that Rachel had a chance to mull it over in the sober light of day, that melodramatic note and the ring from his SEAL team seemed a bit much. The woman had probably known him during his years in the Navy and had decided to take advantage of their connection, that's all. The baby probably had been fathered by someone on his team, and the man had decided to walk out on his family. Men did that, leaving women to cope as best they could.

Her steps slowed. On the other hand, what if the initial conclusion that Rachel had jumped to last night was the correct one after all? What if Charli was Quinn's child? Wasn't it possible that Quinn had sought the company of another woman after Louisa had died? The note and the ring might have been nothing but a ploy to get Quinn's cooperation. Because if the baby's mother had known Quinn well enough to conceive a child with him, she would have known about his strong sense of responsibility....

No, that didn't make sense. If the baby was Quinn's, then why wouldn't the mother simply tell him the truth? If he would assume responsibility for another man's child, wouldn't he do the same for his own? Besides, it was that same sense of responsibility that would have made it unlikely for Quinn to conceive a child unknowingly. As he'd said, he wasn't in the habit of forgetting the women he'd slept with.

The women he'd slept with. Had there been that many? Doubtless they hadn't forgotten him, either. Who would, with a man like Quinn? Even disheveled and exhausted, he still projected an aura of rampant masculinity. She'd felt the restrained strength in his grip when he'd caught her wrist at the garage, and again this morning, and yesterday, when he'd lifted her down from his truck. The touches hadn't been sexual, but they had still set off tingles of warmth.

There was a sudden thunk, followed by the squeak of skin against wet tile. Quinn must have dropped the soap, Rachel thought, her gaze straying to the bathroom door. He was probably stretching down to retrieve it, water streaming across his broad shoulders and glistening on the curves of his muscular arms.

Rachel blew out her breath, impatient with the direction of her thoughts. Okay, she might be over her teenage infatuation with Quinn, but that didn't mean she was immune to the appeal of the present, mature version. Again, it didn't mean anything. She was a normal, healthy thirty-two-year-old woman. Simply because she had noticed Quinn's appeal didn't mean that she was going to slip back into the pathetic fantasies of her youth.

She wasn't the same girl. He wasn't the same boy. As far as she was concerned, they were starting fresh.

Not that she was interested in starting anything. No, not with Quinn. Not with any man.

The sound of the shower shut off abruptly. There was a brief silence, then the bathroom door opened and Quinn stepped out.

Rachel averted her gaze and spun around, but she wasn't fast enough. Although the image was nothing but a blur of white terry cloth, bare skin and tall, lanky male, it was enough to make her pulse thud.

Again, only a natural reaction. Nothing to panic about, no big deal. She was a grown woman; he was a grown man. Their main concern—the only reason she was here—was the baby she was holding.

Oh yes, he was a grown man, all right, every glorious glistening inch of him. "Uh, excuse me," she muttered, heading for the stairs.

"How's the kid?" he asked.

"Fine. I was just walking with her," she said. "She likes that. I don't think she's ready to settle down yet, so I'll take her downstairs for a while."

"Thanks. Give me a few minutes and we'll get going."

"Going?"

"To the garage. For your car."

Right. Her car. Once it was fixed, she was out of here.

Quinn hitched the towel around his hips as he watched Rachel disappear down the stairs. He knew he wasn't a pleasant sight, but if she hadn't been holding that baby, she'd probably have been running.

Shaking his head, he glanced down. The incisions from the series of operations he'd had on his leg weren't anything a woman would want to see. Nor was the puckered skin that stretched down his left side from the middle of his ribs to the top of his pelvis. Aside from the females on the hospital staff, no woman had seen the condition of his body since the accident.

He hadn't given it much thought before. His body was merely a tool, something that he expected would do its job despite the damage it had sustained. Thanks to the stainless steel pins that held his bones together, he had all the mobility he needed for the life he led now. The cane was a nuisance, but in another few months he'd probably be able to get along without it. The skin grafts were blending in as well as could be expected, and as long as he was careful not to move too quickly, the spasms from the ripped-up muscles in his back were tapering off.

At least he was alive. There had been a time when that thought hadn't meant much to him. The past year had taught him that there was a difference between merely being alive and...living. Skilled doctors and blind luck had allowed him to cheat death, but starting to live again was the real challenge.

The aroma of fresh coffee drifted up the stairs along with the sound of Rachel's voice as she talked softly to the baby. For a moment Quinn stood motionless, feeling something loosen inside him as he absorbed the sensation of having a woman in the house. He'd enjoyed the solitude when his sister and her family had left, but somehow Rachel's presence didn't seem intrusive.

He'd always liked her voice, although she used to be too shy to say much around him. Was it shyness that had made her turn away from him so quickly? Or was it repulsion?

Not that it should matter to him one way or the other. The kid was his concern, not the woman who happened to be helping him with her. Clenching his jaw, Quinn limped to his room and pulled on some clean clothes, combed his wet hair back from his face with his fingers and went to look for his nephew's old car seat.

Rachel stood in the doorway between the garage and the office so that she would be able to hear when Charli woke up, but so far the baby was still sleeping peacefully in the infant carrier Quinn had found in the attic. The ride from the Keelor house had lulled Charli to sleep, so rather than disturb her, Rachel had left her in the carrier and had brought her into the office when they'd arrived at the garage.

And now that Charli didn't need her attention, there was nothing for Rachel to do except to wait for Quinn to finish with her car.

She leaned against the door frame, slipping her hands into the pockets of her skirt as she watched Quinn move around under the car. "How bad is it?" she asked.

Metal rang hollowly as he reached up to tap something with the edge of a wrench. "Where did you say this happened?"

"Just outside Springfield. It didn't seem bad at the time."

"You're lucky you made it all the way here before your muffler fell off," he said, giving the car another tap. Something clinked to the cement floor of the garage.

"Great," she muttered.

"I hope you got the license plate of the other guy. What was he driving, a semi?"

"It was a van, and yes, I did get the license plate number. Along with the name of his insurance company and the address of the retirement home where he and his wife live."

Quinn rolled our from under the car and looked up at her. "Retirement home?"

"He appeared to be about eighty years old. He was driving a modified van to accommodate his wife's wheelchair. They were both so upset about running into me that I didn't want to make a big deal out of it.''

"If he's a dangerous driver, he should be off the road, whether you feel sorry for him or not," he said, putting down the wrench to pick up a screwdriver. "Someone could have been hurt."

"Well, no one was. Besides, accidents just happen sometimes."

"Accidents rarely just happen."

Something in his tone made Rachel look at him more closely. Was he thinking about his own accident, the one that had left him with that limp? "What do you mean?"

With a nudge of his foot, he rolled himself back under the car. "There's always a reason."

"Do you think everything is part of a pattern? Like fate?"

"I'm not talking about fate, I'm talking about cause and effect. Any event can be traced back to a cause."

"You're talking about blame."

"Blame, responsibility, call it whatever you want. Any accident can be prevented." There was a gritty, scraping sound, then Quinn emerged from beneath the car once more. He grabbed his cane and levered himself to his feet. "You're going to need a new exhaust system."

"Can't you just clamp it back into place?"

"It's rusted through. You would have needed to replace it soon anyway, so you'd be better off getting it done now."

"Fine. How long will that take?"

He replaced his tools in the red steel cabinet and went over to the sink to wash his hands. "That depends on how long it takes me to get the right parts."

She gestured toward the shelves on the far wall of the garage. "Don't you have anything here that you can use?"

"We don't usually keep imported parts in stock. I'll make a few calls," he said, moving toward her. "We might get lucky."

She stepped back when he reached the door, feeling as if

the small office had suddenly shrunk to half its size. Not that she was running away. She could handle his proximity. There was no reason for her to keep imagining all the naked skin and muscle that was now concealed by his jeans and white T-shirt.

Deliberately, Rachel moved away and busied herself by checking through the bag of baby supplies she'd brought with them. She'd have to remind Quinn to pick up more diapers before she left, and maybe some more powdered formula. Taking a pencil and a small notepad from her purse, she started to make a list.

It only took a few minutes for Quinn to phone the suppliers he knew around the area. When he finished, he turned to Rachel. "I got a definite maybe from one place. They'll check on it and call back."

"And when will that be?"

"Sometime today."

"Do you have a car I can use until then?"

"Sorry. My dad took the spare one so he could leave me the truck. That was him on the phone this morning when you got to the house. He called to let me know he won't be back until the end of the week." He paused. "Are you in a hurry to get somewhere? We could load the kid back in the truck and I could drop you off."

"I do have to meet with the Summer Festival committee, but that's not until this evening."

"The Summer Festival?" he repeated, leaning against the edge of the desk. "I've seen the advertisements for it around town. I'm surprised they're still doing that."

"Oh, it's become a major event in the county. One of the other teachers at the school is the chairman this year, so most of the staff is pitching in to help."

"School? Does that mean you ended up being a teacher?"

"Yes. Kindergarten."

"That figures."

She lifted her eyebrows. "How's that?"

"You're good with kids. And you did a good job teaching me about iambic pentameter back in high school."

"I haven't tried Shakespeare with my students yet."

One corner of his mouth twitched. "If you could get it through my head, you could probably teach anyone."

Was that a smile? she wondered, focusing on his lips. If so, it was the first one she'd seen so far. And it was a far cry from the generous grin he used to flash. "As I recall, it wasn't a lack of ability that was your problem, it was a lack of time."

"Yeah, I'd rather have been on the playing field than behind a desk." He nodded toward the corner where she'd left the infant carrier with Charli. "Our deal was your help with the kid for my help with the car, but it looks like it's going to be a while before I can fix it. Would you mind hanging around until then?"

This was her opportunity to leave. It could be hours, maybe even days before he got the parts he needed. She chewed her lip for a minute, then looked at Charli. "I can stay a little longer. You're still going to need someone to watch her while you work on my car."

"Thanks."

"I've made a list of some things you're going to need to pick up from the store. And you should think about getting a proper crib for her to sleep in."

"I saw one in the attic when I was looking for the car seat. I'll bring it down before tonight, although I doubt if it will make much difference. The kid doesn't seem to want to sleep much, anyway."

"She'll feel better once she settles into a routine."

"I didn't get to that chapter yet."

"Quinn, I think you're going to need to do more than just read that book on child care."

"Maybe you could give me some more pointers, like the way you showed me how to hold her."

Into her mind came the image of Quinn as he had looked yesterday, with the sleeping infant cradled protectively in his arms. Her gaze strayed to the hard biceps that pushed against the short sleeves of his T-shirt. "Well…"

"Consider it another tutoring job."

"I suppose I could, but isn't there anyone you could call to help you out on a more regular basis?"

"I'd prefer to keep this between the two of us. The fewer people who know about this kid the better."

She lifted her eyebrows. "I know you've been away from Maple Ridge for a while, but it's still a small town. You can't possibly expect to keep Charli's presence a secret."

"Good point. That's all the more reason for keeping the number of people involved to a minimum. We need to get our story straight."

"Story?"

"If I'm going to keep the kid safe, I don't want a lot of gossip drawing attention to her or some interfering bureaucrats taking her away. No one else needs to know how I found her."

She hesitated. She still wasn't convinced that the situation was as serious as Quinn thought, but she didn't like the idea of broadcasting the truth, either. If the authorities got involved, Charli would probably be taken away by some nameless social worker and disappear into the foster care system. The baby had already experienced enough turmoil in her short life. "Maybe all of this is unnecessary. Her mother might change her mind. She could be on her way back right now."

"Whatever trouble she's in made her desperate enough to abandon her baby. I don't think her problems are going to disappear overnight, so I'll need a cover story."

"A cover story?" Rachel repeated. "You make it sound so…cloak-and-dagger," she said with a smile.

"We'll keep it simple," he went on, no trace of amusement in his voice. "If anyone asks, I'm taking care of the kid for some friends of mine. That should be enough."

"Why would your friends want you to do that?"

"I owed them a favor."

"No, I mean, what will you say if someone asks why your friends would need to leave their child?"

"A sick relative, a trip overseas, a vacation. That's really not anybody's business. What matters is that no one else knows the truth."

"All right. I won't say anything."

"As long as you haven't already told anyone...?"

She shook her head. "No. I haven't talked to anyone else since I left you last night."

"So you live alone?"

The question shouldn't have bothered her. It was nothing but a matter-of-fact inquiry. "Yes. How long do you think you'll need to keep Charli?"

"That's immaterial. I'll keep that kid as long as necessary."

"Charli."

"What?"

"Her name's Charli. Why do you keep calling her 'kid'?"

He lifted his gaze to hers. "Do you have a problem with that?"

"It just seems so—" she waved her hand "—so impersonal."

"Rachel, I'm taking care of that baby because of my duty to my team, that's all. It won't help her if I let my personal feelings get mixed up in this. For her own good I should stay as objective as possible."

"She's a child, not a...a boat or whatever it is that you're accustomed to dealing with in the Navy."

"A boat?"

"You know what I mean. Charli needs more than just food and shelter, she needs to feel cared for. She needs to feel loved. All children do."

Something flickered in the depths of his gaze. For an instant there was a hint of emotion, of the old Quinn, the one who used to be kind and generous and open. But then the emotion faded and he shook his head. "The kid's gotten to you already, hasn't she?"

"She's a sweet, innocent child. I can't help feeling moved by her situation. Anyone would. I—"

The shrill of the telephone on the desk cut off the rest of what she was going to say. At the sudden noise, Charli whimpered.

Quinn made a grab for the receiver before it could ring again. "Yeah, Keelor's Garage," he said.

Rachel moved to the corner beside the filing cabinet where she'd left Charli and squatted down to check on the baby. Although her eyes were still closed, Charli's mouth was wrinkling into a knot. Rachel reached out and lightly stroked the back of her hand. "It's okay," she murmured. "You're fine, sweetie."

Charli's lips pursed as she made a soft, sucking noise. Gradually her expression smoothed back into sleep. Yet Rachel didn't immediately withdraw her hand; instead she let her fingers rest on the downy-soft skin of the baby's delicate wrist.

In a way, Quinn might have a point. It wouldn't be smart to let personal feelings get involved in this situation. Getting attached to this baby would be all too easy. Charli was Quinn's responsibility only temporarily. And just like her old infatuation with Quinn, Rachel had put to rest her old yearnings for a child a long time ago.

No, the desire for a child wasn't as strong as a yearning. It was just a natural extension of her fondness for children. That's why she'd gone into teaching, wasn't it? Because she enjoyed children so much? Of course, she would love to have a baby of her own, but that wasn't going to happen. A child needed two parents, not one, and Rachel had no intention of trading her independence for marriage. She wasn't going to risk that kind of vulnerability simply for the sake of a baby.

So you live alone?

She frowned. The question *shouldn't* have bothered her. But somehow being around Quinn seemed to shake the control she'd worked for years to achieve. She didn't like that.

"Who is this?" Quinn said, his voice low and harsh.

Rachel twisted around to look at Quinn. She had assumed the call was from one of the parts suppliers he'd contacted earlier, but judging by his tone, this had to be something else.

"Yes, she's fine," he said tightly. "Where—" He scowled, then replaced the receiver.

Pushing herself to her feet, Rachel gestured to the phone. "Who was that?"

"She wouldn't give her name."

Rachel noted the tense set of his jaw. She glanced at the baby, then back at Quinn. "You think it was Charli's mother, don't you?"

He nodded. "Had to be. She wanted to check on whether or not I found the kid."

"Did she say anything else?"

"No."

"Did you recognize her voice?"

"No. Damn!"

"Maybe she'll call again."

"I should get the phone company to hook up a number display so I can trace the next call. Here and at the house."

Rachel paused to think for a moment. "But the phone at the house would be in your brother-in-law's name, wouldn't it?"

"Yeah."

"So unless Charli's mother is from around here, she wouldn't know how to reach you there."

"You're right. The only listings under Keelor in the area would be my father's apartment and this garage. There wouldn't have been any answer at my father's place, so that explains why she would look for me here."

"That's probably why she chose to leave Charli here at the garage last night," Rachel said. "She didn't know where you were living."

"Yeah." He raked his fingers through his hair and looked through the open garage door to the yard outside. "It might be better if she didn't try to call again, or she might lead whatever trouble she's in right back to us.''

''But you still don't have any idea who she is?''

''I'll know more once I trace the owner of that ring.''

''Quinn, about that ring...''

He turned back to face her, his gaze shuttered. ''What about it?''

''I find it hard to believe the trouble Charli's mother mentioned in her note is all that serious. Don't you think you might be overreacting?''

''No, I don't,'' he said firmly.

''Then why don't you just call up the other men from your SEAL team and find out what's going on?''

''I can't do that.''

''While it's admirable that you're so willing to accept this responsibility, hasn't it occurred to you that one of those men could be Charli's father?''

''That would be impossible.''

''How can you be so sure?''

''They're dead, Rachel.''

That stopped her. ''Dead?''

''All of them. They were killed in an explosion during a mission more than a year ago. The baby's less than two months old, so none of them could be her father.''

Her heart contracted at the distance in his tone. It was like the distance in his expression. ''Oh, Quinn, I'm so sorry. That must have been awful for you.''

''Depends on how you look at it. I survived.''

She glanced at his cane. ''Was that what...I mean...''

''Gave me the bum leg? Yeah. It was my last mission.''

The sympathy she'd felt for him last night deepened on a wave of understanding. Not only had he lost his wife, he'd lost his men soon afterward. He'd endured so much tragedy and death in the last few years, was it any wonder that he seldom smiled anymore?

Despite her resolve to keep her involvement with Quinn

limited to the baby, Rachel had an overwhelming urge to reach out to him, to pull him into her arms and stroke the tension from his muscles and kiss the harshness from his face.

He grasped his cane and brushed past her to pick up Charli's carrier. "Let's get started on that list you made. With any luck I'll have word on that exhaust assembly for your car by the time we get back."

"But—"

"You might know all about keeping the kid happy, but that won't be much use if I don't keep her safe."

Chapter 5

"Josh, how are the repairs to the bandstand coming along?"

"Right on schedule, Emily." Josh Winters leaned back in his chair, stretching his long legs under the table. "As long as the weather holds, we'll have the floor finished and painted in plenty of time for the opening ceremonies."

"Great." Emily Townsend, the fifth-grade teacher and part-time vice principal at Rachel's school, made a check mark on the list in front of her. "With Logan's Hardware donating the paint and your company donating their time, we might even come in under budget. Thanks, Josh."

"No problem."

Emily turned to the gray-haired woman who was sitting at the other end of the table. "Hazel, what kind of response have you had so far to the raffle?"

Rachel listened as Hazel McInnes, who was in charge of this year's fund-raising efforts for the county hospital auxiliary, read a detailed account of the ticket sales to date. Afterward, the half-dozen people who were gathered around Emily's dining table made comments and suggestions, but the preparations seemed to be progressing without a hitch.

This was the third year Rachel had been part of the Maple Ridge Summer Festival Committee, and she was always impressed by how well run the event was. The whole town seemed eager to get involved, but that was just the way things were in a small community. They might not have the same excitement or business opportunities of a big city, but it felt good to belong here.

She hadn't always felt that way. Throughout her adolescence, she'd felt like an outsider, but she'd worked hard to overcome that. She'd made a place for herself within the town. She'd established a respected career and a good reputation, and she was very satisfied with the way her life had turned out.

Then why did she feel it necessary to keep reminding herself of that?

It was because of Quinn. There was no use pretending that his return to her life hadn't shaken her up. The easiest thing to do would be to end their association, but because of Charli, she wasn't going to be able to get Quinn out of her life any time soon.

After their shopping trip, she'd spent the rest of the day helping him clean up his niece's room and convert it into a temporary nursery. And then it had seemed only natural that she'd give Charli her bath and her bottle. And then when she'd shown Quinn how to hold the baby to his shoulder and use the warmth of his body to soothe her as he rocked her to sleep, Rachel had wanted to forget about attending this meeting. Instead, she'd wanted to stay with Quinn.

No, it was Charli she'd wanted to stay with.

She sighed with frustration and rubbed her eyes.

"Rachel?"

At Emily's voice, she glanced up quickly. The meeting was breaking up amid a shuffling of papers and a buzz of friendly conversation. "Oh," Rachel said, pushing herself out of her chair. "That went fast."

"We're a well-oiled machine," Emily responded with a grin. "Now, if only our staff meetings could go that smoothly."

"It must be the brownies Hazel brought," Rachel said, gesturing at the empty platter in the center of the table. "All that chocolate must stimulate our brain cells."

Emily laughed and patted her rounded stomach. "I don't know about our brains, but it sure adds a certain something to other parts of my anatomy."

That Rachel could joke about food like this was a measure of how far she had come in the past fifteen years. Relaxing, she smiled at her friend. Barely an inch over five feet, with her sparkling eyes and close-cropped hair, Emily looked like a pixie, although a very pregnant one. "I think that's due more to Junior than to Hazel's baking," Rachel said. "How's he doing?"

"I think he's destined to be a world-class soccer player, if his practice kicks are anything to go by."

"Do you want some help cleaning up?" Rachel asked, moving toward the door as the rest of the committee departed.

"No, thanks, the twins will take care of it. Brad and Brett are in charge of dishes this week while Rob is on call at the hospital," Emily said. "But I was wondering if you could stay for a while. Can you spare a few minutes?"

"Of course. Is everything all right?" Rachel asked, concerned. "This organizing committee isn't too much for you, is it?"

"Oh, no. Now that school's out for the summer and I'm officially on maternity leave, it's great to have something to focus on to keep my mind off the waiting. I just thought we could relax and catch up with each other's news. It's been ages since we had a chance to talk."

Rachel looked at her curiously. "I was over here three days ago."

"Oh, right. But a lot can happen in three days." Emily led her over to the living room and sat down on the sofa. She waited until Rachel had settled beside her, then turned to her and grinned. "Okay, what's the story?"

"What?"

"I heard you're seeing Quinn Keelor."

"*What?*"

"Aren't you?"

"No," Rachel said. "Definitely not. Where did you hear this, anyway?"

"Hazel told me. She heard it from her daughter-in-law, who saw the two of you in Quinn's truck at the mall this afternoon. She'd been so sure it was you, but I guess she was wrong."

"She might have seen me in Quinn's truck, but we're not seeing each other, not the way you mean."

Emily tilted her head. "Ah. Then what way *are* you seeing each other?"

"I took my car in for repairs, and then we went shopping," Rachel said. "I can't believe how fast that news traveled. And I wasn't aware that you even knew Quinn. He'd left town years before you and Rob moved here."

"That may be, but I know who he is. A person can't set foot in the high school without seeing Quinn Keelor's name all over the trophies in the front display case."

"He's changed a lot since high school, Emily."

"Yes, well, I met him when the transmission dropped out of my station wagon last month and he showed up instead of Doug Keelor with the tow truck. Quinn seemed like a nice man, although he was a bit quiet for my taste. What were you shopping for?"

She hesitated, thinking about the cover story that Quinn wanted to use. She hated to lie to her friend, but, considering Emily's condition, it would probably be kinder to keep her out of it. Besides, she didn't really have to lie, all she had to do was to withhold some of the truth. "I was helping him pick up some baby supplies."

"What would Quinn need with baby supplies?" Emily's eyes widened. "Oh, my. How long have you been seeing him? Rachel, you're not..." Her gaze darted to her stomach.

"Good God, no," Rachel said, laughing at the absurdity of what her friend was implying. "Emily, I already told you I'm not involved with him. If Hazel's daughter-in-law had waited to see us get out of Quinn's truck before she jumped on the gossip hot line, she would have seen the baby for herself. Quinn's baby-sitting for some friends of his, that's all."

"That's all? Are you sure?"

Rachel shook her head. "Give it up, Emily. You know that I don't have any interest in getting romantically involved with anyone."

"Not even Quinn?"

"Especially not Quinn," Rachel said firmly.

"Why not? Is there something in particular you don't like about him?"

"Not really. He's just..." What could she say? That he was too intense, too hard, too masculine, and he stirred up old pain and old yearnings she didn't want to remember? "He's just a friend," she finished.

Emily sighed. "I'm sorry, I don't mean to interfere, but when I heard that you and Quinn were—"

"Shopping," Rachel repeated.

"Well, I kind of hoped it would be more."

"I know you mean well, Emily, but I'm simply not like you. I don't need a husband and children to be happy. My independence means too much to me."

Emily looked at her in silence for a moment. "I'll bet you saw your mother recently," she said finally.

"Yes, I saw her yesterday, but what does that have to do with anything?"

"Ann's a wonderful woman, but don't you see that she's brainwashing you into being just like her?"

"No, I don't see that at all."

"Every time you visit her, you come back more determined

than ever to remain alone. You're letting her bad marriage dictate the way you live your life.''

"There's nothing wrong with my life," Rachel said. "And speaking of brainwashing, aren't you trying to do the same thing?"

"I'm sorry," Emily said, grasping her hand. "Blame it on the pregnancy hormones. They're turning me into a match-making marshmallow."

Rachel smiled, well accustomed to her impulsive friend's tendency to speak first and think later. "At least you care enough to nag."

"It's just that I've been so happy since I heard the news about you and Quinn—"

"There is no *news* about us."

"Okay, okay. I'm backing off." She squeezed Rachel's fingers and then withdrew her hand. Sighing, she glanced at her sideways, obviously not prepared to drop the subject entirely. "But I think it's a shame. Quinn seemed like an interesting man."

"Interesting?"

"Still waters running deep and all that. And despite the cane and the limp, he's got quite the hot body."

"Emily!" Rachel exclaimed on a startled laugh.

"Just because I'm married to the sexiest doctor in the state and am waddling around with Junior doesn't mean I've gone blind. Quinn's one impressive figure, even in his overalls, don't you think?"

He was even more impressive when he was fresh from the shower wearing nothing but a towel, Rachel thought. "I'm giving him a hand with the baby he's taking care of, that's all," she said. "Now, can we please change the subject?"

Hanging up the phone, Quinn dropped his head into his hands and focused on the paper in the center of his sister's desk. It had been surprisingly difficult to write down that list of names. Until he'd done that, they had still been alive in his memory. Yet with each letter he'd formed as he'd put the names on the paper, he'd felt the memories change. They were no longer the men who had supported each other through the agony of Hell week, or the friends who had closed down bars together, or the warriors who had executed one mission after another with lethal efficiency. No, they were the names of the dead.

He'd thought that he'd accepted their deaths. And his guilt. But writing this list had brought back the memories that had only been allowed to surface in his nightmares.

It was going to get worse. The deeper he got into this investigation, the more scars he was going to rip open. But he had no choice. If he wanted to help Charli and her mother, he had to start by finding out who they were.

Gritting his teeth, he picked up a pen and drew a line through the first name on the list. Gino Ferrone's mother had been startled to hear from Quinn after all this time, but she had quickly recovered from her surprise and had chatted to him for almost an hour, proving to be as warm and gregarious as Gino had been. If she harbored any resentment because Quinn had survived while her son hadn't, it hadn't been evident in her voice.

Quinn hadn't been sure how to inquire about the ring, so he'd ended up taking the direct approach and had asked Mrs. Ferrone flat out if she had it. She'd claimed that she did. It was in a display case on her mantel, along with Gino's medals and service ribbons and the SEALs' gold trident.

There was no reason for Quinn to doubt her word—if there had been even a whiff of trouble concerning any of Gino's friends and family, Mrs. Ferrone would have detailed it at some point during their conversation. In addition, considering the size and the supportiveness of the Ferrone family, it was unlikely that anyone associated with Gino would be driven to act as desperately as Charli's mother had.

So he could reasonably eliminate Ferrone from the list. One

down and five to go. The odds were improving. And he only had to put himself through this five more times.

"Any luck?"

At the soft voice from across the room, Quinn lifted his head. Rachel stood in the doorway of the study, the baby cradled against her shoulder. And as usually happened when Rachel held her, Charli was mercifully silent. "I'm narrowing things down," he said.

"That's good news."

"Yeah. It's a start."

She hesitated, her gaze on his face. "Are you all right?"

"Me?"

"This is tough on you, isn't it? Having to contact the families of your men."

He could see the sympathy in her eyes and had a hard time looking away. He didn't deserve anyone's sympathy. And he didn't need anything from Rachel, other than her help with the baby. He lifted his shoulders in a stiff shrug. "If I want to help the kid's mother, it has to be done."

"I would have thought that Charli's mother would have called again by now. It's been three days."

"Maybe she's smart enough not to risk it."

Rachel rubbed her hand over the baby's back, not replying.

Quinn knew that Rachel still didn't believe Charli's mother was in real danger. He couldn't blame her for her skepticism, considering the sheltered life she'd led, but what she thought didn't matter as long as she continued to cooperate.

He'd fixed her car yesterday morning. At first he'd been tempted to delay by telling her the parts hadn't yet come in—when he'd been on a mission, he hadn't hesitated to use any available method that would ensure success. But the ruse hadn't been necessary. Since their first shopping trip together, Rachel had been coming over regularly to tutor him in child care and help watch Charli when he was busy at the garage.

He couldn't say the tutoring was like old times, since there was a hell of a difference between handling babies and deciphering Shakespeare. And Rachel was no longer the same shy girl, nor was she afraid to express her opinions.

But then, her personality wasn't the only thing that had changed about her. There were the physical changes that he kept struggling not to notice.

The drop in weight from her teenage years hadn't left her model thin. No, there was nothing angular or coltish about her. Instead, her body carried the kind of generous curves that had been rousing a response in him from the first moment he'd laid eyes on her back at the garage. She was all woman, soft and rounded, blatantly feminine. And the more she was around him, the more he noticed.

It was a natural reaction, this growing interest he was feeling. Just like his slowly improving mobility and the gradual healing of his skin, it was a sign of his return to health. The sexual awareness meant that his body was functioning as it was meant to, that's all.

It had been a long time since he'd had these stirrings. For most of the past year, he hadn't been in any condition to even think about sex, let alone do anything about it. And before that, during the endless months of Louisa's illness, he'd found other ways to express his love for his wife. He'd learned to sublimate his physical drives. He'd managed to control his needs.

But now, as his body recovered, so did his recognition of himself as a man. It was all part of the difference between living and merely being alive. So this was only part of a normal recovery. It wasn't any big deal. And it wouldn't be a problem, as long as he didn't allow his body's interest in Rachel to interfere with the purpose of their association.

He turned the list of names facedown on the desk and rose to his feet. "Okay, what's the lesson for tonight?"

Charli grabbed a fistful of Rachel's hair and pulled it to her mouth. Smiling, Rachel eased the hair out of the baby's grip before she looked at Quinn. "Well, since you seem to be doing all right with feeding and burping, I thought we'd progress to the next step.''

"Which is?''

"Bath time.''

The image took him unawares, springing into his mind full-blown. Rachel, her hair damp and curling around her face, her body naked and surrounded by steamy water as she lounged in a bathtub. Her skin would be flushed with heat, her eyes half-closed and her lips parted with pleasure....

He scowled and focused on the baby. "Sure. Let's go.''

"Dribble some of the water over the inside of your wrist or your elbow,'' Rachel said, gesturing toward the white plastic tub she'd placed on the bathroom counter.

"To check the temperature, right?'' Quinn asked, moving to stand beside her.

"That's right.'' She smiled in approval. "Have you been reading ahead in that book?''

"No, I remembered how you showed me to check the temperature of the formula before I gave her a bottle.'' He extended his arm over the tub and scooped up some water over it with his cupped palm. "Seems okay to me,'' he said. "What do you think?''

She shifted Charli to one arm and held out the other.

Quinn looked at her arm for a moment, then took her hand in a loose grasp. Filling his palm with water once more, he let it drip over the sensitive skin near her elbow.

Rachel caught her breath. Between the warmth of Quinn's fingers clasping hers and the sensation of the water trickling over her arm, her skin tingled with unexpected pleasure.

And that was ridiculous. They were here to give Charli a bath. There wasn't anything remotely sensual about that, was there?

Pulling her arm away from Quinn, she took a careful step back. Not that there was anywhere to go in this small bathroom. Perhaps they would have been better off doing this at the kitchen table so that they would have more space, but the long counter in this room had seemed the most convenient the last two times Rachel had bathed the baby.

But those other times, she had done this alone. She hadn't realized how...intimate this room could feel when she shared it with a man as large as Quinn. Her gaze strayed to the shower curtain that hung over the bathtub. This was where Quinn took his showers. This was where he stripped off his clothes and stood naked under the streaming water....

She rubbed her wet wrist on her skirt, impatient with herself. "The water temperature's perfect, Quinn," she said finally.

"All right. Now what?"

"Now we put her in the tub."

He squeaked his thumb along the plastic rim. "It looks slippery. Aren't you concerned she'll slip under the water?"

"Not if you hold her. Here," she said. "I'll show you." Taking off the towel that she'd wrapped around Charli earlier, Rachel carefully eased the baby into the water. "You can support her by slipping your hand behind her back and holding her arm, see?"

Quinn moved behind Rachel and brought his arm alongside hers, covering her hand. "Like this?"

She nodded. "That's it. Let me move out of the way," Rachel said, starting to withdraw her hand.

Instead of stepping to the side as she'd expected, Quinn stayed where he was, extending his other hand around her to grasp the edge of the counter and cage her between his arms. "Walk me through it first," he said. "I don't want the kid to start screaming."

"I don't think she will. Charli likes baths. Look."

Most babies Rachel had dealt with enjoyed the feel of warm water against their skin, and Charli was no exception. Her plump, pink body was relaxed against Rachel's arm, her chubby legs kicking reflexively as she took advantage of the freedom the water provided. Instead of a pout, her mouth pursed to blow tiny bubbles.

"Yeah, I guess she does like it." Quinn's breath stirred the hair over Rachel's ear, his chest brushing her back as he let go of the counter and angled himself to her side. "You know a lot about babies, don't you?"

"I suppose so." It was disconcerting how the merest contact with Quinn was able to accelerate her pulse. Concentrating on the task at hand, Rachel dunked the washcloth and slowly started to smooth the soap over Charli's chest. "There's no secret to it. Most of it's common sense. They let you know when something's wrong."

"That's for sure," Quinn said dryly. "At least we know there's nothing wrong with this kid's lungs."

"When she cries, it's her way of communicating."

"The trick is figuring out exactly what she's saying."

"That comes with experience, but you're already making a pretty good start," Rachel said, working the lather between Charli's delicate fingers. "You know when she's hungry, or when she's tired, or when she just needs some reassurance that someone cares. I'm going to take my hand away from her back now. Ready?"

She felt him stiffen, as if he were preparing himself for an unpleasant duty. Glancing up, she looked at their reflections in the mirror that covered the wall over the counter. His mouth was set in a grim line, his gaze focused on the baby. But he didn't stop Rachel from withdrawing this time. She slid her fingers from beneath his until he was supporting Charli on his own.

And despite the wary unwillingness on Quinn's face, within another few minutes he had taken the washcloth from Rachel and was completing the bath by himself. Just as he'd done with the other things she'd shown him, Quinn was focusing intently on learning this new skill.

All the while, Charli was studying him with a wariness that almost matched his. Following Rachel's directions, Quinn managed to transfer the slippery baby to the towel without incident and was gently patting her skin dry when the unexpected happened.

Charli looked Quinn in the eye and smiled.

Quinn seemed so startled, Rachel couldn't help laughing. "See? She doesn't cry all the time."

He stared at the child, his movements ceasing.

Gurgling happily, Charli kicked her feet and waved her fists in the air, knocking into his hand where he held the towel.

"Go on," Rachel encouraged. "She wants to play."

"Play? Isn't the kid too young for that?"

"Well, she's not quite ready to go out in the yard and catch a football, but it wouldn't hurt if you gave her some attention."

Quinn tilted his head and leaned closer. And gradually, the corners of his mouth lifted in response.

Charli's tentative smile changed quickly into a toothless grin as her limbs flailed in the air.

"Hey, there," he said softly, enclosing the baby's tiny fist within his.

As had happened so many times over the past three days, Rachel was once more struck by the contrast between the infant's helplessness and Quinn's strength. Yet now she saw more than his strength, she saw...tenderness.

And for some crazy reason, Rachel felt a lump rise in her throat.

She swallowed hard. "I think you've made a conquest."

"The kid's getting used to me, that's all," he said, releasing Charli's hand. Before he could move away, the baby grabbed his finger.

"Charli," Rachel said.

"What?"

"Her name is Charli."

Quinn turned his head to meet her gaze. "Let's not get into that again, all right?"

"She's an innocent baby, Quinn. What harm would it do to loosen up a bit?"

"I already told you, Rachel. It wouldn't be wise to let my personal feelings get involved—"

"For God's sake, can't you at least call her by her name?"

He gently extricated his finger from Charli's grip. "Why is it so important to you?"

She hesitated, unsure how to answer. She thought she understood the reasons he tried to maintain a distance from the baby in his care, and she had accepted the fact that he wasn't the carefree, outgoing boy she used to know, yet this glimpse of a smile, the softness in his voice...it moved her. It made her want to see what else was buried inside the man he'd become.

"Is it because of your father?" Quinn asked.

She started. "My father? What are you talking about?"

"This baby's situation is completely different from what happened to you, Rachel."

The change of topic made her stiffen. "Of course, it's different. I don't know why you'd even mention it."

He looked at her for a long moment, his gaze far too penetrating. What was it about Quinn that made her feel as if he were looking right through to her past, and the girl she didn't want to remember?

Yet were her and Charli's situations that different? Being abandoned by a parent, at whatever age, could wound a child in a way that might not leave physical scars, but that scarred all the same. A child needed to feel secure, she needed to feel loved. Otherwise she lacked the base to build her identity from. She might spend years trying to gain the self-confidence needed to get on with her life, and yet she would still be haunted by feelings of inadequacy and self-loathing...

"Sorry," Quinn said. "That's not any of my business."

Rachel shook her head and stepped back. "No, it's all right. I guess I deserved that, considering the way I'm pushing you about Charli. I know that none of this is easy for you, especially since you have to contact the families of your men to trace that ring. I realize it upsets you. I should be minding my own business, too.''

''I didn't say it to get even, Rachel.''

She waved a hand. ''The comparison is understandable. I thought about it myself when I discovered how Charli had been left, but the big difference is that I still had my mother. This child doesn't have anyone.''

Wrapping the baby in a dry towel, Quinn picked her up and turned to face Rachel. ''You're wrong. Until I can get her back to her mother, she has me.''

That lump was back in her throat, along with a hint of mistiness in her eyes. The determination on Quinn's face, the strength in his stance as he held Charli reminded Rachel of the way he'd looked when she had found him in the study earlier. This situation wasn't easy for either of them. It wasn't fair of her to expect more from Quinn—he was already doing more than most men would.

Blinking hard, she started to clean up the bathroom.

''Oh, hell,'' Quinn muttered suddenly, holding the baby away from his chest. Looking down, he scowled as a dark patch of dampness spread over the front of his shirt.

Obviously pleased with herself, Charli gurgled, kicking her feet free of the towel that had been clean moments ago. Moisture that wasn't due to the bathwater dripped from her toes.

Rachel glanced from Charli to Quinn. And just like that, the tension she'd felt, the echoes of poignancy from their earlier words, dissolved on a burst of startled laughter.

Whatever Charli might mean to Quinn, whatever memories the child might stir up for both of them, she was still just a baby.

A very wet and very happy baby.

Despite his scowl, Quinn's lips twitched. ''So you think this is funny?'' he growled.

''I'm sorry,'' Rachel said, chuckling as she retrieved the washcloth. ''But you have to admit we had it coming.''

"Why?"

"We're both so concerned with what this child means that we tend to forget the fact that she's really just a baby."

He grunted, the lines beside his mouth deepening with the hint of a smile. "Next time I'll make sure to put the diaper on her right away."

"That would be a good idea. Hold still. I'll wipe you off, then we'll put her back in the tub." She dabbed the washcloth against his shirt, following the path of dampness down his chest.

"It's all right, Rachel," Quinn said, shifting Charli against his shoulder with one arm as he made a motion toward the cloth. "You don't have to do that. I'll be changing the shirt, anyway."

"It's so you don't drip in the meantime. Just be glad Charli's a girl. Baby boys tend to be…well…messier."

"You can say that after you saw what the kid did to my niece's room?"

"It's not an insult, Quinn. It's an anatomical fact."

"Rachel," he said, his voice dropping. "I might not know much about kids, but I do know the difference between boys and girls."

She flipped the cloth over and stroked downward. Speaking of the difference between boys and girls… Her fingers brushed the front stud of his jeans and she froze as the manner in which she was touching him finally registered on her brain. She looked at the masculine bulge just inches from her hand.

And the humor she'd been feeling changed instantly to awareness.

Oh, God. How had this happened? She'd only meant to help him. She wasn't trying to take advantage of the situation by getting personal. Her cheeks burning with embarrassment, she snatched her hand away and stepped back.

Unfortunately, in the confines of the small bathroom, her sudden movement brought her elbow into contact with the plastic tub. Water sloshed over the rim, splashing down the front of her blouse.

At the sound of a whispered oath, she looked at Quinn. His gaze was fixed on her chest. She glanced down quickly, then felt the flush on her cheeks deepen. The water had turned her cotton blouse practically transparent. Against the lace of her bra, she could plainly see the dark outline of her nipples.

Before she could reach for a towel, Quinn had one in his hand. He stepped closer, bringing the towel to within a hair-breadth of her breasts. "Want me to return the favor?" he asked.

"Favor?"

"I'll dry you off."

The mere thought of the touch of his hand against her breasts was enough to pucker her nipples. Inhaling sharply, she raised her gaze to his.

Awareness as fast and mindless as her own sparked in his eyes. It didn't seem to matter that they were standing in a bathroom or that he was holding a wet baby. The circumstances weren't the least bit seductive, yet there was no mistaking his expression.

Had she thought she'd wanted to see what feelings were buried inside this man? The heat she glimpsed in his eyes wasn't the kind of feeling she'd expected. Or wanted.

Grabbing the towel from him, she covered her chest and inched past him toward the door. "I think I'll manage, Quinn. It's time I went home, anyway."

Quinn watched her without speaking, then finally turned away and eased the baby back into the bathwater. "Fine. I'll finish up here and put Charli to bed."

Rachel continued to retreat. Maybe it would be better to leave well enough alone. Maybe she should regard this situation with the same distance Quinn did.

The towel crumpled in her fingers as she headed for the

stairs. Yet despite the clammy feel of her wet blouse, warmth spread through her body.

But was it because of the lingering sensation of Quinn's gaze on her breasts? Or because he'd finally said "Charli"?

Chapter 6

Rachel picked up the telephone and wandered across her living room. The clouds that darkened the horizon were bringing an early dusk and the promise of rain. That was good. Perhaps there would be a break in the hot, muggy weather of the past week. The humidity was setting everyone on edge.

No, she couldn't blame her edginess on the weather. She wasn't going to try to fool herself. The tension that had been filling her days wasn't due to any meteorological phenomenon; it was due to Quinn. And the more she saw him, the worse it became.

Any woman would feel a certain tug toward a man as strikingly masculine as Quinn, yet the pull Rachel felt wasn't merely sexual. It would be a lot simpler if it was. But since that day last week when Charli had smiled at Quinn, the baby had been breaking through his reserve more and more often. And each time Charli smiled and Quinn responded, Rachel felt her heart melt a little more.

He'd bought a rattle today. And a delicate butterfly mobile to hang over the crib yesterday, and a music box that was shaped like a rabbit the day before. Naturally he explained the purchases by claiming the toys kept "the kid" occupied so he could concentrate on more important things. That was his way. He still didn't want to get emotionally involved with Charli, but despite his attempts to distance himself, a bond was forming between them nevertheless.

It was obvious to Rachel. Almost as obvious—and unpreventable—as the bond that had begun to form between Quinn and her.

"It's a marvelous opportunity, Rachel. My flight is booked for next Wednesday."

At her mother's voice, Rachel transferred the receiver to her other ear and leaned her shoulder against the window frame. With an effort, she pulled her thoughts back to their conversation. "Congratulations, Mom. It's a real coup to be included in the national meeting so soon after your promotion."

"The company needs someone who isn't opposed to traveling. I'm sure that's one of the main reasons they chose me."

"I think the fact that you're a brilliant accountant might have had something to do with your success, too, Mom."

Ann Healey laughed softly. "Thanks, Rachel."

"How long will you be in New York?"

"At least three weeks. After that, I'll be going to the regional office in Chicago until the end of the month."

"It sounds as if you'll be gone awhile."

"Oh, I'll be linking my laptop to my office computer to keep up with my work." She paused. "Would you like me to give you the numbers of the hotels where I'll be staying in case you need to reach me?"

"I'll be fine, Mom."

"Of course you will, darling," Ann said easily. "You're so wonderfully independent. How is your work on the Festival Committee going?"

"Things are going smoothly so far, probably because Emily's running it this year."

"It must be difficult for her, with that family to worry about."

"You know Emily," Rachel said. "She has energy to burn."

"Mmm. Her maternity leave presents you with an excellent opportunity, though. Taking over the vice principal's duties while she's gone will be a good way to demonstrate your abilities to the school board. It's sure to benefit your career."

"The position's only temporary. I actually prefer to stay in the classroom."

"And you're a superb teacher, Rachel, but don't ignore the possibility of advancement this situation presents. You have a tremendous advantage over your friend Emily."

"She's a terrific teacher," Rachel stated.

"Absolutely. But she's splitting her concentration. She should be focusing on her career instead of expanding her family. Doesn't she realize the serious position she would be in if she had to support those children on her own?"

Smothering a sigh, Rachel shifted the phone to her other ear. She'd heard all of this before—it was the lesson she'd been raised with. A woman had to be independent in order to maintain control of her life. Commitment to a man made a woman vulnerable. "Rob isn't going anywhere," she said. "He's a very decent man."

Ann paused. "In the long run, one can truly count only on oneself. I hate to see a woman wasting her talents that way."

Rachel doubted that Emily would consider staying home to have a third child "wasting" her talents. She was one of those women who appeared to fit perfectly into the role of wife and mother. Then again, Emily hadn't experienced the other side of things. She'd never seen how destructive a marriage could be, and how painful the effects were on innocent children.

Lifting her head, Rachel watched the darkening clouds. Lightning flashed silently, the thunder too remote to hear. She rubbed her free hand along her arm, feeling a tingle from the distant storm.

"Oh, and by the way," Ann went on. "I heard the silliest bit of gossip this morning from Marlene."

"Who?"

"Marlene Winters. Her cousin runs the hardware store in Maple Ridge."

"That would be Josh. He's on the Festival Committee with me."

"That's right. Well, according to Marlene, you're practically engaged to Quinn Keelor."

"*What?*"

Ann's laughter sparkled over the phone line. "I thought you'd find that amusing."

"I can't believe the way the gossip is distorting things. My car was in Quinn's garage for repairs, and now I'm helping him with a child he's baby-sitting for some friends, that's all," Rachel said. "We're not dating."

"Oh, I know you're not," Ann said immediately. "I didn't believe Marlene for a second. I know my daughter better than that. You're far too sensible."

Sensible? Rachel thought. Yes, that was her, all right. Rational, sensible Rachel. "Thanks for your vote of confidence."

"You always have it, darling. I admire the way you're concentrating on the important things in life. You make me proud."

Rather than lifting her spirits, Ann's praise somehow seemed like a burden. "Thanks, Mom," Rachel murmured.

"Well, I'd better get started on the presentation I'll be making in New York," Ann said. "I'll call you when I get back."

"I hope you have a good trip."

Ann laughed lightly. "More important, I hope I have a profitable trip. Bye, Rachel. Love you."

"Love you too, Mom."

A few lazy, isolated drops of rain fell on the window as Rachel hung up the phone. She rolled her shoulders, frowning at the clouds. That vague sense of dissatisfaction, that same feeling of restlessness that had followed her last visit to her mother, had returned.

But she loved her mother. They had the kind of close, supportive relationship that would be the envy of thousands of mothers and daughters.

She's brainwashing you into being just like her.

The words Emily had spoken a week ago niggled at the edge of Rachel's mind. It was true that Ann Healey had repeatedly lectured her on the unreliability of men and how important it was for a woman to maintain control and independence. But the lectures had been for Rachel's own good. It was because Ann loved her and wanted to spare her daughter pain.

It had been devastating to Ann when Owen Healey had walked out on his wife and five-year-old daughter. Devastating both emotionally and financially. Ann had married Owen at seventeen and had become a mother six months later, so she hadn't had the opportunity to further her education or establish a career. She hadn't planned to be anything but a wife and a mother. Suddenly confronted with the sole responsibility for herself and her young daughter, Ann had worked at a succession of low-skilled, minimum-wage jobs during the day while she had taken night school courses in the evenings. Only after years of struggle and self-sacrifice did Ann finally achieve the success that allowed her and Rachel some degree of security.

Ann was a wonderful example of strength and perseverance. And if she hadn't had much time for her daughter during those years of struggle, that was because she'd been doing what was best for both of them. Rachel wouldn't allow herself to resent the way she'd felt neglected as Ann had pursued her career. Nor would she allow herself to resent the pressure of trying to fulfil her mother's expectations. That would be childish and unfair. Ann was Rachel's role model. Rachel loved and admired her, and she would forever be grateful that Ann had been strong enough not to desert her the way her father had.

Rachel wanted to continue making her mother proud of her. She owed her that much, didn't she?

The trees across the street swayed in a sudden gust of wind. Lightning flashed deep in the clouds, and thunder rumbled closer. Rachel leaned her forehead against the window, her thoughts as unsettled as the weather.

The explosion wouldn't end. It kept rumbling in his brain, the flashes stabbing through his eyelids even as he tried to pull himself from sleep. But the nightmare wasn't finished with him yet. Vibrations traveled through the ground where he'd fallen. He clenched his jaw, trying to still the chattering of his teeth as the flames crept toward him. More flashes, more rumbling. Then suddenly the world erupted in a flare of white and an ear-ringing blast.

Quinn exhaled hard and opened his eyes.

Rain drummed against the windowsill. Lightning flickered ghostly pale across the bedroom, followed by a roll of thunder. The sheet was wrapped around his legs, damp from the cold sweat that covered his body. But there were no flames, no smoke, no death. Only a storm.

For a minute he lay motionless, concentrating on his surroundings until reality slowly returned and pushed back the terror of the familiar nightmare. Kicking off the sheet, Quinn rolled to his side and reached for the lamp. Light flooded the room. He rubbed his eyes, gritted his teeth and levered himself out of bed to shut the window. But he didn't return to bed. There was no point trying to get back to sleep after that nightmare—from experience he knew he was up for the day.

Four and a half hours of sleep wasn't anything to complain about. When he'd been going through BUDs, he'd gone for an entire week with less than that. The body could take an amazing amount of abuse, because when pushed to the limits, the body's real strength came from the mind.

Not that he could compare this past week to the hell of basic training, he thought. Sure, Charli's lung power still rivaled an air horn, and her demands could be as arbitrary and rapid-fire as a whistle drill, but he was finally getting the hang of how to handle her.

And as far as instructors went, there was no comparison at all. He much preferred the gentle guidance Rachel was giving him to the sadistic orders of the master sergeants he'd known. Still, in her own way Rachel could be just as obstinate.

Shaking his head, Quinn pulled on his pants. It hadn't taken him long to get his thoughts around to Rachel. That was understandable. She was rapidly becoming a major part of his life. Of course, that situation was only temporary. Just like Charli.

He retrieved the nursery monitor from the bedside table, holding it up to his ear so that he could hear over the noise of the storm. He would have thought the thunder would have awakened the kid for sure. Yet oddly enough, there was no sound.

Immediately the last grogginess of sleep disappeared as Quinn's mind filled with a variety of possible scenarios. Had Charli's mother come back? Or had the trouble she was running from found him here? Instead of buying those baby toys while he was out today he should have given more thought to security. The locks on the doors wouldn't stop anyone for long. He should have backed them up or at least tried to set up a perimeter by installing an alarm.

Or maybe it was simply a matter of equipment failure. One of his primary rules on a mission had been to assume any piece of equipment that could possibly fail probably would. He should check the monitor's batteries before he contemplated turning the house into an armed camp. This was Maple Ridge. Most people didn't bother to lock their doors around here.

Thunder rumbled as he crossed the hall to Charli's bedroom and opened the door. In the amber glow of the night-light, he could see she was on her stomach in the center of the crib, her knees drawn underneath her and her rump in the air, as usual. There was a momentary lull in the thunder, and above the sound of the rain Quinn could just hear the steady rhythm of the baby's soft breathing.

No one had broken in and taken the baby. And there had been nothing wrong with the nursery monitor. By some miracle, the kid really was still asleep.

Quinn rubbed his face, then raked his hair off his forehead and focused on Charli. He was doing it again, worrying more about what the baby represented than the baby herself. He was seeing everything through his military experience. But that's what he was good at, that's what he was trained for. And that's why Charli's mother had brought the kid to him in the first place.

A draft swirled in from the hall, and the plastic butterflies that dangled over the crib fluttered daintily. Leaning back against the door frame to take his weight off his bad leg, Quinn glared at the mobile. Charli had smiled at the dancing butterflies today. So had Rachel. And both smiles had given him more pleasure than he'd felt in years.

He shouldn't have felt anything. He couldn't risk letting his emotions get mixed up in this. He needed to maintain his distance and keep a clear head, especially now that his investigation was gathering speed.

Quinn rotated the silver ring, rubbing his thumb over the engraved initials. He'd been able to cross out Petrosky and Hoffman from his list yesterday, and he'd received a good lead on the whereabouts of Larson's brother, but he wouldn't have the chance to follow it up until he did the laundry and prepared today's supply of baby formula. Instead of standing here wasting time watching the kid sleep, he should be taking advantage of the free time to get a head start on the day.

Pushing away from the door, he was about to move back into the hall when thunder boomed directly overhead, rattling the very foundations of the house. Charli shifted and whimpered weakly but didn't wake up. Quinn frowned. That crash had been loud enough to wake the dead.

His gut tightened with a sickening jerk. Turning around, he crossed the room to the crib.

Even before he touched the baby, he could feel the heat radiating off her body. He felt her forehead. Beneath his fingers, her skin was burning with fever.

He didn't need to be an expert with children to realize this baby was sick. But the routine medical training he'd received in the Navy had concentrated on diving medicine and the treatment of burns, gunshot wounds and field trauma. That wasn't much help now. Jake Simms had been the team's medic. If only Quinn could ask him...but Simms was gone. They were all gone. All that was left of his team were the silver rings and this helpless baby.... Muttering an oath, he scooped her out of the crib.

Rachel yanked the hood of her raincoat over her head and sprinted from her car to Quinn's porch. The front door opened just as she reached the top step.

Quinn stood in the doorway, his large frame silhouetted against the light that spilled from within. "Thanks for coming."

Without slowing her pace, Rachel dashed inside. "Where is she?"

Quinn closed the door behind her. "I put her back in her crib a few minutes ago."

She peeled off her dripping coat and tossed it over the newel post as she took the stairs two at a time. "How's she doing?"

"I'm not sure."

Rachel glanced behind her as she reached the second story and saw that Quinn was right on her heels. Despite his cane, he had managed to climb the stairs almost as quickly as she had. "What does that mean?" she asked.

"I gave her some water and took off her sleeper to help cool her down."

"Did it help?"

"She doesn't feel as hot."

"That's good."

"Yeah, but she went back to sleep practically right away," Quinn said, following her into the bedroom. "That's not like her."

Her heart pounding from a combination of anxiety and her race to get here, Rachel stopped beside the crib and looked at Charli.

The baby shifted fretfully in her sleep. Her face was flushed and her brows slightly puckered while her chest moved with her rapid breathing. Rachel laid her wrist gently across Charli's forehead. "She's definitely running a fever. How long has she been this way?"

"She was fine when I gave her a bottle around eleven." He moved beside Rachel. "I didn't notice anything wrong until I checked her half an hour ago. I got concerned because she slept right through the thunder."

"She's probably too exhausted to want to wake up. Fevers can drain an infant's strength."

"What should we do?"

Rachel stroked the downy hair at Charli's temple, then withdrew her hand and grasped the rail at the side of the crib. She turned to look at Quinn. "We could try bringing down her temperature by sponging her off with lukewarm water. And keep giving her fluids so she doesn't get dehydrated."

"Yeah, that's what I read in one of Leona's books."

"We don't know her history, so I wouldn't want to risk giving her any medication without a doctor's approval."

"Taking her to a doctor could be a problem."

"The emergency ward at the county hospital is only half an hour away. The storm isn't that bad."

"We might have trouble getting her admitted without any record of her identity. There would be too many questions. We'd have to decide on a last name for her and nail down our cover story about her parents' whereabouts."

She parted her lips, intending to give him another blast about regarding Charli as a mission instead a child, but then she took a good look at his face. Even the mellow glow of the night-light couldn't soften the tight set of his jaw or the anxiety that darkened his eyes. He cared more than he wanted to admit. "My friend's husband is a doctor," she said finally. "His patients are far more important to him than hospital administration, so I'm sure he wouldn't mind bending the procedural rules to do a house call. If Charli isn't better by the morning, we'll phone him."

By dawn the storm had tapered off to a steady drizzle. As the watery light that seeped through the window strengthened, so did Rachel's worry. She called Rob Townsend, luckily catching him before he left the house. Just as she'd hoped, he stopped at Quinn's on his way to the hospital.

Unlike his impulsive wife, Rob was carefully methodical in his actions and thoughtful with his speech. He gave Charli a thorough examination before he informed Rachel and Quinn of his diagnosis. "My guess is that this baby has the flu," he said, stepping away from the crib as he replaced his instruments in the backpack that served as his medical bag.

"Guess?" Quinn repeated. "You're not sure?"

Rob lifted his palms. "Without lab work, nothing's a hundred percent certain, but in this case I don't believe further tests are necessary. This bug is going around. I saw three patients with it yesterday."

"What should we do?" Rachel asked.

"Keep her comfortable and try to keep her fever down. You've already been doing everything that I would, so I recommend that you just continue." He dug into an outside pocket of his pack and brought out a small bottle to give to Rachel. "You can also try giving her some of this every four hours. The dosage is on the label."

"We don't know if she has any allergies," Quinn said as they accompanied him to the door. "I'm having trouble contacting her mother."

Rachel glanced at him. He hadn't lied outright to Rob about Charli's identity, but further explanations hadn't been necessary. Thanks to Emily, Rob had already heard the story about Quinn baby-sitting for his friends, and because of Emily's friendship with Rachel, Rob was willing to accept it without question.

"Don't worry," Rob said. "Adverse reactions to acetaminophen are extremely rare, but I'll give you a list of side effects to watch for, anyway." He paused on the threshold. "Apart from the flu, this child appears to be in excellent condition. Her lungs are clear and her heart is strong, so I'm sure she'll be able to fight this off. I have great faith in the natural resilience of babies, but if you have any questions or she gets worse, don't hesitate to call me, all right?"

Rachel gave him a quick hug. "Thanks, Rob. I really appreciate this."

"No problem." He shook hands with Quinn, then smiled and popped open his umbrella. "Don't let it get around, but I'd rather do a house call like this than see the emergency ward cluttered up with babies who would be better off at home."

She watched Rob hurry through the drizzle to his car, then turned to Quinn. "I'll fix some coffee," she said. "I think it's going to be a long day."

Quinn caught her arm before she could move past him. "Can you stay?"

"Yes, I don't have anything else planned."

"No, I meant can you stay until she's better?"

She looked around. "Here? That could be days."

"You can use Pete and Leona's room. They won't mind."

She wavered, all too aware of the place where his fingers curled around her arm. For the past several days they'd been careful not to touch each other. It hadn't been easy, considering the close contact necessary as they shared the child-care duties. How could she even contemplate moving in with him?

But she wouldn't be really moving in with him, not in the sense that they'd be living together. In the same way she wasn't really seeing him in the sense that the gossip maintained they were "seeing" each other.

"It would only be temporary," Quinn went on. "Just until Charli's over the flu."

She lifted her gaze to Quinn's. Yes, it would only be temporary, just like everything else about their association. And it would be best for Charli if she stayed nearby. She shouldn't let her hangups about getting close to a man come before the baby's welfare.

Yet it wasn't only Charli who mattered to her, was it? It was Quinn. It was the worry in his voice that had drawn her from a sound sleep to go racing into the rain. It was the need on his face that kept her here. It was the mere touch of his hand that was accelerating her pulse and had the power to make her want to forget about being sensible and in control and making her mother proud....

"Rachel?"

"I'll stay."

The next two days were a blur of activity as Rachel and Quinn took turns tending to Charli. The baby's initial sleepiness soon wore off, and as the flu progressed, the baby grew fussier. Quinn was glad that he'd convinced Rachel to stay. She hadn't wanted to take the master bedroom at first, arguing that she was short enough to fit on the couch so she could stay in the downstairs office. But he had insisted she take the bedroom, preferring to keep the impact of her presence here as limited as possible.

It had been a futile attempt. Apart from the continuous contact they had because of the baby, even when she was out of his sight, he still felt her presence. Tonight was no exception. He'd dozed off two hours ago, only to be awakened by his usual nightmare. But it wasn't the lingering traces of the dream that bothered him now, it was the thought of Rachel lying all alone in that big bed down the hall.

Damn, it was getting harder to keep his hands off her.

Didn't he have enough complications in his life already? He knew he shouldn't even think about touching her, but he couldn't seem to stop himself. She was just so inviting, so…alive.

Rolling to his back, he flung his arm across his forehead and stared at the ceiling, forcing his mind to ignore the discomfort in the lower half of his body. It was natural. It had no more significance than the way his stomach rumbled when he was hungry. He had far more important concerns. There was Charli's illness, and the question of her identity, and—

There was a rustling noise from the nursery monitor beside his bed. Quinn turned his head to listen. The kid had taken almost half a bottle around midnight and had kept it down this time, so he'd hoped that she would have been able to sleep a little longer. He waited a few minutes, giving her a chance to calm down on her own.

"Shh, sweetie. It's okay."

At the sound of Rachel's voice, Quinn exhaled hard and sat up. It was his turn to get Charli tonight. He should take over so Rachel could go back to bed. He fastened his jeans and shrugged on a shirt, then padded barefoot across the hall.

Rachel was standing beside the crib, her head bent as she focused on the baby cradled in her arms. She was humming softly as she swayed back and forth, her pale nightgown swishing against her calves. In the dim light her hair looked almost black where it tumbled over her shoulders.

She had the warm, disheveled appearance of a woman who had just arisen from her bed. And she had. That big bed down the hall where she'd slept all alone.

But he shouldn't be thinking about that now; he should be thinking about Charli. Stepping into the room, he cleared his throat. "I'll take over, Rachel."

Her curls danced as she shook her head. "She's going back to sleep. I'll put her down in a minute."

"How's her fever?"

She twisted to look at him over her shoulder, a smile working its way across her face. "It's gone."

He straightened up. "Gone?"

"Uh-huh. I think she's getting better."

He strode to her side and reached out to place his hand on Charli's forehead. Sure enough, her skin was cool. At his touch, the baby opened her eyes and looked at him. Her gaze was clear, her expression completely relaxed for the first time in days. That, more than anything else, convinced him that the worst was really over. Relief washed through him. "Thank God," he murmured.

Charli smiled sleepily, her eyelids fluttering shut once more.

"I think she was waiting to see you before she settled down," Rachel said.

"I doubt it. The kid's too quiet for that."

She laughed softly. "Quinn, come on. You know that Charli likes you."

"She'd like anyone who fed her or changed her diapers."

"Sure, Quinn. Then I guess that wasn't you who rocked her to sleep in the rocking chair last night."

He felt a smile tug at the corners of his mouth. "It was the only way to save my hearing."

She shook her head. "All right, have it your way. But you were as worried about her as I was."

"Yeah. I'm glad her fever broke."

"I wouldn't be surprised if her appetite was back by tomorrow. Children often get over illnesses as quickly as they come down with them."

He studied the baby, then moved his gaze to Rachel. "Once the body starts to recover, the appetite does, too. It's only natural."

"I'd better put her down," she whispered. "She'll probably keep us busy tomorrow."

Quinn stroked his fingertips along Charli's cheek. But the light was dim, and Rachel chose that moment to lean forward to put Charli back in the crib. So instead of touching the baby, Quinn's knuckles stroked the side of Rachel's breast.

She jerked back, her eyes widening.

"Sorry," he muttered. "It was an accident."

Tension stiffened her shoulders. She took a careful step to the side to tuck a light blanket around the baby.

But he wasn't sorry at all, he thought, as he watched the way Rachel's nightgown outlined her body with her movements. And he knew that there weren't any real accidents. No, whatever circumstance had brought it about, he'd wanted to touch her. The only surprising thing was that he'd managed to resist for this long. He followed her out the door, his fingers still tingling from that glancing contact.

Rachel pushed her hair back from her face in a nervous motion. "Well, I'd better let you get some sleep," she said, starting toward her bedroom.

"Rachel."

She paused. "Yes?"

"Thanks for your help."

"I did it for Charli."

"Right." There was nothing more he wanted to say. The smart thing to do would be to say good-night and leave well enough alone. But that wasn't what he did. In two strides he was standing in front of her and had taken her face between his palms.

Her lips parted in surprise. "Quinn?"

He lowered his head slowly, giving her the chance to pull away if she wanted, but she didn't. His mouth settled lightly over hers in a kiss as soft as the moonlight that stole across the floor.

It felt good. Better than he could have imagined. It had been so long since he'd kissed a woman, so long since he'd felt this intimate sharing of taste and breath. Part of him knew this couldn't go on, but part of him was rejoicing because he was still able to feel.

Normal appetite, normal hunger…the natural physical re-action of a body returning to health. That's all it was.

Rachel uncrossed her arms and stepped closer, lifting her hands to his shoulders and swaying against him. The hem of her nightgown slid across his jeans in a whisper of cotton as her breasts molded to his chest. And with a murmured sigh, she returned the kiss.

Desire slammed through him, startling in its intensity. He wanted her now. Here, on the floor, against the wall, he didn't care where or how, just so long as he could lose himself in the sexual oblivion she promised. His lips hardened, no longer gentle. His hands slid downward, skimming her shoulders, the sides of her breasts, her hips, until he slid his fingers around to cup her buttocks. Her cotton nightgown crumpled as he tightened his grip and lifted her against him.

She trembled and pulled her mouth from his. "Quinn," she gasped. "Stop."

He barely heard her over the pounding of the blood in his ears. He didn't want to hear her, he didn't want to listen to reason, not when he was holding her so close to where he wanted to be, not when he could feel her heat where he pressed her against the front of his jeans. He drew in his breath, his senses reeling at the sleepy muskiness of her skin.

"Quinn, please."

Exhaling on an oath, he tipped back his head and counted to ten. Mind over body. He could control this. He had to.

"Put me down."

Her voice was as unsteady as his legs. Loosening his grip, he let her slide downward until her feet touched the floor.

She took a step back, her eyes wide as she stared at him. "I don't want you to get the wrong idea. This shouldn't have happened," she said.

He didn't want to talk. And he sure as hell didn't intend to apologize this time. He wanted to pull her back into his arms and kiss her again.

"I think we're both exhausted," she went on. "And we

were both relieved that Charli's getting better and so we…lost our heads. That's all. I'll see you in the morning,'' she finished, turning away.

Her excuses were valid ones. It would be easiest for both of them if they could leave it at that. He'd hate to think there was more to it.

But what he really hated was the way he had to curl his hands into fists to keep himself from reaching out to stop her from leaving.

Chapter 7

Rachel folded her nightgown and placed it under the pillow, then briskly made her bed. Things were looking up. Charli hadn't had any trace of a fever when she'd checked on her at dawn. The baby had taken her first bottle of the day four hours ago with a renewal of her old appetite, and although she was still weak, she'd been playful and alert. Even without consulting Rob, it was a safe bet that Charli was on her way to recovering from her bout with the flu. Once Rachel was certain that the baby wasn't going to have a relapse, there really wouldn't be any reason for her to prolong her stay here, would there?

She sighed, sinking down on the edge of the mattress. She'd been through this before, hadn't she? At first it was just until Quinn got the baby home. Then it was only until he fixed the car, and then only until he could manage on his own. It seemed that she kept setting limits to their association and then disregarding them.

Could there be some other reason why she kept finding one cause after another to stay with Quinn?

Through the bedroom window came the sound of a car engine and crunching gravel. Thankful for the distraction to her thoughts, Rachel went to the window to see who had pulled into the driveway. She recognized the man who got out of the car. With his silver hair gleaming in the sunlight and his paunch straining the buttons of his plaid shirt, Doug Keelor was unmistakable.

Smoothing her blouse into her skirt, she checked her appearance in the dresser mirror. She groaned. She had hoped that she didn't look as much of a wreck as she felt, but it seemed as if every minute of the previous night was written on her face. Her lips looked puffy and her eyes were a little too bright.

She looked like exactly what she was. A woman who had been well kissed and then had spent too many restless, lonely hours lying in bed torn between wishing it hadn't happened and wishing that it hadn't stopped.

Quinn had stolen her breath with the first touch of his lips. It had started out as the kind of tender kiss she'd built her teenage daydreams around. But then she had kissed him back, and things had changed. There had been no mistaking the maturity of the man who had so boldly taken charge of their embrace.

If he'd kissed her like that fifteen years ago, she would have been thrilled to the point of terror. She would have run for the safety of her solitude and probably would have made serious inroads into her secret stash of chocolate bars.

Frowning, Rachel turned her back on the mirror. She didn't need to seek comfort in food anymore. She'd overcome that weakness a long time ago. It was in the past, and that's where it would stay.

Still, she wasn't looking forward to facing Quinn today. Maybe it was a good thing that they had company. At least that would spare her from having to scramble for more inane excuses for their behavior. How could she pretend that the kiss had been due to exhaustion or relief? Even as she'd said those words, she'd known there was a lot more to it than that...at least on her part.

On the other hand, it probably hadn't been the slightest bit complicated for Quinn. He certainly wasn't haunted by any unrequited teenage love for her. And while he appeared to appreciate her help with Charli, he'd feel the same kind of gratitude toward anyone. She shouldn't blow this incident out of proportion. They were two adults, brought together in circumstances that naturally led to a certain amount of familiarity. That kiss had been no more significant than...than the way he'd accidentally brushed her breast...or the way she'd stroked his chest with the washcloth...or any of the dozens of occasions when they'd come into physical contact over the past several days.

Then what was she afraid of?

That was an easy one to answer. She was afraid that if Quinn ever kissed her again, she wouldn't have the presence of mind to stop. She would end up making a fool of herself over him. Again.

Men's voices reached her as she descended the stairs. Taking a deep breath, she followed the sound to the kitchen.

Doug Keelor was sitting at the table, a cup of coffee in front of him. Quinn was seated across from him, but instead of holding a coffee cup, he was holding a baby bottle. Positioning Charli in the crook of his arm, he watched her latch on to the nipple, then looked at his father.

"Leona told me she didn't mind," Quinn said.

"She shouldn't. This house is as much yours as it is hers," Doug stated. "Why didn't you tell me about this before? I would have cut my trip short. Work must be backed up at the garage."

"It wasn't too busy, so I managed to stay on top of most of it, Dad." He moved his gaze to the doorway, looking directly at Rachel. "Besides, I had help."

Despite herself, Rachel felt a flush heat her cheeks when his gaze met hers. And that was stupid. This situation was only as awkward as she would let it be. Squaring her shoulders, she walked the rest of the way into the room. "Hello, Doug," she said.

Quinn's father looked up quickly, his mouth dropping open in shock. He glanced at Quinn and then back at Rachel. "Heck, I was only gone ten days and it's one surprise after another."

"Rachel's been helping me out with the kid," Quinn said, still holding her gaze. "I don't think my friends realized how little I know about babies when they asked me to baby-sit Charli. It's lucky for me that Rachel had some time to spare."

So he had decided to stick to his story with his father, Rachel realized. She nodded to let him know she understood. "Charli's such a sweetheart, I'm happy to help." She moved her gaze to the baby, who was sucking vigorously. "It looks as if her appetite is definitely returning."

"Yeah." Quinn adjusted the collar of the bottle to let the air bubble out more easily. "She's getting better as fast as she got sick, just like you said."

Doug chuckled. "You handle that bottle like an old pro, Son."

"Rachel's been teaching me," Quinn said.

"This is like old times." Doug drained his coffee cup and got up to help himself to more. "I remember how Rachel used to try to get Shakespeare through that thick skull of yours back when you were in high school." He winked at Rachel. "He never liked English."

"He preferred football," she said.

"That's my boy, always one to choose action over words."

Rachel felt her blush deepen. Yes, she knew that Quinn was a man of few words, but he could express himself quite well through his actions. Take that kiss, for example. He hadn't asked her permission, he hadn't discussed it, he had simply acted. "How was your trip, Doug?" she asked, hoping to change the subject.

He grinned. "Following the stock-car circuit was a real bus

driver's holiday. Taking time off from tinkering with cars to go and watch other guys tinker with cars. I guess I'm not happy unless I've got grease on my hands.''

Of course there was no trace of grease on Doug's thick, blunt-tipped fingers—he was as meticulous as his son when it came to cleaning up at the end of the day. Doug was well suited to his chosen line of business. On the occasions when Rachel had seen him work, he'd been reassuringly competent, approaching mechanical problems with the same kind of down-to-earth attitude that was a part of his nature.

By contrast, Quinn was much more...intense about everything he did. He was as knowledgeable a mechanic as his father, but he didn't share Doug's easygoing approach. Quinn tended to concentrate completely on whatever he was doing, directing all his energy toward accomplishing his goal.

That's how he kissed. Intense and focused, with an unmistakable purpose....

Couldn't she forget about that for two minutes? Rachel thought, impatient with herself.

Quinn set the bottle down and transferred Charli to his shoulder. Rachel seized the opportunity and went over to take the baby from his arms. "I'll finish her feeding, Quinn," she said. "You and your father probably have a lot to catch up on."

For a moment Quinn resisted. He didn't want Rachel to leave, not when she was blushing so sweetly, and her expressive eyes were mirroring her thoughts so clearly. As a matter of fact, he'd prefer it if his father left. There were things he wanted to say to Rachel in private.

Who was he kidding? He didn't want merely to *talk* to her. There were things he wanted to *do* with Rachel in private.

Quinn handed the baby over and watched Rachel leave the room, then shifted uncomfortably on his chair. His body didn't seem to care where they were or whether they had an audience. The awareness had been strong enough before, but now that he'd sampled the taste of her lips, now that he'd felt how perfectly her form molded to his...

"That Rachel Healey sure turned into one fine-looking woman, didn't she?" Doug commented, sliding his coffee cup on the table as he sat down. Wood creaked in protest as he tipped his chair back on two legs. "Who would have thought it?"

Quinn frowned, glancing at the doorway. He hoped Rachel was out of earshot. Apart from the night they'd found Charli, neither of them had made any reference to her old weight problem. "Yes, she's changed a lot over the years. We all have."

"I used to feel real sorry for her back then. None of the boys could see past her appearance to the good person she was inside. Except for you. You were always nice to her."

"Dad..."

"Bet you got a surprise when you saw how she turned out," he said, tilting his head to study his son.

"I didn't realize you and Rachel were so friendly."

Doug lifted his shoulders in a shrug. "I see her at church sometimes. She'll be having Leona's youngest in her kindergarten class next year."

"Rachel has always been good with kids."

"I remember the way she used to help out in the church nursery when she wasn't much more than a kid herself. A woman like that seems made for being a mother. Too bad she never married. You know she's single, right?"

"Dad, is there a point you're trying to make here?"

"She's here awful early in the morning. Is that her Renault out in the driveway?"

"The kid had the flu and Rachel stayed over to help me out."

"Uh-huh." He crossed his arms over his stomach. "It's all right, son. You don't have to make up stories on my account."

Quinn's frown deepened. "What?"

"It's high time you showed some interest in a woman."

"That's not what's going on, Dad."

"Then what's making her blush when you look at her? And how come she's got you moving around on your chair like your pants are too tight?"

It had been a long time since anyone had been able to make him feel self-conscious, Quinn thought ruefully. But even when he'd been a kid, his father had had a knack for cutting right through to the heart of the matter—Doug Keelor had always preferred straightforward to subtle. "She's here because of the baby," Quinn stated. "There isn't anything going on between the two of us."

"Why not?" Doug asked bluntly. "You've still got plenty of good years ahead of you. Louisa wouldn't have liked the way you've been keeping to yourself, Son."

"Leave Louisa out of this," Quinn said sharply.

Doug brought the front legs of his chair back down on the floor and regarded him in silence for a while, not even remotely intimidated by Quinn's tone. "When your mother passed away, I had days when I didn't see much point in getting out of bed in the mornings. We'd been together almost thirty years, and I felt as if there was a big hole in my life that I'd never be able to fill again. I'm not telling you to go out and replace Louisa, because that's not possible. But you're still young. You still have a lot of living left."

"Hell, Dad. It's only been fourteen months. You can't expect me to be considering jumping into something with another woman." He gestured roughly toward the cane that he'd propped against the counter. "Besides, I've had other things to deal with."

There was another silence, longer this time. "Sometimes when a customer brings in a car that's been bashed around, I can repair all the surface dents and dings without any trouble, but it's the damage inside that's the real problem. You can't ignore it, not if you want to get the car working again."

Quinn restrained a groan. Whenever his father wanted to

make a point, he spoke in car metaphors. "Dad, I'm not ready for the scrap pile yet."

"And sometimes," Doug went on, "once the damage is repaired, the owner is still unwilling to use the vehicle to its full potential. I try to tell them that sooner or later, they have to take the chance."

"Are you suggesting that I should take Rachel out for a test-drive?"

Doug drained his cup and set it down with a decisive bang. "Rachel? I thought I was talking about cars."

"Right."

Pushing to his feet, Doug clapped his hand on Quinn's shoulder. "Okay, I've done enough lazing around. I'd better get down to the garage and see for myself what damage you've done while I was gone."

A few minutes later, filled with a mixture of amusement and exasperation, Quinn closed the door behind his father and looked up toward the second story where he could hear Rachel moving around as she tended the baby. Doug might mean well with his less-than-subtle hints about damaged bodies and test-drives, but he was oversimplifying things. Quinn wasn't in any position to get involved with a woman, not as long as he was responsible for Charli.

But had that kiss last night really done any harm? He knew that he couldn't afford to let his emotions get mixed up in this situation. Emotions made a man weak. They clouded his judgment. They cost lives.

Yet it wasn't emotional involvement that he wanted with Rachel, was it? It was simple, basic sex. It was sating the appetite she stirred up. It was physical release, mindless escape...

His thoughts were interrupted by a sudden knock on the door. Quinn gritted his teeth and turned around. It was probably his father, coming back for another round of well-meant advice.

But when Quinn pulled open the door, it wasn't his father he saw, it was a ghost.

Quinn gripped the door frame for balance, not willing to believe what he was seeing. "No," he mouthed.

It was impossible. Yet the man was still there. He had the same pale blue eyes, the same beak of a nose, the same straight slash of a mouth....

"Do I have the right house?" the man asked. "I'm looking for Quinn Keelor."

Quinn reached out, grasping the man by the shoulders. This was no figment of his imagination. He could feel hard muscle and bone and warmth beneath the black shirt. As impossible as it was, Gus wasn't scattered across a Central American swamp. He was here. Alive.

The past crashed in on him without warning. Images that he'd tried to relegate to nightmares swirled through his head. For a moment he was back there in the smoke and the blood. "My God," Quinn whispered. "Larson?"

The man jerked. "Oh, hell, you must think I'm Gus."

"What...?" Quinn swallowed hard, his voice failing him. "How...?"

"Damn, I'm sorry." He gave a rueful smile. "I'm Erik Larson, Gustav's brother."

Quinn dropped his hands. "What?"

"I'm sorry," he repeated. "I thought you knew. Gus was my twin. You're Quinn, right?"

He nodded numbly.

"I was talking to Gino's mother last week, and she mentioned that you'd called her. I hadn't known where you'd gone after you left the hospital, and I've been wanting to talk to you about Gus—" He stepped forward, catching Quinn's elbow. "Hey, man, are you all right?"

No, God, no. He felt as if he'd just been kicked in the gut. He inhaled slowly, trying to regain control over his racing pulse, trying to concentrate past the adrenaline that surged through his system. He wasn't seeing a ghost; he wasn't seeing a miracle. Gus Larson was still dead, as dead as the rest of them.

Quinn forced himself to study the stranger in front of him. This man wasn't Gus. There were differences. His hair was the same pale blond, but it was much longer, pulled back into a ponytail. His nose had an extra bump in the center where it must have been broken at one time. And there was no recognition in those eyes....

Dropping his gaze, Quinn focused on where Gus Larson's brother still gripped his arm.

And that's when he noticed the gleam of a familiar silver ring.

Dusk had darkened the corners of the room when Rachel found Quinn in the study. At first she thought he was asleep. Slumped down on the leather couch, with his head resting on the back and his legs stretched out in front of him, he was completely motionless. But as she approached, she noticed the stiffness in his muscles and the tension in his face. His eyes gleamed in the dim light as he regarded her through half-closed lids.

He'd closeted himself here for hours after his visitor had left this afternoon. It was clear that seeing Erik Larson had upset him. This happened each time Quinn made contact with the families of his SEAL team.

And yet he kept putting himself through it over and over in his effort to learn who had entrusted him with Charli.

"How's the kid?" he asked, breaking the silence.

"Fine," she answered. "She settled down quickly."

"No fever?"

"Not a trace. She's doing well."

"Good."

"Did you have anything to eat? There's some leftover chicken and rice in the fridge."

"I'm okay."

Anyone could see that he wasn't okay at all. Concerned, Rachel moved closer. "Is something wrong?"

He made a short noise that was too bitter to be called laughter. "Wrong?"

"What happened?"

He sat forward then, clasping his hands between his knees. At the crinkle of paper, Rachel looked down and saw that he held a handwritten list.

"It's either Simms or Norlander," he said.

"What?"

"The ring we found with Charli. I've narrowed it down."

"That's good," she said carefully. "You're making progress."

"Yeah, progress," he muttered. He stabbed a finger at the lines he'd drawn across the page. "Ferrone's mother has his ring in what amounts to be a shrine to her dead son. Petrosky's parents put his in his coffin along with the parts of him the Navy was able to find. Hoffman's thirteen-year-old daughter wears her father's ring on a chain around her neck, and today I saw Larson's. So that leaves either Simms or Norlander."

The pain in his voice made her heart contract. What did she know about the horror he must have gone through when he'd lost his men? Each time he crossed off another name, he dredged up the grief once more. Sitting down beside him, she took the list from his hand. "Maybe you don't need to do this, Quinn."

"What?"

"Charli's mother still might come back on her own."

He shook his head. "I owe it to the team to try to help."

She knew from her past attempts to comfort him that he wouldn't welcome her sympathy. He preferred to keep his feelings about this inside, bottling them up in the same way he tried to bottle up all of his emotions.

But whether it was her business or not, whether it was smart or not, she couldn't leave him to go through this on his own. If he didn't want to talk about his feelings, then at least she could encourage him to talk about something else. She set the paper on the table beside her and moved her gaze to the ring he wore. With the tip of her finger, she traced the pattern of intertwining initials that were engraved in the silver. "These rings must have been very important to all of you. Are they valuable?"

He slipped the ring off and held it up in the fading light from the window. "The dollar value of the silver doesn't amount to much."

"What made you and your men decide to get them made? Does every SEAL team do that? Is it a tradition?"

"It's not a tradition. It was a reward."

"A reward?" she said encouragingly. "It sounds as if there's a story behind it."

"Yeah. We were on leave in this Mexican dot on the map and we decided to check out the local cantina. A guy had set up a table outside to sell cheap jewelry to the tourists." He studied the ring for a moment, then put it back on his finger. "We stopped him from being robbed, so he gave us the rings."

"That was a brave thing to do. No wonder the rings have such meaning for you."

He hesitated. "We weren't trying to be heroes."

"But you saved that jeweler."

"We were on our way out of the cantina when it happened," he said. "Gino never could hold his tequila. He stumbled into the jeweler's table and fell on top of a scrawny teenager who was holding a knife. Once the kid rolled Gino off and saw the rest of us, he dropped his knife and ran for it."

Rachel blinked. "Gino was drunk?"

Quinn shot her a sideways glance. "He never admitted it. But it took three of us to get him back on his feet."

She smiled. "He sounds like quite the character."

He looked at her in silence for a minute. Then he rubbed his hands over his face and leaned back against the couch. Yet his posture wasn't the same as when she'd arrived. This time, instead of being rigid with tension, his body gradually relaxed into the softness of the leather. "Yeah, Gino was a hothead, but we could always rely on him when the going got rough."

"What about Erik Larson's brother? What was he like?"

"Gus was cool as ice. He was our communications man."

"Communications? You mean he operated the radio?"

"We all had to know how to use the equipment, but he specialized." He paused. "Besides being able to jury-rig an antenna out of the foil from a ration pack, Larson had a talent for picking up languages. That came in handy."

"They must have been interesting individuals to know."

He rolled his head along the cushion to look at her. "They were the best. I know what you're doing."

"What?"

"You're trying to get me to talk about them. I already did the obligatory chats with the shrink before they let me out of the hospital. The Navy's pretty advanced these days when it comes to counseling."

"I'm not trying to be a professional counselor."

"Then what are you trying to be?"

This time she was the one who hesitated. She looked at the way he was leaning against the couch so close beside her. She looked at the way his eyes gleamed as he regarded her in the thickening dusk, and she was struck by an overwhelming need to offer him far more than comfort. Lifting her hand, she stroked a lock of hair back from his forehead. "I'm trying to be your friend, Quinn."

Moving with a swiftness that belied his relaxed pose, he caught her wrist. "My friend?"

She could feel her pulse beating hard against his hand where he held her. "I think you could use one."

"Why?"

She wasn't sure how to answer. "Because you're alone."

"Are you feeling sorry for me?" he asked, kicking the tip of his cane with his toe. It fell to the floor with a clatter. "Because I don't need anyone's pity."

"Quinn, I know all about pity. I got enough of it myself when I was growing up to know better than to offer it to anyone else." She gestured toward his injured leg with her free hand. "And you should know I would be the last person in the world to put any importance on someone else's physical condition. Have you forgotten what I used to look like?"

He gentled his hold, circling his fingers around her arm. "No, I haven't forgotten."

Oh, God. Had she really brought that up? Why would she want to remind him of her old appearance? She didn't even want to think about it herself. She started to pull away but he held her fast.

"I don't need your pity or your sympathy, Rachel."

"But I want to help you, Quinn."

"By getting me to talk about a bunch of dead men?"

"By listening to you talk about their lives. It's no good trying to bury your feelings or run away from a problem. It can wear away at you inside until it's out of control. I know. That's what I did."

"What do you mean?"

"Instead of dealing with the problems I had as a kid, I tried to avoid them. But the method of escape I used was food, and that only made things worse. It became part of the problem. I..." She shook her head. "Well, you know what happened."

"We're two different people, Rachel. I'm not running away from anything. I just don't want to talk about it."

"Then what do you want to do?"

He moved his hand to her elbow and tugged her sharply forward.

Startled, she braced her hands on his chest as she fell against him. "Quinn?"

"I want to kiss you again," he said, his gaze steady on hers. "That's what I want to do."

She knew she shouldn't. Hadn't she spent almost twenty-four hours going over the reasons why she shouldn't?

He slid his arms around her back and pulled her closer. "You said you wanted to help me."

She moistened her lips with the tip of her tongue. "Yes, but—"

"Then help me, Rachel," he murmured against her mouth. "Help me forget."

Chapter 8

Help me forget. She wished *she* could forget, Rachel thought as she felt the first touch of Quinn's lips. If only she could forget the lessons she'd learned, the decisions she'd made and the life she'd chosen to lead. She pulled her head back. "Quinn, I can't."

"Just a kiss, Rachel." He brushed his lips teasingly along the edge of her jaw. "Only a kiss. You can give me that much, can't you?"

She wanted to give him more than that. But what excuse could she use this time? She couldn't blame it on exhaustion or anxiety over Charli. Where could she run to escape these feelings?

But problems never got solved by running away, did they? That's what she'd just told Quinn, wasn't it? They kept building until they burst out of control, unless you faced them head-on.

Quinn moved his hands to her hair, combing his fingers through her curls in a slow, sensuous caress. He wrapped a strand around his finger and brought it to his lips, his eyes half closing in pleasure. "You used my shampoo. It smells different on you."

The intimacy of living here with him struck her all at once, sending a tremor of awareness along her skin. Her hands splayed across the front of his shirt.

The lines beside his mouth deepened. He released her hair and cupped the curve of her cheek. "You have a gentle touch, Rachel. Sometimes when I watch the way you touch Charli, I've wondered what it would feel like to have your hands on me."

"Quinn, I don't think—"

"Ah, that's the whole point of this," he said. "We're not going to think. We're going to kiss."

Under her palm she felt the strong, steady beat of his heart, and her own heart tripped in response. She inhaled unsteadily, striving for reason, but instead she caught the clean, masculine scent of his aftershave. "And that's all," she whispered. "Just this once."

He smiled. "Whatever."

Oh, *God,* Rachel thought helplessly, staring at his mouth. He was *smiling.* Not some sardonic quirk of his lips, or a grudging curl at the corner of his mouth. This was a full, open smile, just like the old Quinn's, like the smile of the boy she'd once loved. His teeth gleamed, his cheeks creased, and tiny lines appeared at the corners of his sparkling eyes.

Rachel could no more resist that than she could resist drawing her next breath. Closing her mind to the voices of reason that were clamoring in her head, she skimmed her hands to his shoulders and closed the distance she'd put between them.

His mouth settled over hers as tenderly as a sigh. It was like the last time, only better. Her lips remembered the texture of his, the firmness, the way they tasted of…Quinn. Her hands rose to his face, her fingertips tracing the hard edge of his jaw up to the surprising, vulnerable softness of the skin beneath his ear. And like his smile, it reminded her of the sensitive soul that was still there somewhere inside the hardened man.

Closing her eyes, she gave herself up to sensation. She didn't resist when she felt his tongue nudge coaxingly against her lips. And when he slipped inside, she welcomed the satisfaction that followed. This couldn't be wrong, could it? How could she have been so afraid of something that felt so natural? Her fingers slid around to his nape, urging him closer.

With a rumbling groan, Quinn shifted on the couch, twisting to lean against the arm as he brought Rachel down on top of him. Her hair fell like a living curtain across his cheek as he tilted his head to fit his mouth more securely to hers. And while her senses were spinning from the feeling of his taut body stretched out beneath hers, he slipped his hand between them and closed his fingers around her breast.

Pleasure shuddered through her. This felt natural, too, having him hold her like this. His touch wasn't possessive, or predatory, it was…right. Like an extension of their kiss. It was warm and sure and oh, so easy.

And she wanted it to go on forever.

But this was Quinn. *Quinn.* Her teenage fantasy, her first love, her weakness…. And the hard stranger who had buried a wife and six friends and only wanted to kiss her so he could forget.

Breathlessly she lifted her head.

Quinn was looking into her eyes, his gaze steady and direct. "One more."

"What?"

He squeezed her breast. "Kiss me again, Rachel. We're not finished."

Blood rushed to every sensitized nerve ending in her body. Her nipples hardened with desire. "Quinn…"

"I can feel what you want," he murmured, moving his thumb in a slow, teasing circle, sending tingles of delight racing outward. With his other hand he opened the buttons of her blouse and unfastened her bra. And just like that, he was cupping her bare breasts in his hands.

The swiftness of her response was staggering. Rachel had

never considered herself a passionate woman. She harbored no illusions about sex. But the desire that surged through her at Quinn's bold caress was like nothing she'd experienced before. She throbbed, actually throbbed with need. Quivering, she arched her back to press more fully into his hands.

"Beautiful," he whispered, his gaze dropping. "You're absolutely beautiful, Rachel." He took the weight of her breasts on his palms, rubbing his thumbs back and forth across the tips. And to her disbelief, her flesh swelled even more. He returned his gaze to her face. And he smiled again.

What else could she do? Leaning forward, Rachel gave him the kiss he'd asked for.

Quinn took what she offered, his hands moving reverently over her flesh as her lips moved sweetly over his. She was so generous, so giving, so primally female. It had been too long since he'd done this, but his body remembered. It was taut and hard and humming with impatience.

And it felt damn good. Too good to stop.

He eased her blouse off her shoulders and tossed it on the floor behind him. Her bra followed. Then Quinn twisted around, reversing their positions to come down on top of her. Sliding downward, he pressed his lips to the delicate skin at the base of her throat.

She trembled, her fingers digging into his back. A twinge of pain shot around his ribs and he sucked in his breath, but the scent of her skin make him forget the pain. More than that, it made him remember. Remember what it felt like to be truly alive.

Sex. That's what it was. The desire for it might have lain fallow for more than a year, but the basic human urge survived, along with all the other appetites.

He slid farther down, pressing his cheek to her breast, listening to her racing heart. He turned his head, his lips grazing her nipple, and he could feel the tiny jerk of her chest as he breath caught. She was so responsive, her body as eager as his for this pleasure they could give each other. Lifting himse on his elbows, he closed his mouth over the hardened bud and gave her another kind of kiss, one she hadn't asked for aloud.

"Oh, Quinn," she breathed, shifting restlessly beneath him. He smiled in satisfaction, tonguing her nipple against the roof of his mouth, then drew her in more deeply and sucked hard.

"Oh!"

It happened to Quinn without warning, too fast to avoid. Rachel arched upward, clutching his back, and the muscle that had merely twinged before went into a full-fledged spasm with a renewed viciousness that could no longer be ignored. He shifted to his side, holding himself motionless in the hope that it would subside.

Rachel smoothed her hand over his chest. "Quinn?"

Her cheeks were flushed, her lips swollen. Her hair was a tangled mass of dark curls that brushed sensuously over her naked skin. And as she looked at him, the desire on her face changed slowly to concern. Her fingers lifted to his cheek. "Quinn?"

He clenched his jaw, somehow managing to hold back the string of oaths that sprang to his tongue. "Sorry," he said through his teeth.

"What happened?" She sat up, her hand fluttering over his thigh. "Is it your leg? Did I hurt you?"

"It's not the goddamn leg."

"You're in pain."

"It's nothing. Just a muscle cramp. It'll go away."

"Where is it?" she asked, her forehead furrowing.

"Forget it, Rachel. It's some damaged muscles in my back, that's all."

"It's from that same accident, isn't it?" She placed her hand gingerly on his side, flicking her hair over her shoulder with a toss of her head that made her breasts sway.

But he knew she wasn't trying to be enticing, even though the lower part of his body still hadn't gotten the message.

"Would it help if I massaged it? Would that make you feel better?"

He bit back another curse and adjusted his jeans to ease the pressure. "Thanks, but that's one part of me that seems to be functioning just fine."

Her gaze flicked down to his groin, then back to his face, her eyes widening. "That's not what I meant. I was talking about massaging your back."

"No, it'll pass."

"Do you need some ice? Or a hot-water bottle? I don't know what you usually do—"

"Dammit, Rachel, I'm not that much of an invalid."

"I didn't mean to offend you," she said softly. "I only want to…help—" She hesitated. Her words echoed her previous offer, the one that had led to their kiss. She began to inch away.

"Damn," he muttered, taking her hand. He pressed her knuckles to his lips, frustrated beyond belief. "Don't you go anywhere. We were just getting started."

As if she were only now realizing that she was sitting in front of him half-naked, Rachel snatched her hand away and quickly crossed her arms. "Oh, no," she whispered.

"Rachel—"

"This shouldn't have happened. I never meant— We shouldn't have—oh, no."

Her attempt at modesty was not only too late, it was futile— her arms barely shielded her curves from his gaze. Again, she wasn't trying to be enticing, but she was. Damn. Gritting his teeth against the pain, he pushed himself up to sit beside her. "It was only a kiss, Rachel."

"We shouldn't have," she repeated.

"Why not?"

The question made her pause, but only briefly. She glanced around self-consciously. "Where did you put my…um…"

It was no use. The mood of moments ago was well and truly shattered. "On the floor beside the lamp," he said.

She stood up quickly and retrieved her clothes, keeping her back to him while she put them on. "I, um... I think I hear Charli."

"I don't."

"I'd better check."

"Rachel—"

"Good night, Quinn."

"Rachel!"

She left without looking back. And Quinn suspected that if the study hadn't been so small, she probably would have been running by the time she got to the door.

This wasn't the first time she'd run from him. He didn't want it to become a habit.

There really was an awful lot of laundry piled up from the past few days with Charli, Rachel thought as she stuffed another load into the washing machine. Yes, this was enough to keep her busy for the next hour at least. Then she'd have to sort everything, and fold it, and tuck it away in the dresser they were using for the baby's things. And then of course there were more diapers to buy. Amazing how many diapers a sick baby went through. And while Rachel was out, she'd have to remember to pick up another few cans of the powdered formula. And then she needed to stop by Emily's to drop off the list of prizes she'd talked the local businesses into donating for the family races at the Summer Festival. And she really could use a manicure....

Slamming the washing machine lid shut, Rachel pressed her fists to her eyes and groaned. This wasn't any good. Eventually the laundry would be done, her errands would be finished, and sooner or later, no matter how hard she tried to put it off, she was going to have to face Quinn.

What an idiot she'd made of herself last night. A complete fool. She'd only meant to comfort him. How had things gotten so completely out of hand?

Yet if they were adult enough to get into a situation like

that, then they were both adult enough to deal with it in a logical, rational fashion, right?

She sank down on a stool and put her head in her hands. Rational and logical were two things she hadn't been. God, what would her mother say if she knew how close Rachel had been to losing control over a man? All he'd needed to do was smile at her and she was all over him like some oversexed teenager.

Except she'd never been an oversexed teenager, had she? Her mother's constant lectures about the evil of men, as well as Rachel's weight problem and the low self-esteem that had been part of it had kept her from experiencing what amounted to a rite of passage for most girls. No, there hadn't been any groping, steamed-up evenings at the county drive-in for Rachel, no furtive tumbles on a sofa with the boy next door, no sneaking a boyfriend into the house where she was supposed to be baby-sitting....

She laughed ruefully. Well, maybe it was coming fifteen years too late. She'd just had a furtive tumble on a couch in the house where she was supposed to be baby-sitting, hadn't she?

No, she couldn't say it had been furtive. Quinn had been very straightforward about what he'd wanted. And to call it a tumble would be like calling a 7.9 earthquake a mild shake-up. And technically, they hadn't even done anything all that intimate...other than the way Quinn had used his tongue and his hands and his lips on her bare breasts.... Oh, God. Just thinking about what he'd done was enough to have her tighten with excitement.

It had never been like that for her before. The one and only time she'd taken a lover had been in her senior year at college. She'd been away from home, separated from her mother's influence long enough to realize there was nothing to stop her from satisfying her curiosity over what the fuss was all about. The experience had been disappointing and disillusioning. Worse, it had bordered on boring. She'd assumed it was due to her own inexperience or her lack of ability to feel passion. She'd been half-right. It had been due to her lack of ability to feel passion for the computer science major she'd chosen to be her partner.

Her attitude would have been far different if her first lover had been Quinn.

But that would have been impossible, Rachel thought. When she was in college, Quinn was already engaged to Louisa Gunnerson. As a matter of fact, the night Rachel had decided to take a lover was the very date of Quinn's wedding.

It hadn't been a coincidence. It had been a deliberate attempt to get him out of her heart once and for all.

Yet she hadn't succeeded, had she?

But it was only a fantasy she held in her heart, wasn't it? A memory of the teenager she'd adored. She hadn't really known him back then, and she didn't know him now. He was now scarred and distant, not a boy but a man. A virtual stranger.

A stranger who bought plastic butterflies for an abandoned baby, who could smile with the openness of a seventeen-year-old, who evoked responses from her body as no one else ever had.

"No," she whispered, shaking her head. "God, no."

"Good morning, Rachel."

Quinn's voice rolled over her in a wave of warmth. She looked up to see him leaning against the door frame, his hair damp and slicked back from his face, his cheeks taut from a fresh shave. His arms were bared by a sleeveless olive-drab T-shirt, and his legs were hugged by faded denim.

He looked different today, she realized. Oh, she'd seen him freshly shaved and showered before, and she'd seen him in those clothes before, too, but this morning there was something different in the set of his shoulders and in the way he held his head. He was more…at ease. Not relaxed by any means—his gaze still had that intense edge to it—yet now he seemed more…approachable.

Was it because of her, because of what they'd done? Had their kisses helped to drive the haunted expression from his eyes?

Despite the utilitarian surroundings of the laundry room, despite the heap of soiled baby clothes at her feet and the tedious *shush-whump* of the washing machine, Rachel felt her pulse thump and her breath catch and desire tingle through her veins.

Stupid. Pathetic. Hadn't she learned *anything?* Next thing she knew, she'd probably start gorging herself on chocolate bars.

"I've got to pick up some more diapers," he said. "Can you think of anything else we need while I'm out?"

Yes. Fudge brownies. Cherry cheesecake. Jelly doughnuts with an inch of powdered sugar. Or maybe some greasy fried chicken and a big order of fries and gravy. Rachel frowned and got to her feet. "I have a list in the kitchen. I'll get it."

She reached the doorway and paused, waiting for him to move out of her way. But he didn't. Instead, he put his hands on either side of her waist, pulled her forward and kissed her.

Helplessly she melted against him. There was no other word for it. Everywhere they touched, she felt the heat they generated molding her body to his. Her lips parted, drinking in the familiar taste of him. His tongue dipped inside to stroke along hers in a brief, slick suggestion of mating. Then he nipped gently at her lower lip and pulled back his head.

She cleared her throat. "You shouldn't have done that."

"Why not?"

That's how he'd responded last night. And just like the last time, she didn't have an answer she could give him. What could she say? That they shouldn't kiss because it made her feel seventeen and painfully, pathetically in love again? She shook her head. "Quinn, what we did was a mistake."

He studied her, his gaze far too penetrating, as always. Finally he slid his arm around her shoulders and steered her through the kitchen toward the back door. "Come outside with me."

"But Charli—"

"The windows are open, so we'll be able to hear when she wakes up."

"But—"

"Rachel, we need to talk."

He was right. Avoiding a problem was no way to solve it. They were adults. They could deal with this. She let him lead her to the cool green shade of the backyard. When he tugged her to sit down beside him on a wooden bench near a bed of petunias, she drew up her knee under her skirt and turned to face him.

Before she could say anything, he leaned forward and brushed a lock of hair back from her face, his fingertips a whispering caress across her cheek. "Rachel, I'm not going to apologize for what happened between us."

"I hadn't expected you to."

"Good."

"But it can't happen again, Quinn. I'm not looking for a serious relationship."

"Neither am I."

The swiftness of his agreement startled her. She withdrew from his touch and squeezed farther into the corner of the bench. "Well, that's good. You see, I like my life the way it is. My career and my independence are what matter most to me."

"I can understand that."

"I'm glad. Because we both know our association is only temporary."

"That's right."

Did he have to agree so readily? Only a matter of hours ago she'd been writhing in his arms. Only a matter of minutes ago he'd given her a good-morning kiss that had melted her knees. Couldn't he have seemed a little more disappointed at the prospect of not repeating their embrace?

This was stupid, she told herself. She should be thankful that he was giving up so easily. Because it was getting more and more difficult to concentrate on all the reasons why she had to continue resisting the pull she felt toward him.

"Are you seeing anyone else?" Quinn asked.

"What?"

"I remember that you told me you live alone, but I was asking whether you're dating anyone."

"No, I don't date."

He stretched his arm along the back of the bench, his hand resting casually on her shoulder. "Good. Tell me something, Rachel. Last night in the study, did I do anything that you didn't like?"

The question took her off guard. She could feel heat rise in her cheeks. "I can't see much purpose discussing this since we're not going to repeat it."

"Who says we're not?"

"I thought that was the point of this conversation."

He moved closer, his thigh nudging her knee. "No, Rachel, that's not the point I'm trying to make at all."

"But…"

"The way I see it, we're both unattached adults. And we've got some serious chemistry going on between us."

"Chemistry?" she repeated.

"Uh-huh." He trailed his fingertips along the curve of her neck, then toyed with the top button of her blouse. "I liked what we did. As a matter of fact, I enjoyed it very much. Didn't you enjoy it, Rachel?"

She inhaled sharply as his knuckles brushed the bare skin at the base of her throat. It would be so much easier if she could lie, she thought as she shook her head. "Whether I liked it or not isn't important."

"It's important to me."

"Quinn, I like my life just the way it is. That's why this…thing between us can't go on."

He studied her in silence for a moment. "I don't want to

change your life, Rachel. I'm not in the market for another marriage or any kind of long-term commitment. I want to take you to bed, that's all.''

Amid the ordinary backyard sounds of rustling leaves and chirping birds, Quinn's bold words seemed all the more jarring.

I want to take you to bed. As if that *wouldn't* change her life. As if it wouldn't be the fulfillment of every fantasy she'd ever had of a lover. There it was. Out in the open. The words she would have given anything to hear back when she'd loved him.

But she hadn't loved him. She'd loved the ideal he'd represented. And she didn't love him now, no matter how drawn to him she was. Because he wasn't talking about love. He was talking about sex.

If she'd needed any more reminders that Quinn was no longer the boy she'd adored, this was it. Because the old Quinn never would have been so...crass. The old Quinn had treated Louisa with the kind of love and respect that had bordered on chivalrous. Seeing it had fed Rachel's lonely fantasies of someday being loved like that....

But that was just it, wasn't it? Quinn had loved Louisa. And Rachel wasn't Louisa.

He put his hand on her knee, his long fingers splaying over the top of her thigh. And through the folds of her flowered cotton skirt, the heavy warmth of his touch sent awareness zinging across her skin. He'd said he wanted to kiss her to help him forget. Was that also why he wanted to make love? To forget? To satisfy his body while his heart still belonged to his dead wife?

And God help her, on some level Rachel didn't care why Quinn wanted her as long as he did.

Where was her pride? Where was the self-esteem she'd fought so hard to gain? If this was what happened when she'd merely kissed him, how much further back would she slip into her old insecurities if they actually made love?

But it wouldn't be love. It would be nothing but lust.

Flicking his hand off her knee, she rose to her feet. "I said I would be your friend, Quinn. That's all."

"Rachel—"

"Although your invitation is hard to resist," she bit out, "I'm afraid I can't accept."

"Invitation?"

"Taking me to bed, as you so gallantly put it."

He stared at her. "You're angry."

"Not only is he gallant, he's perceptive," she snapped, stalking back into the house.

Quinn was on his feet and following her before the door could close behind her. "I was being honest," he said.

"Honest," she muttered. "What do you think I am? Some kind of easy—" she struggled for a word "—there's no polite term for it, is there?"

"There's nothing wrong with two unattached adults enjoying a physical relationship," Quinn said. "It's a natural part of life."

"Yes, but did you have to be so blunt about it?"

"Would you have preferred it if I lied?"

"No, of course not."

"Because if you want the dinner and movie first—"

"God, Quinn. You're making it worse." She strode back to the laundry room and dumped the first load of clean clothes out of the dryer and into a basket. "I can't believe this technique worked on all the other women you've slept with."

"What are you talking about?"

"You claimed that you weren't in the habit of forgetting any of them, or wasn't that true?"

"Look, I was pissed off when I said that. I already apologized for thinking Charli was your kid and you were trying to pass her off as mine."

"Well, excuse me for not jumping at the chance to be another name on your list."

"What list?"

She brushed past him and headed for the hall with the laundry basket. "Of women."

"Woman."

"What?"

"There's only been one."

That stopped her. Clenching her hands on the handles of the basket, she turned around.

"Only my wife," Quinn went on. "Only Louisa."

No. She didn't want to hear this. She didn't want to see that flash of vulnerability on his face as he said his dead wife's name. She didn't want to see him as faithful or chivalrous or in mourning for the love of his life. She wanted to hang on to her righteous indignation over his crude invitation to have sex.

He raised his hand to rub the back of his neck. "Damn, I didn't mean to offend you, Rachel. I just wanted to get things straight between us."

"Well, you've succeeded. I got your message loud and clear. As far as I'm concerned, the subject's closed."

His gaze locked with hers, pinning her in place. "Is it?" he asked quietly.

She swallowed hard. But she was saved from having to answer—from having to lie—when the telephone began to ring. Seconds later an angry wail echoed from upstairs.

Without another word Rachel turned and fled.

Swearing to himself, Quinn watched her go. Again. This was getting to be a pattern. He strode across the floor and grabbed the phone. "Yeah?" he answered gruffly.

"Hello? I'm looking for Quinn Keelor."

He didn't recognize the man's voice, but the slow, west Texas drawl was somehow familiar. "You found him."

"Mr. Keelor, I heard you've been trying to contact me. I'm Milt Simms."

At the sound of the name, Quinn braced himself for the surge of guilt, waiting for the edge of the nightmare to strike him the same way it had the other four times.

But instead of seeing Jake Simms's smoldering body, Quinn saw an image of Jake as he'd shared his rations with a half-starved dog that had strayed into camp one time. Jake with his brown eyes unwavering behind his wire-framed glasses as he told one of his long-winded down-home stories while he calmly stitched up a ten-inch gash in Hoffman's forearm. And Quinn realized he was seeing Simms as he'd lived, not as he'd died.

And the wave of pain wasn't as strong this time.

Was it because he was getting accustomed to it? Or was it because of the way he'd been able to lose his pain in Rachel's kiss?

He closed his eyes and leaned his forehead against the wall. No. He knew what he wanted Rachel for, and it didn't have anything to do with his emotions. It couldn't. He wouldn't let it.

Chapter 9

"It's Norlander's," Quinn said to Rachel, turning the ring around so that he could rub the engraving with his thumb. "All the other rings are accounted for."

"Is that what the phone call was about?"

"Yeah. It was Jake Simms's cousin."

"So it has to be Norlander's ring."

"Right."

Charli wriggled on the changing table, fretting restlessly. Rachel fastened the diaper and lifted the baby to her shoulder.

"What's wrong with her?" Quinn asked. "Is she having a relapse?"

"No, I don't think so. She's just a little fussy today," Rachel said, rubbing Charli's back. She forced down a twinge of guilt. She knew what the problem was. Charli was a sensitive child, and as she'd done before, she was picking up on the tension around her.

And as far as tension went, there was enough around to make anyone restless.

Quinn shoved his hands into his pockets and leaned against

the bedroom door. "Norlander's ring would have gone to his widow. I figure she's probably Charli's mother."

"His widow?"

"Darlene Norlander. They'd been married for about a year."

"But that would mean..." Rachel hesitated. "The baby would have been conceived less than two months after her husband's death."

"That's right." He looked at her. "It's not impossible. Appetites recover, whether we want them to or not."

Rachel knew which appetite he was talking about. There was no apology in his eyes, no shame. Only a simple, honest awareness that he refused to hide.

And despite herself, Rachel felt her body respond.

No, she thought, clenching her jaw angrily at her lack of control. She wasn't going to let it happen again. She had told him the subject was closed, and that's how it would stay.

Charli bumped her head against Rachel's neck and cried wearily. Rachel swayed back and forth in an effort to soothe her. "If Darlene Norlander is Charli's mother, then who do you think the father is?"

"I have no idea. In the note Darlene said he was gone."

"That could mean anything. He could have walked out on her, or he could have died, or he could already have been married."

"Whoever he is, he's out of the picture." He frowned. "Unless he's the one she's running from."

She tried to remember the exact wording of that cryptic note. "She didn't give that impression."

"No, she didn't. But I won't rule it out."

"What was Norlander's wife like?" she asked.

"I didn't know Darlene very well," Quinn said. "That last year I was too busy with Louisa to socialize much when I was on leave."

Of course, she thought. Louisa's illness would have taken up all of Quinn's time. There had been the chemotherapy and then the search for a bone marrow donor. He must have gone through hell…

No. She was not going to let herself feel sympathy for him, either. "Would you recognize Darlene's voice?"

"I can't say for sure whether or not it was her voice on the phone that morning in the garage. It could have been."

"But do you think she would have abandoned her child?"

"Given the right circumstances, people are capable of just about anything."

She couldn't disagree with that. The last twenty-four hours had proven to Rachel that even she was capable of acting irrationally.

"It's not too much of a stretch that she would have come to me," Quinn continued. "She might only have been married to John for a year, but she would have known how tight everyone on the team was."

"What are you going to do now?"

"Concentrate on finding Darlene," he stated. "If she's not Charli's mother, then she'd know who is. And once I get some answers, I can get on with solving her problem."

Rachel's hold on the baby tightened. "What if you can't help her? What if the situation isn't something you can resolve?"

"For the sake of my team, I'll find a way."

There was a note of steel in his voice. It was the same determination she heard every time he spoke of his men. His loyalty was admirable. But then, Quinn was a loyal man. He'd been loyal to Louisa all his life.

Yes, he'd loved his wife. He'd supported his men. He had taken responsibility for Charli. But there was nothing noble or admirable about the nonchalant way he wanted to have sex with Rachel.

Her anger stirred once more, and she welcomed it. She didn't want to admire him. She didn't want to sympathize with him. And she didn't want to fantasize. Her mother was right. No good could come of getting close to any man. "And once you settle Darlene's problems," she said, "you'll give Charli back to her."

"That's the general idea."

Right, she thought. His involvement with Charli was temporary, just like the involvement he wanted with Rachel. He had no intention of getting attached to either one of them.

And that was the only smart way to handle this situation. Rachel would be a fool if she did any different.

"Here," she said, thrusting Charli toward him.

Automatically he withdrew his hands from his pockets and took the baby. "What are you going to do?"

She squeezed past him to the hall and headed for her room. "Pack my things."

He followed. "Why?"

"I agreed to stay until Charli was over the flu," she said, taking her bag from her closet and placing it on the bed. "She was over it yesterday."

"What if it comes back?"

She hesitated, then grabbed her nightgown, rolled it up and stuffed it in her bag. "Call Rob Townsend. I'll leave the number by the phone."

He was silent while she gathered the rest of her belongings. Charli whimpered, and Quinn put his hand on the baby's back, rubbing gently. "Is this because I kissed you?"

"You've learned enough about taking care of babies to manage on your own," she said, not answering him directly. "It's time for me to go."

"Because if you're worried that I'm going to jump you or something, don't be. When we make love, it's going to be mutual, the same way that kiss was mutual."

She kept her gaze down, her fingers tightening on the edges of her bag. *When* we make love, she thought. Not *if.* "Quinn, I told you already. That subject is closed."

"Rachel..."

"For Charli's sake, I'm going to try to forget you said anything."

His silence lasted longer this time. For a minute the only sound in the room was the baby's restless whimpering. When Quinn spoke again, his voice had cooled. "Will you still be coming over when I have to go in to the garage?"

She nodded curtly. "Let me know your schedule, and I'll do my best."

"All right. Thanks."

Zipping up the bag, she turned to face him.

And immediately wished she hadn't. He was standing less than a step away, one knee bent as he kept his weight on his good leg. The lean muscles of his arms, bared by his sleeveless T-shirt, flexed tautly as he shifted Charli from one shoulder to the other, his long fingers splaying protectively over the infant's back.

A sudden stab of longing took Rachel unawares, but it wasn't just for Quinn. It was a longing for both the man and the baby. And her arms felt so...empty. She clutched her bag to her chest. "Quinn, if you think you need me..."

Something flashed in his gaze. For a moment he seemed to sway toward her. But then his expression closed and he stepped aside. "No, Rachel," he said. "I don't."

"If you put any more torque on that bolt, you're going to snap off the head, Son."

Quinn glanced at his father across the width of the car. "I know what I'm doing, Dad."

"Uh-huh." Doug lifted a soda can to his lips and took a long swallow, then wiped his forehead with the back of his hand. "Weather getting to you?"

"It's not too bad."

"The humidity's always harder to take than the heat, isn't it? Can make a man edgy."

Quinn turned his attention back to the carburetor he was installing. "Is there a point you're trying to make here?"

"Just talking about the weather," Doug said, draining the soda. He tossed the empty can into the trash and shoved his hands into the pockets of his coveralls. "You know, sometimes when a customer brings a car in with a bad rattle, it's hard to pinpoint the problem. You try checking all the obvious sources, and then tighten everything else up, but there's still a rattle."

"Mrs. Budge's car wasn't rattling. It needed a new carburetor. I'm putting one in."

"Uh-huh. It's usually the stuff you don't want to look at," Doug continued. "Places that are too hard to get to, like the gear cable. Remember how long it took to replace the sleeve on that old Chrysler we had in here last week?"

"Gear cables don't rattle," Quinn pointed out.

"It was just an example."

"Of a rattle?"

"Of problems we don't like looking for."

Metal scraped on metal as Quinn fitted the wrench back in place. He gave the bolt one last, vicious twist. The head snapped off, bounced against the engine block and pinged to the floor. Swearing under his breath, Quinn ducked out from underneath the hood and straightened up.

"That's the third time that happened to you this week," Doug commented, shaking his head. "Must have been a whole box full of faulty bolts."

The wrench clattered onto the bench as Quinn snatched up a rag to wipe his hands. "Yeah, must be."

"Or maybe there's something wrong with that wrench."

He snorted. "Right."

"Want a soda? You look like you could use some cooling off."

Quinn nodded, then went over to the sink in the corner and splashed water on his face. The cold water felt so good that he ducked his head under the faucet. But Quinn knew it wasn't just the July weather that was bothering him.

It had been a long, frustrating week. His search for Darlene Norlander was getting nowhere. In the year since the accident, she had moved around constantly, not staying in any one place for more than a few weeks. Every time he thought he had a lead, it turned into another dead end. It was like trying to track down a ghost.

He'd done all he could do from here. He'd used every resource he could think of. He'd even contacted the families of his team once more, hoping that they might have kept in touch with Norlander's widow. Gino's mother had tried, and her tip had led to the best source of information so far, a landlady in Duluth who had rented a room to Darlene in March. Quinn had called the woman yesterday. He hadn't learned where Darlene had gone, but he had learned that she had definitely been pregnant.

There was no longer any doubt in Quinn's mind that Darlene was Charli's mother. And judging by her pattern of keeping herself on the move, she was obviously on the run. That fitted in with the panicked tone of the note she'd left with the baby.

But why was she running? And where was she now?

"You coming up for air anytime soon?"

At his father's voice, Quinn shut off the water and grabbed a towel. "Sorry about that bolt, Dad," he said, wiping his face. "I'll bore it out."

Doug handed him a soft drink. "It's getting late. You might as well let me finish the job."

Quinn raked his wet hair off his forehead and popped the top on the can. "It's my problem. I'll fix it."

"Sometimes even the best mechanic needs to ask for help."

His father was warming up for another one of his convoluted car metaphors. Quinn knew he meant well, but there was no way Quinn was going to involve him in this business with Charli. Rachel was the only one he trusted.

He hesitated, then tipped the can to his lips. Yes, he trusted Rachel. He hadn't really had any other choice, since she'd been there when all of this had started. "Thanks, Dad. I'll keep that in mind."

Doug placed his hand on Quinn's arm. "Son, why don't you go home?"

"There's too much work—"

"And you're making more. It's Saturday night. You've got a woman waiting for you at home. What are you hanging around here for?"

"Rachel isn't waiting for me. She's baby-sitting."

"You think my brains are addled from inhaling gasoline fumes or something? You might think the rest of the town swallows that story, but don't expect me to."

"It's the truth. Rachel comes over to help me with Charli, that's all."

"Ah," Doug said slowly. "So that's why you've been snapping heads off bolts all week."

Leave it to his father to point out the obvious. There was a lot more to Quinn's state of frustration this week than the dead ends he'd hit with his search for Darlene.

Since she'd moved back to her apartment, Rachel had been scrupulous about keeping her distance from him. She made sure to arrive just before he left and leave the moment he returned. The kid hadn't had a relapse of the flu. As a matter of fact, ever since she had recovered, Charli had dropped her 2:00 a.m. feeding and had regularly been sleeping through the night. There had been no reason for Rachel to stay. There were no more lessons in child care, no more intimate conversations at dusk, no more smiles or touches.

Damn, he hadn't realized how much he'd miss her. He'd grown accustomed to hearing her around the house, humming a lullaby or laughing at the baby's antics. Or looking at him with those expressive hazel eyes, urging him to share his pain.

"None of my business," Doug said, giving Quinn's arm a squeeze before he dropped his hand. "But whatever's going on between you two, it's good to see you taking an interest in something again."

"What do you mean?"

"I know you were looking for peace and quiet when you

came home. So did Leona. That's why she didn't change her plans about that sabbatical in France. She figured you needed some time on your own.'' He tucked his hands back into his pockets. ''I think we were wrong. Meeting up with Rachel again and taking in that baby were probably the best things that could have happened.''

Quinn frowned. His father didn't know the whole story. Rachel and Charli were merely means to an end for him. Charli was the key to atoning for his failure to help his team. And Rachel was…

Rachel was making him feel alive. Maybe Doug wasn't completely wrong after all. Even the frustration was better than nothing.

The house was quiet when Quinn let himself in the front door. He paused on the threshold. Rachel hadn't said anything about taking Charli out this evening. Lately she was practically waiting by the door for him so that she could leave as quickly as possible. Had something happened?

He eased the door shut behind him and looked around, a twinge of foreboding tightening his stomach. He'd been as discreet as possible while he'd been trying to trace Darlene this week. Had he tipped off whoever she was running from? Had the trouble she was in rebounded here?

A low laugh drifted down from somewhere upstairs, followed by the sound of splashing water.

Quinn blew out his breath and moved toward the staircase. From the sound of things, Rachel was giving the kid a bath. She wouldn't have heard him come in.

''It feels good, doesn't it, sweetie?'' Rachel said, a smile in her voice. ''You're still a bit too young for a shower, but this is the next best thing.''

There was more splashing, then the sound of Charli's delighted gurgle.

''Want some more?'' Rachel murmured. ''Okay, here goes.''

Quinn reached the second floor landing, but before he could call out a greeting, Rachel spoke again.

"Next time, we should try out the big tub. What do you think about that? It would be almost as good as a swimming pool."

What was it about Rachel and tubs, Quinn thought? It was one of his frequent fantasies, Rachel in the water, her skin slick, tendrils of hair teasing her cheeks and her nape as the steam swirled around her.

"Oh, you like it when I pour water on your tummy, don't you?"

Charli made a cooing noise and Rachel laughed again. "Go ahead and splash, sweetie," she said. "It's so hot, you're doing me a favor."

It was good to hear Rachel laugh, Quinn thought, stopping in the bathroom doorway. He knew that as soon as she saw him, she'd probably clam up as she'd done all week, so he remained silent, leaning one shoulder against the door frame as he watched her with the baby.

She had fastened her hair back into a ponytail today, but some strands had pulled loose, curling damply down the side of her neck. In the mirror over the counter, he could see that her full lips were curved into a soft smile and her eyes were glowing with humor as she cupped water in her hand and let it dribble out in a slow stream. And as her hand lowered, he saw that the front of her coral-pink T-shirt was soaking wet and clinging to her curves like a second skin.

Quinn's gut tightened, but it wasn't from worry this time. He knew he should look away. He was only tormenting himself. The last time she'd soaked her shirt that way, it had been difficult enough for him to keep his distance. But now that he'd felt her, tasted her...

There was just something about Rachel's breasts. He'd never been overly concerned about that part of the female anatomy before, but with Rachel, it was different. They were so generous, so...ripe. So female. He could easily imagine himself spending the night with his head pillowed there. Or seeing them swell with the purpose they were meant for as she held a baby of her own.

He must have made some noise. In the next instant, Rachel's gaze met his in the mirror and she gasped.

"Quinn!"

"Hello, Rachel."

"What are you doing here?"

"I live here."

"No, I mean why are you here so early? I wasn't expecting you to come home for another hour."

"My dad kicked me out." He nodded toward the baby. "Do you want me to take over?"

"No, I'll finish. We're almost done."

"Want some help?"

Charli grinned and kicked her feet, scattering more water droplets in a glittering arc. Rachel glanced down, then quickly looked at Quinn, her cheeks flushing. She had obviously noticed the state of her clothes.

"Don't worry," he said, crossing his ankles as he settled more comfortably in the doorway. "I've seen them before."

She frowned. "Quinn..."

"With and without clothes."

"Would you mind leaving?"

"As a matter of fact, I would. I find that I'm enjoying the view too much."

Pressing her lips together, she lifted Charli out of the water and wrapped her in a towel. She patted the baby dry, put a diaper on her and handed her to Quinn. "Fine," she said. "If you're not leaving, I will."

Charli wriggled in Quinn's grasp, waving her fists as she grinned at him. He tucked her in the crook of his arm. "Where were you planning on going?"

"I have some things to pick up," she replied tersely.

"Like that?"

"Like what?"

He nodded his chin toward Rachel's wet shirt. Against the soaked cotton, her nipples pushed outward in defiant little buds. "Unless fashions in Maple Ridge have changed since I've been gone, you're liable to cause a riot."

She quickly grasped the fabric in her hand and held it away from her breasts. "This isn't funny."

He smiled. "I'm not thinking of laughing. I'm thinking of doing something else entirely."

"Quinn, I thought I made myself clear about this."

"Sure, you did. I did, too. We just didn't agree, remember?"

Water trickled down her wrist and dripped to the floor. She let go of her shirt and crossed her arms. But just like before, the gesture didn't hide much. She tightened her jaw. "Could you lend me something to wear? I'll bring it back tomorrow."

"Sure. Here, hang on to the kid for a minute," he said, handing Charli back to her.

"But I'm all wet."

"It's hot. I don't think the kid will mind what that water does for you any more than I do."

She hesitated, then uncrossed her arms and took the baby.

Quinn reached for the buttons on his shirt.

Her eyes widened. "What are you doing?"

"Giving you something to wear," he said, unfastening the buttons.

"But…I meant something you're not already using."

He enjoyed seeing her flustered like this. He'd only meant to tease her, but then he felt her gaze on his bare chest, and his pulse thudded hard. He wanted to see the spark of desire come into her eyes as she looked at him the same way he was looking at her. He wanted to give her this shirt that still bore the warmth and the scent of his body and know that it was touching her naked flesh. He wanted to be the one to shelter her and protect her.

No, dammit. He wanted to sleep with her, that's all. His smile fading, he stripped off his shirt and held it out.

After a moment of silence, she took the garment he offered. Her fingers brushed his, and her hand trembled from the contact. "Thank you," she murmured.

"Anytime."

She stood motionless, her gaze moving over him like a slow caress. Her eyes darkened and her lips parted, but she made no sound.

This wasn't a good idea, Quinn realized, feeling his breathing quicken. His shirt dangled from her hand, the baby bumped against her shoulder, and Quinn could still see the luscious outline of her breasts. What if he carried the baby to her crib, then took Rachel to his room and peeled her wet clothes off her body and eased her down on the bed and...

"Oh, God," she breathed.

For a moment he wondered whether she'd somehow guessed what he was thinking. But then he saw that her gaze was riveted to his side. And it wasn't desire that darkened her eyes now, it was shock.

She dropped his shirt and extended her arm, her fingertips barely grazing his skin. "I hadn't realized..."

He stiffened. He knew what she saw. How could he have forgotten about those scars? How could he have bared himself to her sight like this?

"Oh, God," she repeated. "No wonder I hurt you."

"It looks worse than it feels."

She traced the edge of the skin graft in a featherlight touch. "How..."

"Shrapnel. Mostly burns. My leg was busted up too bad for me to move away."

Her lower lip quivered. She drew it between her teeth and stepped closer, skimming her hand around her ribs to his back.

His hands curled into fists. He didn't want her to feel sorry for him. He didn't deserve anyone's pity.

And that wasn't the place on his body where he wanted her to put her hand.

But it felt good. Better than he would have guessed. Gentle. Healing.

"It must have been horrible," she whispered.

Memories stirred. Flames. Smoke. Noise. Pain. "I survived."

Rachel's fingers smoothed over the lumpy tissue as she lifted her gaze to his. There was no repulsion or pity in her expression. Instead, he saw compassion. Caring.

And slowly the memories faded.

"You've been through so much," she said softly. "And you've done it alone. I wish I could—"

Her words were cut off by a sudden pounding on the front door. At the noise, Charli tensed and let out a wail. But Rachel didn't move away. She jiggled the baby against her shoulder and shifted her hand to Quinn's arm. "Thank you for your shirt, Quinn."

He stepped back, retreating from her touch. "I'd better see who that is."

Rachel's vision blurred as she watched him move away. She swallowed hard, her heart crying out at the evidence of what he must have endured. Just when she'd thought she had steeled herself against him, just when she'd believed she was getting her feelings under control, she was right back where she'd started.

He'd taken her by surprise, that's all, she thought as she squatted down to retrieve his shirt. She hadn't been prepared for the way he had so openly acknowledged the sexual attraction between them. And she certainly hadn't been prepared for the sight of his body.

God, she must be twisted. Those scars hadn't repulsed her. On the contrary, they were as much a part of who he was as the sleek muscles that bulged in his arms or the blond hair that kept falling over his forehead or the rare, precious smiles she looked forward to seeing.

And despite an entire week of keeping her distance, she

wanted to take him into her arms and give him whatever he asked for, whatever he needed.

Straightening up, she shook her head. What she needed was dry clothes. She carried Charli to her room and set her down in her crib, then listened to make sure Quinn was still downstairs. Quickly she stripped off her wet T-shirt and bra and shrugged on Quinn's shirt.

The washed-soft chambray was still warm, and it smelled like soap and fresh air and Quinn. She pressed the collar to her cheek, indulging herself for a moment as she inhaled his essence. The cotton brushed her skin like an echo of Quinn's touch, and her nipples hardened.

Rachel exhaled hard and started on the buttons. Definitely time to go. Quinn could give Charli her bedtime bottle. The faster Rachel got out of this house, the better. She had things to do, people to call, a life to lead. A full life, a happy life....
The inside of her wrist brushed Quinn's shirt against her breast as she fastened another button. And she shook with a sudden desire to feel Quinn's hand there instead.

Frowning, she wound up Charli's rabbit music box and gave the butterfly mobile a spin to keep the baby occupied for a few minutes, then rolled her wet clothes into a ball and went downstairs.

Quinn was at the open door, talking to a man who was standing on the porch. As Rachel drew closer, she realized the man was wearing a uniform. She glanced outside and saw the rack of a light bar glinting from the top of a police car.

Her steps faltered. Why would the police be here? Unless someone had finally become suspicious about Charli and had alerted the authorities. She paused, glancing behind her. No, they couldn't take her away now. Not yet. Please.

Quinn nodded at something the officer said, then stepped back and closed the door. He pressed his palm against the wooden panel for a moment, then took a deep breath and turned around. The teasing smile he'd had earlier was gone. So was the wary watchfulness that had tensed his features when he'd revealed his scars. His expression was carefully blank, his feelings hidden behind what Rachel had come to think of as his warrior face.

He was withdrawing into himself, as if he were preparing for a mission. He was once more the distant stranger.

"What did he want?" Rachel asked. "Was it about Charli?"

"It's Darlene."

"What happened?"

"She's in Buffalo."

"And she wants Charli back? Just like that? After abandoning her without any thought to her welfare, she just sends the police to you and—"

"Rachel," he said. "Darlene's been in a car accident. She's in a hospital in intensive care and she asked her doctor to notify me. He sent the police."

She lifted her hand to her mouth. "Oh, no. Is she going to be all right?"

"They won't speculate," he said flatly. "She's in serious condition."

"What are you going to do?"

"I have no choice. I have to go to her."

"When?"

"Now. Tonight."

"What about Charli?"

His gaze slid to the staircase. The tinkling notes of a music box blended with the baby's happy noises. The sounds seemed too ordinary. Quinn clenched his jaw. "It's her kid. She'll want to see her."

"But it's so…sudden."

"It's been almost three weeks, Rachel. It had to happen sometime."

No, she thought. Not yet. *Not yet.*

But this was for the best, right? She had that full, happy life to get back to. And there wasn't really any place in it for a brooding, wounded warrior or a strange woman's abandoned baby, right? *Right?*

Yet despite the conflicting feelings rolling inside her, despite her ongoing struggle to maintain her distance from this man, it didn't take more than a second for Rachel to make her decision. Even if it was only for a few more hours, she would have them both. "I'm coming with you."

Chapter 10

Rachel came awake slowly, her body stiff from being in one position too long. She tried to turn over, but something was pinning her down. She opened her eyes blearily and saw a road sign whizzing past. Tires hummed on pavement.

Of course. They were in her car. Blinking, she grasped her seat belt to ease the pressure on her chest and turned her head.

Quinn was behind the wheel, his face tinged with the slanted golden light of sunrise. His hair was tousled, his shirt wrinkled, and morning stubble bristled along his jaw. He looked hard and masculine and...adorable. Rachel wanted to reach out and smooth the hair back from his forehead, stroke the wrinkles from his shirt and run her fingertips over his beard. Or maybe greet him with a kiss...

Quinn glanced at her. "Good morning."

She swallowed a yawn. "Hi. What time is it?"

"Almost seven." He palmed the wheel to steer around a curve. "We should be there in another forty minutes."

"I thought we were going to take turns with the driving," she said, straightening up. "Why didn't you wake me?"

"I don't need much sleep."

"But—"

"And if I had stopped the car, the kid might have woken up."

Rachel twisted to look over her shoulder. Strapped securely in her infant carrier, Charli was still sleeping peacefully. She was surrounded by bags of clothes and toys, diapers and baby formula. It had been after midnight by the time they'd finally left Maple Ridge, due in large part to the incredible amount of paraphernalia involved in transporting a baby.

This must be what it would be like to be a real family, Rachel thought, leaning her head against the back of the seat. Packing their clothes, gathering the items their child would need to keep her fed and clothed and happy, those would be the kinds of preparations parents would make for a trip. They could be going on vacation, or maybe visiting distant relatives. A family unit, bound by ties of shared love and responsibility.

She rubbed her eyes, then turned her gaze to the windshield. Fields blurred past, flat expanses of green behind wire fences. Houses and barns dotted the landscape while herds of cows stood in distant knots of black and white. This wasn't a vacation. This car didn't hold a family. And when they returned to Maple Ridge, this car might hold one person less.

Maybe she should have said goodbye at the house. Quinn didn't really need her help with the driving. And Charli had slept the entire time. Once Darlene recovered from her injuries and Quinn settled whatever trouble the woman believed she was in, he would return her baby to her. And that would be it. The end. Finished.

But what if Darlene didn't recover? Her condition was serious enough for her to break her long silence and contact Quinn. What if she couldn't take her baby back? What would happen to Charli then?

And what would happen to Quinn? He'd seen so much tragedy and loss already.

Rachel pushed the possibility out of her mind. Three weeks

ago, when she'd first held Charli, she'd been sure that the baby's mother would return any day. And despite the way Rachel abhorred how the baby had been abandoned, and despite her own fondness for the child, she didn't want to think that Charli would never see her mother again. Children needed their parents' love. Even if it was only one parent, even if the parent wasn't perfect. Darlene would get better. Medical science could do almost anything. Just look at the injuries Quinn had managed to recover from.

Then again, Quinn was an exceptional person. He had just driven all night in order to reunite a mother with her child because of his fierce loyalty to six dead men.

She looked at his strong hands, at the competent way he gripped the wheel, at the gleam of silver on his finger, and her heart gave a little lurch. As she had done for the past week, Rachel tried to summon up her anger, but it was no use. Regardless of Quinn's lack of tact when it came to their personal relationship, she couldn't continue to be offended by his honesty. It was all part of the man he was.

And one way or another, their association was almost over. Whatever happened to Darlene, the responsibility for Charli would soon be out of their hands. Hospitals meant forms to sign and official records of medical history. And once the authorities learned about Charli, she would in all likelihood be taken away.

It was inevitable. It had been since Rachel had stopped Quinn from finishing his call to the police that first night in the garage. Quinn's painful search for the owner of the ring, the child-care skills he'd learned, even the toys he'd bought were all for nothing. They had merely delayed the end.

Quinn had been right. She shouldn't have let herself get attached to the child. She should have called her "kid."

Rachel closed her eyes against the sunrise. Not because she wanted to sleep but because she didn't want to watch how fast the miles were slipping by.

* * *

Quinn felt the sweat break out on his forehead the moment he stepped through the doors. It was the smell that got him first, that mixture of chlorine and boiled sheets and misery. Then there were the sounds. Crepe-soled shoes squeaking on tile, the clatter of gurney wheels, the ringing phones and mumbled condolences. It seemed as if he'd lived the past two years in hospitals, first as a visitor, then as a patient. When he'd walked out of the last hospital, two and a half months ago, he'd hoped never to set foot in one again. He didn't want to do it now.

Rachel put her hand on his arm in a touch that made the memories lose their power. How did she do that? What was it about her that sent the nightmares away? He didn't want to need her—he didn't want to need anyone—but he was grateful she had refused to be left behind.

"Over here," she said, nodding toward the bank of elevators.

Squaring his shoulders, he forced himself to walk forward.

The woman sitting at the nurses' station beside the ICU looked at them with weary eyes as she gulped down a plastic tumbler full of coffee. "Visiting hours don't start until two," she said.

"I'm here to see Darlene Norlander," Quinn said.

The nurse put down her coffee and picked up a clipboard. "How do you spell that?"

Quinn resisted the urge to wrench the clipboard from her hand. He spelled Darlene's name. "We were told she had been brought here yesterday."

"No," she said, running her nail down the list. "We don't have anyone by that name now."

"Check again," Quinn insisted.

She put down the clipboard. "Sir, if her name isn't here, we don't have her. She must have been discharged."

Quinn gripped the edge of the counter in front of him. "Then check your computer."

Covering a yawn with the back of her hand, the nurse swiveled her chair toward the monitor beside her. "Norlander," she mumbled, clacking at the keyboard. She looked at the screen for a moment, then glanced up quickly. "I'm going to page Dr. Lassiter," she said, picking up the phone. "You and your wife can take a seat in the—"

"What's going on?"

"I'm sorry, but you really should speak with the physician who handled—"

"Look, lady. I'm not in the mood for this. Either she's here or she isn't. Now if you don't tell me—"

"Is there a problem here?" A man dressed in surgical greens was walking toward them.

"I'm looking for Darlene Norlander," Quinn stated.

He glanced at the nurse and then back at Quinn and Rachel. His gaze lingered on the baby for a moment, then he stopped in front of Quinn. "You must be Mr. Keelor."

"That's right."

"I'm Abe Lassiter," he said, holding out his hand. "I was on call when Mrs. Norlander was admitted. I see the state police managed to track you down."

"How's Darlene?" Quinn asked immediately.

The doctor led them over to a cluster of chairs that was grouped in front of a coffee machine. There was a brief silence.

And even before the doctor spoke, Quinn knew what he was going to say. He'd seen that look before. He'd heard the speech before. Too many times. Too many places. Damn, when would it stop? Why couldn't he stop it?

"Mrs. Norlander was brought here late yesterday after a motor vehicle accident," Lassiter said finally. "Her condition was very serious. We used every available method to treat her injuries, but I'm afraid the damage was too severe. In spite of all our efforts, we were unable to save her."

Rachel raised her hand to her mouth, muffling a sob. She clutched Charli to her shoulder, her eyes moist as she looked at Quinn. "Oh, no."

I've failed, Quinn thought, clenching his fists. *Again.*

He should have found her sooner. He should have tried harder. She'd asked him to keep the baby safe until she came back. Now she would never come back.

"I'm sorry," Lassiter said. "I had hoped that she would be able to hang on until she saw her child."

Quinn started. "What?"

"This is Mrs. Norlander's baby, isn't it?"

His gaze met Rachel's. And in a flash of sudden clarity, he realized that he wanted to lie. Make it last, he thought. Make her stay. Keep them both in his life—

No. He wanted them gone.

Didn't he?

The moment passed. And at the doctor's next words, Quinn knew covering up the truth would have been futile.

"When she regained consciousness, she asked to see her daughter. She told us where to find you." The doctor glanced at Charli, then back at Quinn. "From what Mrs. Norlander said, you were taking care of her baby temporarily, is that right? But you're not a blood relative?"

Again, lying would be pointless. "That's right."

"She told me the child's father is dead. Because of the circumstances, Child Services have already been notified. They'll decide what's best for Mrs. Norlander's daughter."

Rachel bit her lip and looked away.

Quinn stared hard at the doctor. "Darlene gave the responsibility to me."

"That's not for me to determine. That would be up to the courts." He pulled off his green cap and sighed. "I'm sorry. I realize this is a shock."

It was all going so fast, Quinn thought. And he was helpless to stop it. It couldn't end this way, could it? "How did the accident happen?"

"Excuse me?"

"The police officer that notified me didn't give me any details, except to say it was a car accident."

Lassiter paused. "Mrs. Norlander was struck as she was crossing a downtown intersection. The police are investigating, but as far as I know, they're still looking for the driver."

Quinn's gaze sharpened. He'd been wrong. It wasn't over yet. Not by a long shot. "You mean it was a hit-and-run? They haven't found who killed her?"

"Not yet." The doctor looked at Rachel and Charli for a moment, then returned his gaze to Quinn. "I'm sorry."

"There are no accidents," Quinn said.

At the hollow tone in his voice, Rachel pushed aside her untouched salad to stretch her arm across the hospital cafeteria table and grasp his hand. "What happened to Darlene was out of your control, Quinn. You did everything you could to find her. She didn't want to be found."

"She asked for my help."

"To keep Charli. You did that. And you did that wonderfully." Rachel looked down at where Charli sat in her infant carrier beside the table. The child was batting happily at a string of colorful beads. Charli didn't know that she no longer had a mother. She didn't know that by the end of the day she would be just another statistic in some social agency's file. Rachel's eyes filled, but she blinked the impending tears away impatiently. "You did all you could, Quinn. No one could expect more."

"I'm going to find out who killed her."

"Quinn, the police—"

"They haven't made any progress."

"But—"

"I wasn't able to save my men," he said, lifting his gaze to hers. "I couldn't save Darlene. The least I can do is bring her killer to justice."

His fingers felt cold beneath hers. She squeezed them firmly. "Quinn, how can you solve that hit-and-run when you don't even know where to start?"

"She was in trouble. When I find out what it was, I'll find out who killed her."

It took a moment for his words to sink in. When they did, Rachel felt what little appetite she had desert her. "Quinn, you don't believe that her death was…deliberate, do you?"

He pulled his hand from hers. "She was scared. She was running from something that frightened her enough to make her leave her child. Now she's dead. It doesn't sound like a coincidence to me."

Until now, Rachel hadn't really believed that Darlene's problems could be as dire as Quinn had thought. She'd believed he was overreacting, regarding the situation through the filter of his experience with the military.

But what if Quinn had been right all along? What if that melodramatic note Darlene had left with Charli had in fact reflected the truth?

What if Darlene Norlander really had been running for her life?

No. It had to be Quinn's paranoia, that's all. Darlene's death was a tragic accident, nothing more. Perhaps Quinn's unwillingness to let this drop was all part of the responsibility he felt toward his team. He didn't want to accept the vagaries of fate, he didn't want to admit that he'd been powerless to help. He preferred to regard everything as a mission—as a way to handle his emotions.

"You can drive back to Maple Ridge without me," Quinn continued. "I don't know how long it's going to take for me to get the answers I want."

She hesitated. "Are you saying you want me to leave you here?"

"Our agreement was that you'd help me with the kid. That's all."

His gaze was steady on hers. He didn't need to say the rest. Dr. Lassiter had arranged for a representative from Child Services to meet them in his office within the hour. They both knew what that meant. Depending on how the meeting went,

Charli might be placed in a foster home. After all, Rachel and Quinn weren't a real couple. And courts didn't usually decide to grant custody to a single man.

But Rachel wasn't staying with Quinn just because of Charli. Deep down inside, she'd known that for weeks. Even if the court decided to take the child away by the end of the afternoon, she wasn't going to leave Quinn to face this alone.

Rachel could see that Darlene's death—this entire situation—was ripping him apart. Logically he couldn't have done anything to prevent it, but he was considering it his fault, anyway. She wanted to help him, to comfort him and take him into her arms and hold him until that haunted look faded from his eyes. She wanted to love him....

Love? No, she couldn't have been that much of a fool, could she? She couldn't have fallen in love with him now, when the excuse for their association was about to be taken away.

"Let's not make any plans until we talk to the authorities," she said. "They might not have a place for Charli immediately. It could be days. Or maybe longer..." Her lips trembled. Pressing them together firmly, she looked away.

"All right," Quinn said quietly. There was a silence, then Rachel was startled to feel the touch of Quinn's fingers on her cheek.

It was a brief caress. It wasn't sexual. But somehow it was a more intimate connection than they'd had before. And it moved her far more than she would have liked. Rachel blinked hard, hoping he would mistake the reason for the moisture in her eyes.

Oh, God. She couldn't be in love with him, could she?

"Excuse me, Mr. Keelor?"

A woman stopped beside their table. It was the nurse who had been at the ICU when they'd arrived at the hospital. She glanced at Charli, her expression softening, then held out a large white plastic bag to Quinn. "Dr. Lassiter said you'd be here. These are Ms. Norlander's personal effects. What would you like done with them?"

Quinn took the bag, waiting in silence as the nurse walked away.

The moment of closeness was gone. Rachel focused on Darlene's belongings and yanked her thoughts away from the dangerous direction they were taking.

There wasn't much in the bag. The clothes Darlene had been wearing, or what was left of them, and a large black patchwork leather purse. Quinn looked at the purse for a moment, then cleared the dishes off the table and emptied the purse in front of him. Loose coins and a lipstick case clattered to the table, along with a set of car keys, some crumpled tissues and a pair of sunglasses, the kind of odds and ends that one would expect to find in any woman's handbag.

Rachel glanced around, but no one seemed to be paying them any attention in the crowded cafeteria. "What are you looking for?" she asked.

Quinn poked through the pile. He paused when he flipped open a small plastic folder that held a picture of Charli, but then he set his jaw and continued his methodical search through the rest of the items. "No key to a motel room anywhere," he said. "She must have been on the move again." He pushed aside some tissues and picked up a tattered map. He studied it for a moment, then looked at Rachel. "This is a road map of Ontario. She must have been heading for Canada."

"Canada? Why?"

"That would be a good place to go to disappear."

"Could she have had relatives there?"

"Not that I know of, but it's possible." He frowned as he picked up the car keys. "If she didn't have a motel room, the rest of her things would still be in her car. It would probably be parked near the intersection where she was hit, unless it's been towed away by now. We'll have to check it out in case there's some indication of who she was running from—" He stopped abruptly and looked more closely at the purse. "Damn, I almost missed it, just like before."

"What?" Rachel asked, leaning closer.

"That pocket in the lining."

"Most purses have a zippered compartment like that."

"When she left Charli, that's where she put the ring," he said, dropping the keys on the table as he thrust his hand into the pocket.

Rachel waited, not really expecting him to find anything more than a few folded bills, or maybe a spare car key. But to her surprise, when Quinn withdrew his hand there was a dark rectangular object on his palm. It was a cassette tape.

And written across the label, in the same loopy scrawl Rachel recognized from the note that had been left with Charli, was Quinn's name. Her gaze flew to his. "It's for you," she said, unwittingly echoing the words she'd said that first night.

He nodded, his mouth set into a grim line. "Yeah."

"But what...why..."

"There's only one way to find out."

Afternoon sunlight streamed past the potted ferns on the windowsill of Lassiter's office, sending striped shadows across the small tape recorder on the desk. The sunshine seemed too cheerful, the office too ordinary, to hear a voice from the grave.

Rachel took a deep breath and settled Charli into the crook of her arm to give her her bottle. There was no point getting maudlin now. Dr. Lassiter would be back here in thirty minutes for their meeting with the Child Services worker—there would be plenty to get miserable about then.

Quinn took the chair beside hers and reached out to draw the tape recorder closer. He fitted the cassette into place and turned to Rachel. "You ready?"

"Yes."

He nodded and pressed the play button.

A quiet, hesitant voice came from the speaker. "Quinn, I don't care what happens to me as long as Charli is all right. I'm sorry I didn't say anything when I called. I love my baby too much to—'' There was a sob, then a click on the tape where the recording had been interrupted.

Charli drew noisily on her bottle, slapping it with her palm. The baby showed no sign of recognizing her mother's voice. Had she already forgotten her? Somehow, it made Darlene's death seem all the more poignant. Rachel bit her lip. She'd told herself she wasn't going to get maudlin, but how could she help it?

Seconds later, the voice on the tape began again. ''I don't know how to tell you this, Quinn. I hoped I wouldn't need to, but things are getting worse, and I'm really afraid now. You need to know the truth so you can protect Charli. I'm in trouble, Quinn. Bad trouble.''

Rachel was struck by how young and scared Darlene sounded. She glanced at Quinn. He was leaning forward in his chair, every muscle tensed as he kept his gaze on the tape. Again, he didn't seem bothered by the melodramatic overtones of the situation. And now that she was hearing for herself the fear in Darlene's voice, Rachel didn't want to dismiss it, either.

''John made me promise that if anything happened to him, I would come to you for help,'' the voice went on. ''He wanted to tell you the truth himself when things started to go wrong, but you were still in the hospital, and we wanted to get out of the country—''

Quinn hit the pause button, then rewound the tape and listened to the last few seconds again. Scowling, he let it continue.

''...and by then Charli was on the way. Quinn, John hated what happened. He didn't mean for anyone to get hurt, but it was the only way he could get out of it. We were going to make a new start, but then something went wrong with the timer and...''

There was another click and a pause. Quinn didn't move, his face like stone. But beneath the surface of his expression, Rachel could see a terrible, dawning awareness.

She couldn't believe what she was hearing. Darlene must have been mixed-up. From what she was saying, it sounded as if her husband were still alive. Not only that, it sounded as if he'd *deliberately*—

No. The possibility was too horrible to contemplate.

"It started when the team was on that mission in Panama," Darlene continued. "These people promised to pay John half a million dollars to help get some packages back to America for them. I wanted him to take the money, but I didn't know it was drugs. Once it started, there was no way to stop. They said they'd kill me if he didn't keep doing those deliveries, so he planned to rig an accident so it would look like he died...."

Quinn stared at the tape recorder, his eyes dark with shock. "No," he breathed.

"...John got away, just like he planned, but when he heard what happened to everyone else, he just about went crazy. The guilt ate him up. He gave away the money to a drug rehab place. He was so sorry, Quinn, but there was nothing we could do to bring your men back."

"No," Quinn repeated, pain vibrating through his voice. "No."

"The gang never believed John had died. They caught up to us in Vera Cruz last Christmas," Darlene went on, her words coming faster now, as if she wanted to get the story over with as quickly as possible. "I didn't know where to go after they killed John. And after Charli came, it was harder than ever to keep moving. That's why I thought you could keep her for a while. But yesterday I saw the man who killed John. I don't know how they found me, but I want you to know who they are in case...in case they try to get to me through Charli."

Unconsciously, Rachel tightened her hold on the baby. Oh, God. Quinn had been right all along. She hadn't believed him. Charli's mother really had been in trouble. She hadn't been dramatizing things to win his sympathy. She really had been in fear for her life. Quinn's paranoia about safety, his determination to help, all of it had been justified.

This was a nightmare.

But for Quinn, it had to be absolutely unthinkable. The accident that had killed his team had been no accident. One of his own men had betrayed him.

Rachel was filled with an overwhelming urge to stop the tape before he could hear any more, before he could be hurt any deeper. He'd already been through so much.

"You've got to stop them, Quinn," Darlene said. "That's the only way Charli will be safe. The notebook I'm sending you is John's. He said it would be my insurance. Please use it." There was a long pause. "And there's a paper in the notebook I want you to use in case I don't...come back." Another pause. "Please kiss my baby goodbye."

That was it. The tape wound silently for another few seconds. Suddenly Quinn moved, stabbing the stop button with such force that the tape player skidded across the desk. He surged to his feet and pulled the tape from the machine.

"Quinn?" Rachel said, reaching out to him.

He spun away and strode to the door, flinging it open. It slammed against the wall, shuddering on its hinges.

Alarmed, Rachel rose from her chair. "Quinn!"

He stood in the doorway, his body shaking. The muscles in his arms stood out in ropy ridges as he clenched his fists. He didn't utter a word. But the low sound of pain that was wrenched from his throat said everything.

Chapter 11

He was too quiet, Rachel thought, watching Quinn as he stood at the motel room window. After his burst of temper in Lassiter's office, he'd regained control over his emotions to an extent that was almost eerie. He was *too* controlled, deceptively calm, his every movement teetering on a knife-edge of restraint. He hadn't dealt with his feelings, he'd only succeeded in suppressing them. Sooner or later they were going to come out.

And she knew that he was going to need her when they did. It might be the most foolish thing she'd ever done, and she would probably end up regretting it later, but she hadn't insisted that they get separate rooms.

She could no more leave him alone tonight than she could have remained in Maple Ridge yesterday. Or looked away when he'd revealed his scars. Or stopped him when he'd wanted to kiss her.

Maybe Quinn wasn't the only one who was refusing to face their feelings.

Rachel sighed. This wasn't the time to get into all of that.

After weeks of waiting, events were cascading forward at a bewildering pace. She and Quinn had found Darlene's car in a pharmacy parking lot half a block from where the hit-and-run had taken place. Using the keys that had been in Darlene's purse, they had retrieved the rest of her belongings. And stuffed into her suitcase was a small, lined notebook that bore John Norlander's name.

Darlene had said the notebook was insurance. It was. Or at least, it would have been if she had had the courage to use it. Names, dates, places, everything John had done was recorded there.

It was still too much for Rachel to grasp completely. Murder, betrayal, drug smuggling—that kind of thing wasn't supposed to touch the lives of people from Maple Ridge.

Dammit, she'd only wanted to get her car fixed. If she hadn't decided to visit her mother, if she hadn't been rear-ended by that senior citizen in the van, if she hadn't decided to leave her car at Keelor's Garage overnight...

Cause and effect. Quinn had always maintained that there was no such thing as an accident. Everything that happened could be traced to a root cause.

And when it came to the accident that had killed his team, he'd had no idea how right he'd been.

Her hand unsteady, she picked up the document that had been tucked inside the notebook. Darlene had known precisely what she was doing when she'd left Charli on Quinn's doorstep. This paper proved it. Whatever flaws there were in the woman's character, her main concern had been her child. Three days ago, she had again put into writing her request for Quinn to watch over Charli, only this time Darlene had gone to a lawyer and had had the request properly signed and witnessed.

Rachel's gaze went to the crib that had been set up at the foot of one of the double beds. Charli had fallen asleep ten minutes ago, blissfully unaware of what was happening around her. They had been late for the meeting that Dr. Lassiter had arranged with the Child Services people, but once it had started, it hadn't lasted long. Once the document naming Quinn had been verified to be genuine, he had been granted interim custody, pending a final hearing.

So, barring an objection from one of Darlene's relatives, and assuming the court would follow Darlene's wishes with respect to her daughter, it looked as if Quinn was going to be the baby's legal guardian.

The baby whose father had betrayed Quinn and killed his men.

Another man might have rejected the child because of the parents, and no one would blame him for feeling resentful. An ordinary man would have felt under no obligation to follow the wishes of a pair of criminals.

But as Rachel already knew, Quinn was no ordinary man.

He was accepting his custody of Charli with the same grim determination he'd shown from the start. If it became permanent, it would mean a drastic change to the solitary life he'd chosen to lead, but his sense of responsibility hadn't wavered. Any inner turmoil associated with his new obligation was buried along with the rest of his emotions.

She let the paper fall to the night table and walked past the beds to the window. "What are you going to do now?"

Quinn continued to stare outside. Dusk had fallen. On the highway beyond the motel parking lot, headlights tracked through the gloom, the sound of passing cars whining into the distance. It wasn't much of a view. But Rachel knew Quinn was looking at something else entirely.

A muscle twitched along his tightly clenched jaw. "I'm going to take John's notebook to the Navy."

"The Navy? What about the police?"

"We take care of our own," he said.

"And Charli?"

"Until the people who killed John and Darlene are in custody, the baby isn't safe."

"But what reason would they have to go after an innocent child?"

"She's connected to me. I'm connected to the Norlanders. It won't take them long to figure it out. They won't know how much Darlene told me, and I don't want the kid used as leverage." He closed the drapes over the window and turned to look at her. "It's good that you didn't argue about staying with me tonight."

A hint of pleasure tingled through her at his determined tone. He wanted her to stay. He needed her. But the pleasure winked out at his next words.

"It's for your own safety. I've put in some calls to people I know. I'll get us somewhere more secure tomorrow."

"Us," she repeated.

"You're connected to this case just like Charli is now, so you'll have to stay with me. Once the gang is caught, you'll be able to leave."

She felt like shaking him. Didn't he see how much she cared? Didn't he want her to care?

But when they turned out the light, he treated her with the distance of a stranger and took the bed opposite hers. It was still a mission to him, she realized, staring at the ceiling in the dark. That's how he distanced himself from the pain.

He'd known the nightmare would come. It always did. But tonight it was worse. The flames were hotter, the screams were louder, the smells stronger. As if it had been only days since he'd left that swamp instead of more than a year.

"Larson, Norlander. Report," Quinn muttered. "Simms, Petrosky, Hoffman, Ferrone."

The litany of names rolled past his lips. And this time Norlander was there, standing over Quinn as he tried to drag himself back from the flames with useless legs. Standing there. Watching. Doing nothing.

And that was the sharpest pain of all.

The second explosion came. As it always did. Quinn felt

himself lifted, flung through the air, tossed on the shock wave along with the fragments of metal and the pieces of his men.

And amid the rushing air and crackling debris, there was Norlander, like a phantom on the wind, his face as insubstantial as the smoke that surrounded them. His blue eyes full of regret, his dark blond hair framing his round face. Charli's face. The resemblance was so clear now. Quinn should have seen it before. But it was impossible.

No, it was real. The nightmare was real. John had betrayed them.

A new sensation was added to the pain and the panic. Quinn felt his blood pound and his muscles clench. It was more than terror, more than anguish. It was anger. Fury.

Norlander. He had done this. He had planned it.

Quinn wanted to kill him.

"No," Quinn growled. *"No!"*

Hands were touching him, moving like claws over his charred flesh. He rolled away, moaning at the agony in his side where the shrapnel had torn away the tissue and cracked the bone. No, he couldn't want to kill Norlander. That was unthinkable. John was closer than a brother. He was part of the team.

"Wake up, Quinn."

The voice tangled with his nightmare, blending with the face in the smoke.

"Quinn." Fingertips on his brow, on his temples. "It's okay. It's only a dream."

His eyes snapped open. A shadow loomed over him. Acting on reflex, he jackknifed upward. In one lightning-smooth move, he had positioned himself behind his attacker and hooked his arm around the shadow's throat.

With satisfaction, he felt the weak attempt to pry his arm away. He'd always been faster than John. Bracing his knees on either side, he grasped his wrist to lock his arm in place and yanked the phantom's body back against his chest.

An elbow jabbed him in the ribs. The sharp stab of pain

from the old wound brought him fully awake before he could complete the motion and snap John's neck.

No. Not John. Couldn't be John. John was dead.

He blinked and shook his head. Gradually he became aware of the soft mattress beneath his knees. The humming of tires on a distant road. The snuffling whimper of the baby as she settled back to sleep. The scent of motel soap...the silky brush of hair against his chin...the slight weight of the body that trembled against his.

Not a dream. Not a phantom. Rachel.

He released the pressure on her throat immediately and grasped her shoulders. "Damn. Did I hurt you?"

She gasped unsteadily. "No, I'm...I'm okay."

He sat back on his heels, running his hands up and down her arms in helpless apology. "I'm sorry, Rachel." He inhaled slowly in an effort to calm his pulse. He'd moved instinctively, the rage of his nightmare and his years of training dictating his actions. "I'm sorry. I never meant—"

"I know. I could see you were dreaming."

Slipping his arms around her, he held her in a careful embrace. "I thought you were someone else."

She shuddered, her chest rising and falling in quick, shallow breaths. She laughed nervously. "Whoever it was, I'd hate to be him."

He pressed his cheek to the side of her head. "When I think of what could have happened... Oh, God."

She lifted her hand to the side of his face, holding him there as they both trembled. Then she twisted around to kneel in front of him. "I shouldn't have startled you, Quinn," she said, pitching her voice low to keep from disturbing the baby. "I know this whole situation must be horrible for you."

In the dim light that filtered through the curtains, her face was a pale blur, but he knew the expression he would see there. It would be the same concerned sympathy he'd seen before.

"It has to come out eventually," she murmured.

"What?"

"You can't avoid your feelings forever. After what you've been through, anyone would have a nightmare."

He reached out, gently stroking his fingertips over the delicate column of her neck. He didn't want to think of how close he had come to hurting her. He hadn't meant to. It had been an accident....

Was this how Norlander had felt? Darlene had said John was so sorry that he'd almost gone crazy with guilt. Quinn knew what that guilt could do to a man. He'd lived with it for more than a year.

No. There was no comparison between him and Norlander. John had betrayed them. He didn't deserve anyone's understanding. He deserved anger and scorn, Quinn thought. "God, I'm sorry," he repeated, brushing Rachel's hair from her cheeks.

She turned her head, her lips grazing his palm.

And instantly the anger and adrenaline that still pumped through his system changed direction. The last fragments of the nightmare faded away. The memory of death was overpowered by the resurgence of life.

And Quinn knew exactly how he would be able to forget the pain.

But this wasn't why he'd wanted Rachel with him, was it? It had been the only practical way to keep both her and the kid safe until he could get them someplace more secure. He knew how dangerous it would be to let his emotions get mixed up in this situation. Emotions made a man vulnerable, they weakened his judgment. The last time he'd allowed his feelings for a woman to interfere in a mission, the result had been the deaths of six men—

But it had been Norlander, not him.

Hell, this wasn't the time to be thinking of all that. Not with Rachel already in his bed.

"Do you want to talk about it?" Rachel asked softly.

"No." He slid his hand into her hair and cupped the back of her head.

Her eyes widened. "Quinn?"

"I don't want to talk. I want to kiss you."

She moistened her lips. "All right."

"I want to feel your skin against mine."

A tremor went through her. "Quinn..."

"I want to be inside you."

Her breath hitched. "I..."

"You make me feel alive, Rachel." He put his other hand over her heart, then spread his fingers to feel the feminine weight of her breast. "Let me show you."

For an endless moment, she didn't move. Then with a whispering sigh of consent and a dip of her head, she swayed into him.

He didn't give her a chance to say anything more. Holding her steady, he brought his mouth down on hers.

At the first touch of his lips, Rachel knew she was lost. It had been a week since she'd kissed him, seven long days since she'd felt his touch on her body. The desire he'd kindled so easily before flared to instant heat. Her heart swelling with pleasure, she slipped her arms around him and pressed against his chest.

His hands, the same hands that had moved so lethally in his sleep, smoothed down her back and around her waist with a tender urgency. He broke off the kiss to pull her nightgown over her head and toss it to the floor. His briefs followed. Rachel had no time to feel self-conscious at their sudden nakedness. It felt too natural, too necessary.

And then he was kissing her again, the bold sweep of his tongue making her part her lips greedily for more. The power that could have choked her five minutes ago now sent thrills throughout her body as he grasped her by the waist and lifted her to straddle his thighs.

It was happening too fast to think about, too fast to stop. She could feel the thread of violence beneath the surface of his actions, yet she felt no alarm. He needed this, she thought. Basic human contact, simple physical release. It would drive his nightmare away.

But what about her? she thought hazily. How could she explain her own craving for the sensation of his body joined to hers? Because as rapidly as this was happening, as powerfully as Quinn was driving this forward, she knew this wasn't one-sided. She wanted him with as much urgency as he wanted her.

And for her, it wasn't all that sudden. It had been building for weeks. Perhaps years. He had been the man she had compared all others to, he'd been the one she must have been waiting for, even when she had believed she had driven him from her heart.

He smoothed his palm along the sensitive skin of her inner thighs, brushing his fingertips over nerves that were screaming for his touch. He pressed higher, firmer, using his thumb, using his rapid, murmured, shocking words as he told her what he wanted.

Rachel didn't need to answer aloud. They could both feel the reply her body was making.

Quinn muttered an oath and leaned over to reach for something beside the bed.

Rachel inhaled sharply, shivering with frustration from the sudden withdrawal of his touch. "Quinn?"

There was a rustle of clothing, the rasp of denim, then he was ripping open a foil packet and smoothing on a condom with enough force to make the latex snap as he put it in place. He lifted her again, fastening his mouth to her breast.

Clutching his shoulders, Rachel wrapped her legs around his waist and arched into his kiss. He sucked harder. She moaned his name. And he slid inside her with one long, sure stroke.

She hadn't known it could be like this. And yet part of her had known all along. The situation they were in, the memories of the girl she used to be, all of it was submerged by a wave of sensation.

He moved his hips. "Rachel."

She looked at his face. Even in the dim light she could see his smile. Her eyes burned with tears she didn't want to acknowledge. Yes, she wanted him. But she wanted more than he was offering. She wanted this to be more than a frenzied coming together in the dark. She didn't only want his body, she wanted his heart. And that smile made her hope that it might be possible.

But he hadn't spoken words of love. He'd spoken words of need. Bluntly. Explicitly. With a sob, she hooked her ankles behind his back and pulled him down to the bed on top of her.

The end came quickly. They were both too close to the edge to wait. Skin slid against skin, slick and hot, as her cry of release was swallowed by his kiss. He went rigid, straining, shuddering, then tightened his arms around her and collapsed.

The sound of their labored breathing seemed loud in the room. For long minutes neither spoke. Quinn rolled to his back to take his weight off Rachel, drawing her with him as their legs lazily entwined. He stroked her hair, his hand gentle, soothing, as their heartbeats slowly returned to normal.

Rachel pressed her cheek against his chest, closing her eyes as she savored the lingering traces of their lovemaking. Tingles, tiny aftershocks of the pleasure that had shaken her, still stole over her skin. Despite the swiftness of their passion, her body was completely sated. Tomorrow would be soon enough for all those regrets and second thoughts. For now she was going to enjoy the moment.

"I was dreaming about the accident," Quinn said, his voice a low rumble.

She lifted her head to look at him, trying to hide her surprise. Not with what he'd said—she'd already guessed what that nightmare must have been about, since she'd heard him mumble the names of his men in his sleep—but with the fact that he'd said it. How many times over the past few weeks had she tried to get him to talk? Now, without any prompting, he was willing to open up.

"I've had the dream practically every night since it happened," he went on. "I keep reliving it to find out what I could have done to stop it."

"It wasn't your fault, it was John's."

"I hadn't known that until today."

His simple statement barely hinted at the untold anguish he must have felt at the revelations on Darlene's tape. Quinn had blamed himself for the accident that had killed his men. Even though he had never put it into words before, Rachel had known he would feel that way, since that was the kind of man he was. It hadn't been only duty or loyalty to his team that had dictated his actions with Charli. It had also been guilt.

Was it any wonder that he looked haunted? That he tried to close off his emotions? She splayed her hand over his chest, feeling the strength that sheathed the pain. "All this time, you've been torturing yourself over it needlessly."

"Looks that way."

"You have a right to be angry. Anyone would be."

He was quiet for a while, his fingers toying with the ends of her hair. "When I woke up, I thought you were Norlander," he said finally. "I wanted to kill him."

"You wouldn't have," she stated. "I know you."

He wrapped her hair around his fist and brought it to his mouth. His breath hissed out on a sigh. "John was like a brother. We were all like brothers. He could have asked us for help. We would have found a way to get him clear of the trouble he was in. No one had to die."

"From what Darlene said, he regretted what happened."

"Regret won't bring them back. I know."

"It was a tragic accident, whatever the cause. Now that you know the truth, maybe you can lay it to rest."

"It's never going to be over. I could have snapped your neck tonight, Rachel," he said hoarsely.

"But you didn't."

"No, I didn't." He released her hair, skimming the back of his knuckles over the slope of her breast, his ring a glinting silver reminder of his tie to the past. "But I did something else."

She sat up and cradled his face between her hands to be sure he was looking at her. "What we did, we *both* did, Quinn."

"Yeah." He turned his head and drew her thumb into his mouth. He tongued it lightly, then grazed his teeth over the tip.

The desire she'd thought was sated stirred back to life. But it wasn't sex he needed right now, she thought. She moved her hand back to his chest, tunneling her fingers through his mass of springy curls. "Tell me about the last mission, Quinn."

"Why?"

"Because I want to know. And I think you need to put it to rest, or you're going to keep reliving it in those nightmares every night."

There was a silence. Beneath her hand she could feel his muscles tense, as if he were starting to withdraw once more. "Let it go, Quinn," she urged. "You've been carrying this on your own long enough."

"I've already talked to the shrinks."

"You didn't know the truth then."

"No. I didn't."

"And I'm not a shrink. I'm…" She hesitated over the word. His friend? She felt like more than that. His lover? Did only one time make a lover? "I'm here."

"Yeah, you are." He rubbed her nipple. "And I can think of better things to do while we're lying on this bed."

"Quinn," she murmured, batting his hand away.

He sighed. "There really isn't all that much to tell you. We were stationed in Panama," he said. "We weren't on official Navy business. We'd been sheep-dipped."

"What?"

"Loaned to the CIA. Acting as private citizens so the government wouldn't be held responsible for our actions if something went wrong. Our objective was to reconnoiter and destroy a warehouse that was a link in a smuggling pipeline."

"Drugs?"

"Yeah. Cocaine from Colombia that was coming through Panama. The government wanted to use us because we were tight, we were a unit. We couldn't be bought or coerced." He laughed without humor. "They were wrong."

"It wasn't your fault," she said again, because he needed to hear it again.

"The warehouse was heavily guarded and in the middle of a swamp," he went on. "We landed three miles down the coast and made our way up a river the night before, then spent the day in the water up to our necks while we watched the place and waited for dark. It was supposed to be quick and clean—get in, plant the charges, get to the coast and signal for an exfiltration. Something went wrong with the timers."

"Norlander."

"Had to be. We built our missions on redundancy. We had triple-checked everything. There shouldn't have been any mistakes. The dreams keep replaying it over and over in my head, like I'm trying to figure out what I'd missed, what I'd done wrong. All along it had been John. He must have deliberately recalibrated the fuses to cover up his escape." He paused to take a deep breath. "The first explosion caught us within two yards of the building. Then something inside the warehouse went up like a rocket and there was nothing left. I don't remember anything after that."

She thought of the scars on his body, the cane he still used. It was probably a mercy that he didn't remember the rest. "Do you think it was a trap? Could they have known you were coming?"

He paused. "I don't want to think that John could have betrayed us to that extent."

No, she thought. There was only so much pain he could take.

"I was too doped up with painkillers to contribute much to the investigation. There were operations to put the pins in my leg, some more to patch up the missing chunks on my side and back, then the months of rehab." He shifted, as if to turn himself away from the memory. "The government kept the details from the public, said it was a training mission. Training. They couldn't admit what we were really doing."

"That must have made it worse, to have the truth denied that way."

"Truth," he muttered. He rubbed his face roughly. "Why didn't John come to us? None of it had to happen."

She moved her hand down his arm, feeling the firm curve of muscle, thinking of Quinn as well as John. "Maybe it's hard for someone who's been trained to be tough to admit that he needs help."

"I should have noticed that something was wrong with him," Quinn said bleakly. "I should have paid closer attention but I was too—" He broke off.

"Too what?"

"My mind wasn't on the mission. I had buried Louisa only a month before."

Rachel felt her heart clench at what he'd just revealed. This was the real reason behind his nightmare, she realized suddenly. This was the root of his pain. The explosion, the loss of his men, his own horrific injuries, they were all connected in his mind to his wife's death. And to the feelings he'd had for her.

Why hadn't she seen it before? Of course he would believe there was a link between the two events. They had happened within weeks of each other.

And it was possible that he was right, that he *had* been distracted by his grief during that mission. It would be only natural. He'd just lost the woman he'd loved since childhood. But that would be no excuse to someone with Quinn's sense of duty. And so he blamed himself, and he blamed his love for Louisa.

And that, more than the accident, more than Norlander's betrayal, was the real reason he did everything he could to wall off his emotions. Even knowing that someone else had been directly responsible for the tragic explosion didn't completely absolve him. His grief and his guilt were all tangled together.

He'd loved Louisa. He'd already stated what he wanted from Rachel. He'd spelled it out clearly a week ago and again tonight, and it wasn't love. Nothing had really changed between them. He was still using her to forget the pain. The pain of the accident and the pain of losing his wife.

She could sense the tension returning to his body. She stretched out on top of him, anxious to keep from losing the new closeness they'd established. Yet even though they had been as close physically as a man and woman could be, he was still holding part of himself back.

He ran his palm over her hip and gently squeezed her buttock. "Rachel," he said, nuzzling his nose against the top of her head. "If you plan to go back to your own bed, you'd better do it now."

"No."

"Because if you stay here, we're going to make love again."

She felt the heat grow between their bodies, could feel him swell against her belly, and she no longer wanted to talk, either. She would rather be like him, losing herself in the passion they generated.

But he was wrong. Both of them knew that they weren't going to make *love*.

Chapter 12

"Rachel, where on earth are you?"

Cradling the receiver to her ear, Rachel sank into the armchair and leaned back with a sigh. The long day of phone calls and meetings and hurried flight arrangements was finally over, and she was exhausted. And it didn't help that neither she nor Quinn got more than a few hours of sleep last night. "Coronado," she answered finally.

There was a startled squeak, then Emily's voice blasted across the miles and the time zones. "What? California? Why?"

"It's kind of complicated," she said, smiling wearily at the extent of the understatement.

"Does this have to do with Quinn Keelor?"

"Yes."

"Oh. Well, then."

"We're on his old naval base."

"I see."

Rachel rubbed her forehead. How could she explain this to her friend when she was having trouble grasping it all herself?

"Quinn's involved in something. An investigation. We're staying here until it's over."

"Uh-huh."

"It's only temporary." Even as she said the words, she felt a pang. Only temporary. How many times did that make it now? It seemed to be the pattern of her relationship with Quinn, a pattern that he was determined not to change.

"Mmm. Does this have anything to do with the cop who was looking for Quinn?" Emily asked.

"What?"

"Well, Mrs. Budge was picking up her car when Doug Keelor happened to be talking to some policeman who was looking for Quinn because of some medical emergency, so she told us all about it when Hazel heard you missed the committee meeting the other night."

"Good old Maple Ridge," Rachel said, shaking her head.

"Quaint, isn't it? What was the emergency?"

After almost a month of lies, how could she explain the truth? Rachel wondered. But there had already been too much deceit. She wasn't going to keep adding to it. "It concerned Charli's mother," she said, giving Emily the bare facts of the hit-and-run that had resulted in Darlene's death.

"Oh, good Lord," Emily murmured. "How horrible. What's going to happen to the baby?"

"Quinn will continue to take care of her."

"Take care of her? As in custody?"

"Darlene signed a guardianship document. According to the lawyer Quinn retained before we left New York, it appears to be only a matter of time before his guardianship is official."

"Wow. Why would Quinn want to take on that kind of responsibility...." There was a pause. "Rachel, maybe I'm stating the obvious here, but have you considered the possibility that Charli might be Quinn's baby?"

"I did wonder at first, but Charli definitely is not his biological child," she stated firmly. "There are circumstances..." She sighed. "As I said, it's complicated. I'll explain it all when I come home. I just didn't want you to worry about the way I disappeared. I hope to be back in time for the Summer Festival.''

"Don't concern yourself with that. We'll muddle through somehow. And I wasn't really worried about you, Rachel, since I knew you were with Quinn."

"The whole town probably knows."

"Don't let it bother you. Quinn's a good man. Rob likes him."

"Rob finds something to like about everyone. That's what makes him such a good doctor."

"Yes, but Rob isn't living with him."

"I'm not—'' She couldn't complete the automatic denial. As of last night, she and Quinn had progressed far beyond the roommate stage. She was indeed living with him in the sense that the Maple Ridge gossips had tried to link them weeks ago. There were only two bedrooms in this small apartment— one with a crib, one with a double bed.

"The question is," said Emily, "how do *you* feel about Quinn?"

"It doesn't make any difference. Our living arrangement is only temporary. I have a life to get back to, a career—"

"Rachel, for God's sake, you're sounding just like your mother."

She frowned. "My mother?"

"Okay, I'm going to say this fast before you finally lose your temper with me and tell me to mind my own business and slam the phone down on my ear as I probably deserve but—'' Emily took a deep breath. "There's more to life than how you make your living."

"I know that, Emily. I do have a social life."

"Yes, but no love life. Until now."

Again, Rachel couldn't voice the automatic denial. She was getting tired of lying.

"Rachel, ever since Quinn and Charli have come into the picture," Emily continued, her voice softening, "you've had a glow about you. You've opened up to possibilities you've been telling me for years are impossible. No matter how it started, you've ended up taking a man and a child into your heart."

"But—"

"And your life hasn't self-destructed. You're still the same person."

"Emily, this situation I'm in with Quinn isn't some kind of romantic holiday, it's…complicated." There was that word again. "You're just letting your pregnancy hormones do your thinking for you."

"Pregnancy, shmegnancy. It's a friend's intuition," Emily persisted. "Forget your mother's example. Look at mine and Rob's. All I'm saying is give it a chance."

Give it a chance? Rachel thought as she hung up the phone a few minutes later. Emily made it sound so simple. And to her it was. Love, marriage, motherhood, it all came naturally to other people. Emily had told her that she'd fallen in love with Rob on her first day at college, and they had been inseparable since then. They were meant for each other. Everyone said that. Just like Quinn and Louisa.

Quinn had lived on this base with Louisa, Rachel thought, looking around the modest living room. Of course, if they'd had an apartment like this, Louisa would have decorated it to make it more of a home. She'd always had a talent for that. Perfect, charming, lovable Louisa.

This place was spartan, with only the basic furnishings necessary to make it livable. With space on the base always at a premium and Quinn not on active duty anymore, he had been fortunate to get any accommodation for them at all, so she wasn't complaining. It would only be theirs for ten days, until the arrival of the officer and his wife who had been assigned these quarters. They'd have to reassess their situation after that.

Ten more days. Another time limit. It didn't seem nearly long enough to make Quinn change his mind about love.

Love. There. She'd finally acknowledged it. Rachel closed her eyes and let her head fall back against the chair. It hadn't taken Emily's irrepressible romanticism to put the idea in her head. It had been there all along. And after the incredible night she'd spent with Quinn, Rachel could no longer ignore the truth.

She was in love with Quinn. Thoroughly, hopelessly, shamelessly in love.

Again.

Except this time it wasn't the innocent, idealistic infatuation of youth. She loved Quinn for the man he was now, scars and all, even the scars that didn't show. And she loved him for the sensitive soul that still shone through the bitterness and tragedy he'd endured.

Her feelings weren't cause for celebration. They were only going to make things worse when the time finally came for her and Quinn to part. But at least now she could stop trying to scramble for excuses to explain her behavior. She was staying with him because she loved him. She had slept with him because she loved him. She fully intended to sleep with him again tonight and for as long as they were together, because she loved him.

And then...

Impatiently she wiped at the moisture on her cheeks. It was great timing, wasn't it? She figured out she loved Quinn just as she finally understood why he was so determined not to open up his heart. For Quinn, love had brought disaster and pain. And so he was turning all his formidable strength to ensuring he wouldn't love anyone again.

In a way both Emily and Ann were right. Emily rejoiced in the potential of love, and Rachel could understand that, because she loved Quinn. But Rachel's mother said that a woman needed to maintain her independence because loving a man could leave her too vulnerable. And Rachel understood that, too, because she loved Quinn.

Bracing her hands on the chair arm, she pushed to her feet

and headed for the kitchen. Despite her fatigue, she was suddenly hungry.

Ten days were better than nothing, she told herself as she picked up a doughnut from the box Quinn had left on the counter. He might think he only wanted her for sex and sympathy, but maybe it was time for Rachel to think about what *she* wanted. There had to be a way to balance her mother's and Emily's views. There must be some way to love Quinn without, as Emily put it, having her life self-destruct.

Quinn nodded to the yawning clerk and walked into the base commander's office. The military hadn't changed, Quinn decided. It was still hurry up and wait. After calling in every favor he was owed and pulling all the strings of any connections he still had, in order to get Rachel and Charli safely ensconced on the base, he'd been left cooling his heels in the outer office for hours. Night had fallen. The watch had changed. Commander Mikita should have had time to commit John's notebook to memory by now.

"Shut the door, Keelor."

Quinn did as he'd been told, then left his cane against the back of a chair and stood at attention. Old habits died hard.

He watched Myron Mikita tap out his pipe and fill it from the tin of tobacco he kept on his desk. The leisurely movements had the air of a ritual for Mikita. It was deceptive. While his hands fiddled with his pipe, his mind was clicking away with the ruthless logic of a computer.

"At ease, Keelor. You resigned, remember?"

"Yes, sir."

"You were one sorry mess the last time I saw you," Mikita said, puffing a cloud of fragrant smoke toward the ceiling. "You're looking better."

"The doctors did their best."

He waved impatiently toward the chair in front of his desk. "You might as well sit. You're making my neck ache."

"Thank you, sir," Quinn said, taking the seat. "I assume you've had a chance to look over the notebook."

He nodded. Not a strand of his steel-gray hair moved out of place. "Why did you bring it to me? Why not the police?"

"I thought that this was a Navy matter."

"Because of Norlander."

"Yes, sir." Quinn grasped the handle of his cane between his hands, needing something to hang on to. Because with his next words, he was going to unlock a topic he'd done his best to close off a year ago. "I also brought you the notebook because the investigation into the accident in Panama will have to be reopened."

"The training mission."

"You know damn well what it was."

Mikita lifted an eyebrow. "Ah. Good to see that civilian life hasn't knocked the fight out of you after all."

Quinn leaned forward. "Both John and Darlene Norlander were killed by the same group that succeeded in coercing him into smuggling drugs. In addition, because of this group, John's actions led to the deaths of five innocent men. My men."

"You resigned."

"They'll always be my men," Quinn said. His thumb moved across his palm, the tip rubbing the band of the silver ring he still wore.

"Mrs. Norlander's death doesn't fall under our jurisdiction."

"Yes, it does. The same people who killed John killed her. The criminals involved should be brought to justice."

"And they will be. But as far as the investigation into the training mission accident," Mikita said, his steady gaze daring Quinn to object to his word choice, "we don't need to reopen it."

"Why? With this new evidence—"

"It was never closed."

"What?"

"We know it was sabotage. And that Norlander was behind it. We've known it for a year."

Quinn felt as if he'd just been sucker punched. He drew in his breath. "Could you explain that?"

"We never found Norlander's body. Most parts of everyone else's, yes, but not his. No teeth, no fingers we could get prints from, not even a bone fragment we could run a DNA analysis on. And we were very thorough when we dragged that swamp."

"You listed him as missing and presumed dead. The final report said his body had been carried downriver to the sea."

"That's right."

"Why?"

"To facilitate the investigation."

"Do you mean that the Navy has known the truth all this time?" Quinn asked incredulously.

"Not all of it. We weren't able to locate Norlander after he and his wife disappeared to Mexico." Mikita took another long drag on his pipe, then used the stem to point to Norlander's notebook. "This is going to give us what we need to bring the matter to a close. I appreciate your cooperation."

Quinn felt his shock turn to anger. Strange, how quickly his emotions were getting stirred up lately. After more than a year of deliberate numbness, he was struggling just to maintain control. His grip on his cane tightened. "You should have told me."

"Information was given on a need-to-know basis. You didn't need to know," he said, as if that were a sufficient enough explanation.

"Dammit!" Quinn pushed to his feet. "You left me hanging in my own guilt."

"It was your choice, Keelor. It was clear that you didn't want anything to do with the accident investigation from the start."

"After the explosion I was too doped up—"

"That's no excuse. You woke up eventually. But instead of

resuming your duties and pursuing the truth of what really happened, you chose to go running home to some godforsaken crossroads in Ohio. So don't start crying foul now when you finally decide to get involved.''

Mikita was right. Quinn had been so certain of his guilt, he hadn't wanted to deal with his memories of the accident or anything else. He had turned his back on the Navy the minute he'd been able to walk out of the hospital.

If he hadn't resigned, if he had dealt with his memories instead of burying them, would he have learned the truth sooner?

Quinn's anger mounted, a good part of it directed toward himself. "I still had a right to know. And all this time you let me believe it was my fault."

"It was," Mikita said calmly.

Another blow, this time from another direction. Quinn gritted his teeth.

"Your fault, my fault," Mikita continued. "The fault of every person who failed to notice what was going on with John Norlander. Don't try to fool yourself, Keelor. Casualties are never inevitable. They happen because someone screwed up.''

It was the philosophy that had been woven into the fabric of his life, Quinn thought. It was the SEAL tradition. Total responsibility. No excuses. It was what kept the unit strong, what led to the fact that in over thirty years, no SEAL had been left behind on a mission or taken prisoner. They took care of their own. And if they didn't...

If they didn't, people died. Cause and effect.

There would be no redemption here, Quinn thought, looking at the commander's closed expression. And he should know better than to expect any. Mikita was merely stating what Quinn already believed. There were no accidents.

But instead of the guilt he knew he should be feeling, Quinn continued to feel anger. Sure, he had resigned, but out of human decency, Mikita could have told him about Norlander. If

Darlene hadn't sought him out, Quinn could have gone the rest of his life bearing the full burden of his men's deaths. He felt betrayed a second time.

He wanted to smash something. The need for action to release his rage was growing by the second.

Damn, the numbness had been so much easier.

Rachel jerked awake when she heard the sound of a key in the lock. Picking up the book that had fallen to her lap, she brushed the cookie crumbs off the sheet and sat up. A quick glance at her watch showed it was after midnight—no wonder she had fallen asleep waiting for Quinn to come back. Pulling on her robe, she went to greet him.

He was pacing the width of the living room, the tension seeming to roll off him in waves. He had unbuttoned his shirt, the sides flapping open at each restless stride, fluttering against stomach muscles that were tensed into washboard ridges. His hair was tousled, as if he'd been running his fingers through it, and the shadow of a beard darkened his tightly clenched jaw.

He looked hard and dangerous. A trained warrior, fully capable of snapping a man's neck if the need arose. And for a moment Rachel faltered. The gulf between their experiences seemed wider than ever. So much had happened to him since he'd left Maple Ridge. What did she know about Navy policy or gangs of drug smugglers or tragic deaths?

But this was Quinn, the man she loved. She wouldn't turn away when he needed her. "What happened?" Rachel asked.

Quinn spun around and looked at her. "I thought you'd be asleep."

"I woke up. What's wrong? Weren't you able to meet with the commander?"

"Yeah, I saw him. The bastard already knew, Rachel. He knew about Norlander." In a few terse sentences, Quinn related what he'd learned.

Rachel raised her hand to her mouth. "Oh, God," she murmured. As if Quinn hadn't been betrayed enough, he had been deceived again. She understood the reason for his renewed anger. What surprised her was that he made no effort to conceal it.

"I feel cheated," Quinn said, pacing to the other end of the room. "Duped."

"Of course you would. Anyone would."

"I feel as if I've been going in circles. I thought I'd moved back home to get away from what happened, but I'm right back where it all started."

"All of this must be incredibly hard on you."

He paused, bracing his fist against the wall. "Do you remember what you told me about running away?"

"When was that?"

"In Leona's study, after I'd seen Larson's brother." He hit the wall, then turned to face her. "You were so determined to get me to talk. You said it was no good trying to run away from a problem."

She remembered that particular conversation vividly. It had been the first time she had referred to her old weight problem. "I hadn't known what I was talking about then, Quinn. I can't compare my own teenage insecurities to the tragedy you went through."

"The principle is the same."

"But not the scale." She fastened her belt and moved toward him. "So what if my father deserted me? That shouldn't have had any bearing on who I was. It took me a long time to figure it out, that's all."

"Because you had buried your feelings. You said they ate away at you inside until they were out of control."

"You're not out of control, Quinn." Reaching out, she took his fist between her hands and brushed a kiss across his reddened knuckles. "If you were, you would have punched a hole through that wall."

He shuddered at her caress. "I've spent the last hour walking around. I thought I could work this off."

"You've tried so hard to keep your emotions bottled up, it's going to take more than a brisk walk to let it out, Quinn."

"Then what do you think I should do?"

"You can let me help you."

He held her gaze. "Fine. Here?"

"Well, if you like."

Before she realized what he intended, he grasped her wrists and pushed them behind her back. "You sure you wouldn't rather do this in bed?"

"I thought you'd need to talk."

"There you go again with the talking," he said, pulling her against the front of his body.

She thrilled to the power she could feel within him. He looked more dangerous than ever. Because despite the edgy restlessness of his body, there was a smile on his face. A purely masculine smile. The tension that had pulsed from him when he'd arrived had changed to raw, sexual energy. She felt her joints go weak with an instant response. "Quinn," she said unsteadily. "There are other ways to channel your anger besides sex."

"Yeah, but none of them as enjoyable."

"Quinn..."

"We couldn't turn the light on last night," he said. "Because of the kid."

A tremor went through her. "Charli's asleep."

"Is her door closed?"

Breathless, Rachel nodded.

He turned around with her and backed her against the wall. He released her wrists, the weight of his body holding her in place. "I want to see your face this time, Rachel. I want to know what color your eyes look when you close yourself around me."

His words, the taut, hard feel of him as he molded against her, sent desire throbbing through her.

"I've always thought you had beautiful eyes," he murmured, running his fingertips across her cheek. "They're so expressive, they show every emotion you're feeling."

"Do they?"

"Oh, yeah. Always have. So do these," he said, lowering his hand to one breast. He circled his fingers around it, gently squeezing the tip.

Her knees buckled. Quinn slid his leg between her thighs to help support her.

"You have beautiful breasts," he murmured, covering it with his hand. "They fascinate me. They're like you, so warm and generous and womanly." He tugged open her robe, parted the buttons on the front of her nightgown and pressed his palm to her bare skin. His eyelids drooped with pleasure. "I've seen them before, but I want to see them again, watch them swell and quiver when you come apart in my arms."

She moistened her lips. "Quinn..."

"That's another thing. Last night we couldn't make any noise."

Noise? She shivered at the memory of his urgent, whispered words, the low, hoarse sounds he'd made in his throat, the slick slapping of flesh on flesh... "We weren't completely silent," she murmured, her cheeks flooding with heat.

"Yeah, I could feel those little cries you made against my tongue," he said, brushing a kiss along her jaw. He sucked lightly on her earlobe and moved his leg. "Know what else I'd like to feel against my tongue?"

Her nightgown slid upward along the warm denim that covered his thigh. How did he do this so quickly? she wondered, feeling sudden, moist heat pool between her legs. "Uh, Quinn..."

He grazed his teeth along the side of her neck.

Pleasure shot outward from the gentle abrasion. She grasped his head between her hands and pulled back. "Quinn!"

He caught her little finger between his teeth and nipped lightly. "Uh-huh?"

"I thought you didn't want to talk."

He smiled, his eyes gleaming as his gaze dropped to her chest then rose to her heated cheeks. "I also like seeing you blush, Rachel."

"Oh-h." Deciding that perhaps there was nothing wrong with haste, she stretched up and kissed him.

His tongue swept into her mouth as he took charge of the kiss, and Rachel could feel the smile on his lips spread to the rest of his taut body.

She pushed his shirt off his shoulders, splaying her fingers over his chest, as eager for him as he was for her. She raked her nails downward, dipping her fingertips beneath the waistband of his jeans as she shifted sensuously against his thigh.

His breath hissed out on a mumbled curse, and he grasped her by the waist.

She broke off the kiss to look at him, a question in her eyes.

"It's my damn leg," he said, easing her weight off him. He set her on her feet, holding her hips to keep her steady. "I should have known better than to walk so far."

His leg? Of course. The one he'd broken, that was held together with pins. She'd been squirming on top of it. Her flush deepened. "I'm sorry. I didn't think—"

"Hey, it still felt good."

"Should we stop?"

"Hell, no," he growled, pressing closer. "The rest of me's still functioning."

That much was obvious, she thought, leaning back against the wall. Her knees still felt like jelly.

"But I think we need the bed after all," he said.

She tightened her grasp on his waistband. "The floor's closer, Quinn."

With a low chuckle, he carried her down to the carpet with him.

He was using her again, she thought distantly. But she didn't care. If he could use passion to forget, then so could she. Moving her hand lower, she opened the top button of his fly. She had just started on the second when she heard a muffled wail.

Quinn cursed again. "Don't stop," he breathed, his lips on the curve of her breast.

"What?"

"Maybe she'll go back to sleep."

"Yes," Rachel whispered. "She'll go back to sleep."

"She should. She did yesterday."

"She was even more tired-out today."

"Right."

They waited, their pulses pounding, their breathing harsh and rapid, their bodies throbbing from restraint.

Another cry, more insistent than the last.

Quinn lifted his head, his eyes meeting Rachel's, passion and frustration swirling in his gaze. A muscle ticked in his clenched jaw. "She's not going back to sleep."

"No."

He lowered his head quickly, giving Rachel a kiss that sent sparks all the way to her toes. Then with a resigned sigh, he pushed himself to his feet and held out his hand to help her up. "Remember where we left off," he muttered, refastening his jeans as he headed toward Charli's room.

Rachel pressed her hand against the wall to steady herself, amazed that her legs could actually bear her weight. Desire still coursed through her, every nerve ending sensitized by Quinn's touch.

Oh, heavens, she thought, raking her tangled hair out of her face as she glanced at the floor. Was he serious? Remember where they'd left off? With the condition her body was in right now, it wasn't likely to let her forget.

She listened as Quinn murmured quietly to the baby. Charli's wails gradually tapered off to sleepy whimpers. Keeping her hand against the wall for support, Rachel moved to the doorway of the baby's room.

And the sexual desire that pounded through her changed to something far deeper, far more elemental. Quinn was standing by the crib, holding the infant gently against his broad, bare shoulder. The large hands that had been trained to kill and had triggered shivers of delight in Rachel moments ago now soothed protectively over the baby's back. The deep voice that was capable of exciting her with no more than a few whispered, shocking phrases now hummed an off-key lullaby. And the thick blond hair that she'd run her fingers through blended with the baby's wispy pale strands as he leaned his cheek against the top of Charli's head.

Quinn's strength had transformed to tenderness. And he had never looked more masculine or more desirable.

Rachel's heart swelled with a burst of longing that was painful in its intensity. Oh, God, she thought, biting her lip as she leaned against the door frame. Just when she'd believed she was coming to terms with her feelings, how was it possible to love Quinn more?

Chapter 13

Lights bobbed on the waves offshore, quick winks of brightness from the dark shapes on the water. The evening was warm, but the salt-tanged breeze brought a chill from the ocean, causing some of the tourists who had wandered down from the hotel to retreat from the cliff. Many remained, though, probably friends or relatives hoping to glimpse a familiar face among the SEAL trainees that made up the boat crews.

The surf broke loudly against the rocky shore below. Quinn leaned down to check on Charli. Nestled into her stroller, with a light blanket tucked around her sides and a lacy bonnet covering her ears, she appeared to be enjoying the fresh air. Hopefully, the outing would encourage her to sleep more soundly tonight.

"She's fine," Rachel said.

Quinn turned the stroller so that it faced away from the wind. The baby grinned at him and shoved a plastic teething ring into her mouth. He studied her with concern. "The books say that babies get their first tooth around six months," he said. "She's too young to be starting that, isn't she?"

"Two months is probably a bit early for teeth. She just likes to use her mouth to explore things."

"Yeah, I noticed that." He tickled the baby under her chin. She dropped the toy and grabbed his finger, clamping down on it with her gums.

Rachel laughed. "On the other hand, one of these days you'll have to start counting your fingers after she does that."

He retrieved the plastic ring and tucked the blanket more securely around her. The baby immediately kicked her feet free.

"She'll be fine," Rachel repeated. "It's not that cold."

Quinn replaced the blanket, anyway, then straightened up. He was going to need to get some more books if he wanted to do this job right.

In the week since they'd come to the base, he had begun to realize how much he still had to learn about babies. Not only babies, but children. Because Charli was going to grow up eventually.

He still hadn't been able to wrap his mind around that concept. It was hard enough to get used to the notion that he was going to be responsible for the kid for the foreseeable future. Thinking about her growing up, becoming a little girl, then a woman, that was too large an idea to take in all at once.

Yet he'd find a way to handle it. She was his responsibility. His duty. It was up to him to make sure he didn't screw it up.

A sudden cheer went up from the people nearby, drawing Quinn's attention back to the water. One of the dark shapes had broken away from the others and was heading toward the shore.

"What's going on?" Rachel asked.

"They have to land the boat."

A wave struck the rocks at the base of the cliff, sending a plume of spray almost to the top. "Good Lord," Rachel murmured. "In that?"

"Night landings are a necessary part of the training. They're lucky. The ocean's fairly calm tonight."

"They'll be lucky if they're not smashed to bits."

Quinn shook his head. "Injuries are the last thing the master sergeant wants at this stage. If he thought the conditions were dangerous, he'd call off the exercise. It should be perfectly safe, as long as the teams time their approach properly. Holding the end of a line, one man jumps from the bow of the IBS to the rock and plants himself. The rest follow."

"IBS?"

"Inflatable Boat, Small," Quinn explained. "The rubber dinghy. Also known as Itty Bitty Ships."

Rachel smiled. "I thought the Navy didn't have a sense of humor."

"It helps get through Hell Week," he said, keeping his gaze on the first team of recruits. The lead man mistimed his jump, sliding from the slick rock into the water. Yet even as a few spectators gasped in dismay, the team had hauled him back into the raft and were positioning for another try.

Loud laughter and catcalls, amplified by a bullhorn, came from the instructors who were gathered near the base of the cliff.

"I take back what I said about the Navy's sense of humor," Rachel said. "That's terrible. They sound as if they want those recruits to fail."

"On the contrary," Quinn said. "The goading is all part of the program. It's a psychological ploy to weed out the men who will crack under pressure. The recruits have to learn how to partition off their emotions and concentrate on the task."

Rachel paused. "So you're actually trained to do that."

"Emotions can skew a man's judgment," Quinn went on, watching the team make a second attempt. This time the raft came too close, crashing into the side of a rock and spinning sideways before the lead man had a chance to jump. "Those recruits are hungry and tired and dirty, but if they can't close off their feelings, they'll never make it."

"It seems...brutal."

"It's how they survive."

"By walling off their emotions," Rachel said.

Quinn lifted one eyebrow as he glanced at her. "It's the only way to do the job. When lives are at stake, there's no time for the getting-in-touch-with-your-feelings stuff that you're so fond of."

"I guess not."

"Look," he said, pointing to the boat. It had withdrawn to a safer distance from the shore and the men were changing positions. Another recruit had taken up the line and was poised in the bow. This time the man wedged himself securely between two boulders and the team landed successfully.

The instructors had no praise for the team. Instead, only hoots of derision over their lack of finesse came through the bullhorn.

Undaunted by the jeering, a woman near Rachel pumped her arm up and down in a quick victory sign, then turned away and walked back up the slope toward the hotel.

"Do you think she knew someone on that team?" Rachel asked, turning to Quinn.

"It's a safe bet she's someone's wife."

"Did Louisa..." Rachel hesitated for a beat. Then she lifted her chin and finished her question. "Did Louisa watch you from here when you went through this training?"

This was the first time Rachel had brought up the subject of Louisa, Quinn realized. It was strange. He should feel disloyal, or at least uncomfortable, talking about his late wife with his lover. Especially here, on the edge of the cliff where he had said his final goodbye.

And yet, apart from the usual pang of loss that he experienced whenever he thought of Louisa, he didn't feel any awkwardness. Rachel seemed to have a knack for getting him to talk. He looked away, focusing his gaze on the next boat to make the assault on the cliff. "Yes, she did."

"It must have been hard on her."

"She knew I could do it."

"She must have been very proud of you."

"I suppose." He was silent for a while. "Being a Navy wife isn't easy. The attitude of the military is that if they wanted you to have a wife, they would have issued you with one."

"Still, you two managed all right."

"We were apart a lot of the time, but Louisa had plenty of friends. Wherever we were stationed, it didn't take her long to establish a support group of other wives."

"She was always very popular."

"Yes, she was."

"When we were in high school, Louisa was in every club," Rachel said. "She even was president of the Student Council one year."

"That's right."

"I heard that in our senior year, no one was willing to run against her for prom queen. Everyone liked her too much."

He felt his expression soften with the memory. It was easier to remember the early years instead of the suffering at the end. "Yeah. She was—" All of a sudden he realized what Rachel had said. She had *heard* about the prom. Of course, she hadn't attended. No one would have asked her.

A second boat crew managed a successful landing amid a round of cheers from the knot of spectators. Quinn turned his gaze to Rachel. And although he didn't want to do it, he couldn't help comparing her to his wife.

There were obvious physical differences. Louisa had been a tall, willowy blonde. Although Rachel was no longer as plump as she used to be, she couldn't be described as slender. Womanly was the word that came to Quinn's mind. From her thick dark hair to her generous curves, she had a lush beauty that never failed to excite him. They'd made love more times and in more ways in the past week than he and Louisa had ever considered.

But that was only because of the circumstances, he told

himself. And it had been such a long time without sex for both of them. The physical attraction had been strong from the start, and now that they were forced into close proximity because of the small apartment, it was only natural that they couldn't keep their hands off each other.

He frowned, shoving his hands into his pockets. It was getting more and more difficult for him to maintain his objectivity about their situation, to prevent his emotions from interfering with his judgment. Seeing the trainees tonight reminded him of the importance of keeping his feelings under control. No matter how stimulating Rachel's company was proving to be, her safety was still his primary concern.

She had chafed at his first attempts to keep her and Charli confined to the base, so he had compromised by making sure he accompanied them whenever they went out. This excursion to watch the night landing was fairly low risk, since they were only a short drive from the base and within shouting distance of a few dozen highly trained Navy men, should any threat arise. But he could tell that Rachel was getting restless.

Well, it would all be over soon. According to Mikita, the CIA was working with the Navy on the Norlander case now, and things were progressing quickly. A few key arrests had already been made, primarily underlings who were the most likely to testify in exchange for lighter sentences. It was only a matter of time before the whole drug-smuggling network was brought down.

And then there would be no more reason for Rachel to stay with him, would there? Once they got back to Maple Ridge, things would change. Although he had no doubt that their enjoyment of each other was mutual, he and Rachel couldn't continue to sleep together each night—and frequently during the day—as they were now. He knew what would happen if they flaunted their affair in front of the small-town gossips. Back home, attitudes still clung to the old double standard. It would be Rachel's reputation that suffered, not his. She had already endured the ostracism of her peers during her childhood because of her weight problem. He didn't want to cause her more misery. So unless they took extra pains to be discreet, or he decided to marry her—

Quinn drew back, alarmed by the direction of his thoughts. What was wrong with him? He shouldn't confuse his libido with his heart. He'd grown up knowing he would marry Louisa, and his feelings for Rachel were nothing like that easy certainty he'd felt with his wife.

Besides, they'd already gotten this straight. He'd been completely up-front about his intentions weeks ago, and she'd told him then that she didn't want a permanent relationship, either. She'd said that her career and her independence were what mattered the most to her. And that was fine with him. Actually, that was great. Perfect. He didn't need her. He didn't need anyone. He'd just make sure to buy some more books on child care after he went home.

"I guess it's time to go," Rachel said, taking hold of the stroller handles.

Quinn started. *No. Not yet.*

"The last crew made it," she said. "And Charli's fallen asleep."

He looked around. The other spectators were already moving away, as were the weary recruits and their instructors. Rachel and Charli's position here on the cliff top seemed suddenly too exposed, too vulnerable. He'd have to get them somewhere safer. He'd let his attention waver. Instead of concentrating on his duty, he'd been thinking about Rachel. He had to try harder. He didn't want to lose her, too.

But whatever he did, he was going to lose her anyway.

Gripping his cane in one hand, he looped his other arm around Rachel's shoulders and held her close as they walked toward the parking lot. The gesture was out of duty, not affection. The breeze was cool. He wanted to make sure she was warm. And the ground was uneven. He wanted to be sure she didn't stumble. And he wanted to get the kid safely tucked into her crib as soon as possible so he and Rachel could make the most of the time they had left.

Rachel carefully eased Quinn's hand from her breast to her waist, smiling at the way his forehead wrinkled briefly in protest. But within seconds his features relaxed back into sleep, his chest rising and falling soundlessly with his steady, even breathing.

The nightmare hadn't troubled him for three nights now. Maybe he was finally beginning to put the past behind him.

On the other hand, maybe he was simply too exhausted by their regular nocturnal activity to have the energy left to dream about anything.

She blew a tendril of damp hair off her forehead, her smile turning wistful. Who would have thought that a bathtub could be such an erotic location? It had been Quinn's idea. With the soft music playing from the radio and the half-dozen candles he'd placed around the room flickering warmly and the scented steam rising from the water....

Her stomach contracted with an echo of the pleasure he'd brought her. He'd told her that it had been something of a fantasy for him, seeing her in the tub that way. But he hadn't merely looked. He'd touched. And he'd tasted. And it was a good thing that the fresh air had tired out the baby sufficiently to sleep through the noise because the sounds Quinn had wrung from Rachel should have been enough to wake up the entire building.

She ran her palm up Quinn's arm, curving her fingers around his biceps. After a week of the freedom to admire him openly, her fascination with his body hadn't dimmed. He was classically sculpted, a study in lean, firm muscle. Only when he was asleep did she have the chance to look her fill. Because when he was awake, it didn't take long for those muscles to tense, and then to move, and then he'd be overloading her senses with more pleasure than she'd thought was physically possible.

So why wasn't she satisfied?

Her smile faded. She knew why. As enthusiastically as Quinn was taking to the change in their relationship, he was determined not to take it any further than the physical level. Maybe she was only fooling herself to think there might be a chance of unlocking his heart. Maybe it wasn't him. Maybe it was her. Because she wasn't Louisa.

Biting her lip, she looked at Quinn's face. Oh, how she loved this man. More every day. And there wasn't anything temporary about it.

She shifted backward, sliding from beneath his arm. His fingers splayed as his hand fell to the mattress, as if he were seeking her in his sleep. She stood at the side of the bed, tempted to slip back into his embrace and wake him up so they could once more stir the passion that could keep her from her troubling thoughts.

But that's what she'd done for a week. And it was no longer working.

Turning her back on the bed, she picked up his shirt and slipped it on, then walked to the kitchen. The fluorescent ceiling fixture was unmercifully bright, so she switched on the light over the stove. In the dim, bluish glow, she could see the flowered candy dish she had bought yesterday on a trip to a nearby mall with Quinn. It had been a completely unnecessary purchase, but she'd liked the colorful flowers that had been hand painted on the china. She'd thought the kitchen could use some brightening up. She'd hoped the dish would be the kind of little touch that would make the place more of a home.

Oh, God. What was she doing? Trying to compete with Louisa?

Rachel sank down into a chair and pulled the candy dish across the table toward her, running her fingertip along the rim. She was no decorator. She didn't know the first thing about making a house a home. She had grown up knowing that a life of domesticity wasn't for her. Only as a teenager caught in the throes of her hopeless crush on Quinn had she dared to envision marriage and family and happily ever after.

She was living out a fantasy. It might not be as straightforward as Quinn's desire to see her in the bathtub, but it was a fantasy nonetheless. Loving Quinn, staying with him, it was like the fulfillment of a teenage dream.

But ultimately it was just as unreal.

Despite their physical intimacy, despite the time they were spending together, she knew he was still holding part of himself back. He didn't love her.

Naturally. Why would he love her? she thought, picking up a piece of toffee and twisting off the wrapper. He'd already experienced the one great love of his life. Perfect, lovable Louisa, who had cheered for him as he'd done his SEAL training just as she had cheered for him when he'd played football. Had Louisa waved her little pom-poms on that cliff top? Had she done a few perky jumps and cartwheels?

Ashamed of her unkind thoughts, Rachel popped the toffee in her mouth. She hadn't been able to compete with Louisa when they'd been teenagers. She hadn't even considered trying. She'd known it was hopeless. Rachel couldn't have made Quinn love her any more than she could have made her father love her. Maybe that was one of the reasons she'd focused so much of her affection on Quinn. He'd been unattainable, and so in a roundabout way, he'd been safe.

Impatiently Rachel ate another candy, then pushed away from the chair and crossed the floor to open the fridge. She reached for a carton of juice, then changed her mind and picked up the foil plate of leftover fried chicken and carried it back to the table.

How long was she going to let this situation continue? Was the physical pleasure Quinn was giving her worth the growing heartache? Physically he was no longer unattainable, but his love remained out of her reach. Back in high school she had known she couldn't measure up to the popular, athletic, model-thin Louisa, so she had been content to live out her pathetic crush on Quinn in secret.

And now the pattern was threatening to repeat. Night after night, Rachel was keeping silent about her feelings. She was willing to give Quinn whatever he asked for, whatever he needed, and she was happily accepting whatever he gave in return.

Where was her pride? Where was the self-confidence she'd fought so hard to build? So what if her father had deserted her? So what if Quinn didn't want to fall in love with her? It didn't mean she was unlovable, did it?

Did it?

Rachel wiped her fingers on Quinn's shirt, then looked around the kitchen. She went to the counter and lifted the plastic wrap from the pan of brownies she had baked that morning. Determinedly she pried the largest piece out of the pan.

No, there was nothing wrong with her, she thought fiercely, licking the fudge icing off the top of the brownie. She'd come to terms with that more than a decade ago, and she would never get caught in the trap of depending on someone else for her own self-worth again. Owen Healey's problems had been a weak character and a lack of responsibility. He'd barely had enough time to get to know his daughter before he'd deserted her. She and her mother had probably been better off without him. As Ann always said, loving someone left a person too vulnerable. That's why it was so important to maintain control of her life. Depending on anyone else was too dangerous. It could only lead to—

Rachel choked as she tried to swallow too quickly. She coughed, dislodging a piece of pecan that was stuck in her throat, then filled a glass with water and took a hurried drink. And as she set the glass down, she noticed the smears of chocolate that her fingers had left. Automatically she lifted her hand to her mouth and began to lick off the brownie crumbs.

And suddenly, the taste of the chocolate was too bitter, the icing too cloying. Her stomach lurched.

What was she doing?

In dawning horror, she glanced around the kitchen, at the pan on the counter, at the greasy chicken bones on the table, at the pile of empty candy wrappers.

"Oh, my God," she whispered. She looked down at the traces of food on Quinn's white shirt. And in her mind she saw her body expand, saw her thighs enlarge, saw her hips balloon, saw the old image that had reflected the unhappiness she had felt with her life, with her self.

It was starting again. The pattern was repeating. She was slipping back into her old behavior.

"Oh, *God!*"

With a sweep of her arm, she cleared off the table. Chicken bones scattered, candy bounced across the floor, and the hand-painted dish broke into a dozen jagged pieces.

Her vision blurred with tears as she stared at the smashed china, seeing the shattered fantasy of her teenage yearning for Quinn. She wouldn't let it start again. She had come too far. She was no longer the same girl. Her life was under control. She wasn't unlovable.

No, she wasn't unlovable. She had just picked the wrong person to love. The very worst person to love. Because she had known from the start that loving Quinn was going to open up all the old wounds. She'd known it was going to push her right back into the old insecurities.

And yet she'd done it, anyway.

And now she was turning to food once again as a way to escape what she didn't want to face, a way to compensate for the love she felt she lacked.

"Rachel?"

Quinn was there, standing in the doorway, one side of his hair flattened from the pillow and a red sleep wrinkle pressed into his cheek. His chest was bare, his jeans riding low on his hips and a patch of dark hair showing below his navel at the open stud of his waistband. And dammit, he looked adorable and sexy and more appealing than the whole plate of chocolate brownies.

And ultimately, just as bad for her.

"What happened?" he asked, doing a quick survey of the kitchen. "Are you all right?"

"No."

He strode across the floor, kicking aside the shards of broken china. But when he would have reached for her, she held up her palms and stepped back.

"No," she repeated. "Keep away from me."

"What—"

"Don't touch me."

His gaze was keen as he searched her face. "What's wrong, Rachel? Did I do something earlier—"

"Did you do something?" She laughed. "No, you didn't do anything, Quinn. Nothing at all. You've been completely predictable."

"What are you talking about?"

"You, me. Us. I'm not going to go through it again."

"Rachel, I don't understand."

"No, you wouldn't," she said, blinking hard, willing herself not to cry, although she could feel her eyes heat with helpless tears. "But I'm not going to watch my life self-destruct again."

He reached past her upraised palms and stroked her cheek. "Talk to me, Rachel. Tell me what's going on."

"I ate the chicken."

He glanced at the bones on the floor. "So? You were hungry. We both worked up an appetite earlier tonight."

"Don't you dare make light of this, Quinn."

His hand dropped to her shoulder. "All right. I'm sorry. Tell me what's wrong."

What's wrong is that I love you, she thought, staring at his face, leaning into his touch. And she felt the familiar tingles of awareness spread through her body.

She was pathetic. Absolutely without pride. Even knowing how destructive her love for Quinn was to her self-confidence, she couldn't stop it. Grasping his face between her hands, she kissed him with a pent-up frustration that was part anger, part desperation.

She loved him. And right now she almost hated him.

He pulled back, his eyebrows lifting in surprise. "Rachel?"

"That's right. I'm Rachel," she said. "I'm not Louisa."

"Of course not. I never thought—"

"And I'm not Lardo or Beluga or Blimp." Her fingers curled into fists as she uttered the names she'd been tormented with. "And I won't be ever again."

Gently he enclosed her fists within his hands. "No, you've come a long, long way. You're a different person now."

"Yes." She glared at him in challenge. "I'm different. I won't let the pattern repeat."

"One midnight snack doesn't necessarily mean—"

"It's not just the food, Quinn. It's not my appearance I'm worried about. It's what it means here," she said, pulling her hand free to point at her chest. "Inside."

He looked at her in silence for a moment. "Why did you eat tonight?"

"Because I've been so worried about your feelings that I buried mine."

"And what do you feel, Rachel?"

This was it, her opportunity to finally tell him the truth, to reveal the secret that she had carried throughout her teenage years, to share the realization she had been living with for a week, to end the fantasy.

Her throat went dry. Despite the words that clamored in her head, no sound passed her lips. Why couldn't she do it? Why couldn't she take the chance?

Because she didn't want to risk losing him altogether, that's why.

The declaration she wanted to make hung in the air between them, thick and heavy in the silence of the dimly lit kitchen.

And as each second passed, Rachel saw her chance slipping away. She pressed her lips together briefly, then exhaled hard. "Let's talk about this in the morning."

There was no mistaking the expression that flashed across Quinn's face. It was relief.

Well? What had she expected? She knew how difficult it was for Quinn to deal with emotions. The Navy had trained him to suppress his feelings, and his personal tragedies had only reinforced the pattern. Did she think that a few short weeks and a few dozen romps between the sheets would change that?

Patterns. They each had their own. Were they doomed to keep repeating them?

Without warning, Quinn brought his mouth down hard on hers. It was like the kiss she had just given him, full of frustration and anger. But then it changed. The pressure of the kiss eased until he was stroking her lips softly, tenderly, giving instead of taking. His hands cradled her cheeks as if she were something precious, someone to be treasured. Maybe even loved.

No. No more fantasies. Reaching between them, she thrust her hand down the front of his jeans.

But if she'd thought to lose herself in their passion, Quinn had other ideas. He caught her wrist, gently lifting her hand to press it to his chest. And when she would have pulled him down to the kitchen table on top of her, he twined his fingers with hers and led her back to the bedroom. Carefully, reverently, he brought her to the edge of oblivion, again and again. And when he finally gave her body the release it craved, he made no mention of the tears he licked from her cheeks.

And again Rachel knew that they weren't really making love. No, this time, it felt as if they were saying goodbye.

Chapter 14

"What's wrong with her?" Mikita demanded. "She's not sick, is she?"

Quinn paced to the other side of the office, rubbing Charli's back. "She's fine."

Balfour, the shorter of the two CIA men who sat in the chairs in front of Mikita's desk, shifted to follow Quinn's movements. "Could be colic," he said, raising his voice to be heard over the din. "My youngest was like that."

"She's fine," Quinn repeated, making another circuit. "Just hungry."

"Then feed her," Mikita snapped.

"She needs to calm down first or she will be sick," Quinn said.

"Good set of lungs on her," the Judge Advocate General lawyer commented. He brushed at a wrinkle in his white uniform. "She's got a bright future in the military. Reminds me of a certain sergeant I once knew."

"Hell of a way to conduct a meeting," Mikita said, reaching for his pipe.

"Sir, I'd prefer it if you didn't smoke," Quinn said immediately.

Mikita scowled and crossed his arms. "You should have left the kid at the apartment."

Quinn set his jaw as his ears rang from another wail. He would have preferred to have left Charli with Rachel, but Rachel had decided to go jogging just minutes before Mikita's aide had arrived. And after eight days of waiting, there was no way Quinn was going to miss the opportunity to be present at this meeting. So he had stuffed a bottle into the baby's diaper bag and had carried Charli out to the commander's jeep. The baby had been quiet on the ride. But the moment they had stopped, she had started to cry.

Rachel had had difficulty settling her down earlier, too. She'd said it was because Charli was picking up on the tension around her.

And there'd been plenty of that in the apartment this morning. Something had changed last night. It was as if the comfortable bubble he and Rachel had built around themselves was collapsing, and there was nothing he could do to stop it. Instead of the sweet giving he'd grown accustomed to, there had been a desperate edge to Rachel's lovemaking.

What do you feel, Rachel?

She hadn't answered him when he'd asked her that. And the hell of it was, Quinn hadn't really wanted an answer. He wanted things to go on the way they were. She'd said they'd talk about it in the morning, but the cranky baby had needed attention, and then Rachel had decided to go out, and the opportunity to talk hadn't come up. And he'd been glad that it hadn't.

He knew what he was doing—he was running away again. It was so much easier to bury the emotions instead of dealing with them.

Yet this wasn't the time or the place for worrying about his relationship with Rachel. He had more immediate concerns. With an effort, he focused his thoughts on his present situation, his gaze going over the men who were gathered in Mikita's office.

Except for Quinn, they all wore uniforms. Although the dark suits of the men from the CIA weren't as obvious a uniform as the Navy's dress whites, the purpose they served was the same. They were symbols of authority. And judging by the atmosphere that was crackling around them when Quinn had arrived, not one man here wanted to acknowledge the authority of another.

It wasn't any mystery why the investigation into the explosion and Norlander's involvement in the drug ring had been going on for more than a year. It had been caught in the no-man's-land of cross-agency rivalry.

"This is ridiculous," Mikita snapped. "I'll have my secretary take the kid—"

"No, she's my responsibility," Quinn said, lifting the baby in front of him. He waited for her to take a breath, then blew gently into her face. Startled out of the rhythm of her crying, she inhaled sharply and blinked at him.

Encouraged, he did it again.

Charli hiccuped, her chin trembling. But the next breath she drew was almost silent.

"Those SEALs have a truly amazing range of skills," the second CIA man, the taller one, drawled. "Are you teaching them how to be nursemaids before you show them how to blow up warehouses, Mikita?"

The commander picked up his pipe again. He glanced at his tin of tobacco, his scowl deepening, then clamped the cold pipe stem between his teeth. "My people are the best," he said. "Whatever job they take on."

"They're a bunch of overrated loose cannons," the CIA man muttered.

"You don't mind using them for jobs you pencil pushers don't want to dirty your hands with," the JAG lawyer said. "And if your intelligence was half as reliable as you claimed it was—"

"Gentlemen," Mikita growled. "We've already covered this."

The CIA man appeared to be preparing to retort when Charli snuffled loudly. He frowned at the baby, then pressed his lips together and drummed his fingers against his knee.

Quinn ignored the bickering and went over to get the bottle out of the baby's bag, then took the last remaining chair and settled Charli in the crook of his arm.

Mikita narrowed his eyes, watching in silence for a moment as Quinn fed the baby. "All right. Let's get on with this."

"Good idea." Balfour conferred briefly with his partner, then reached beside his chair, swung a briefcase onto his lap and unlocked the clasps. "All right. As agreed, here are our files on the individuals we have in custody."

Mikita leaned across his desk to take the folders. He glanced through them, nodded, then handed them to the lawyer. More papers were grudgingly exchanged and examined, along with terse summaries of the status of the case.

As Quinn had guessed when he'd received Mikita's summons, matters were drawing to a close. Enough evidence had been assembled to arrest the key people in the smuggling operation. A predawn raid this morning had made a clean sweep of the rest of the criminals. It was no longer either Navy or CIA jurisdiction. Now it was up to the courts.

And that was that.

Somehow Quinn hadn't thought the end would feel so anticlimactic. Darlene's desperate abandonment of her child, her futile attempt to escape the criminals, the pain of John's betrayal, the terrible deaths of the team...it didn't seem right that it had all been reduced to a group of well-dressed men having a meeting.

But of course, why shouldn't it be like that? Emotions had no place in this kind of situation. Emotions only messed things up.

There was a round of curt handshakes, then the two government men left with the Navy lawyer. Quinn picked up the diaper bag and lifted Charli to his shoulder, preparing to follow them, when Mikita called him back.

The commander's mouth thinned. He regarded the baby for a moment before he lifted his gaze to Quinn. "The Navy appreciates your cooperation, Keelor."

"Thank you, sir."

"The Norlander case is finished. The investigation into the incident in Panama will be officially closed."

"I gathered that, sir."

"That means you've got no more reason to remain on the base," Mikita stated bluntly.

More than the investigation was over, Quinn knew. His time here with Rachel was over, too. He'd known it would happen eventually, but having it end like this also seemed too... anticlimactic.

"I'm aware of that," Quinn said finally. "We'll be moved out of the apartment as soon as possible."

"There is another option for you to consider."

Quinn lifted his brows. "What?"

"We can always use instructors in the BUDs program. That bum leg of yours wouldn't stop you from training the recruits."

Rejoin the Navy? Quinn paused. "I hadn't considered that possibility."

"What else would you do?" Mikita asked.

"I intend to return home."

"And be some second-rate mechanic in a small-town garage? That's a hell of a waste of the education the Navy gave you."

"I have other responsibilities now." Quinn felt Charli draw her knees up to her chest. He rubbed his fingertips lightly between her shoulder blades, and the baby obliged immediately with a loud burp.

Mikita swore under his breath. "Keelor, you don't have to keep that kid."

Quinn's hand splayed over Charli's back. "Darlene Norlander made me her daughter's guardian."

"The investigation is finished, so your obligation to Norlander is over. That guardianship paper wouldn't hold up if you contested it. Any good lawyer would be able to get you out of this."

Mikita was right. Legally there was nothing compelling Quinn to assume the duty of raising this child. That's what the lawyer he'd hired before he'd left New York had told him, too. If he chose, he could turn his back on this entire situation.

And if he thought about it, that would be the logical thing to do, wouldn't it? Why should he take on this responsibility? Child rearing wasn't what he was trained for. Any debt he owed his team had been canceled by John's betrayal, hadn't it?

He rubbed his thumb over John's ring. No. He still had a duty to his men. It wasn't over.

And as long as he had the baby, there would still be a reason to keep Rachel in his life.

Rachel paused outside the apartment door to catch her breath and leaned over to brace her hands on her knees. She was out of condition. For the past two months, she'd let her usual exercise regimen slide. It had been almost two weeks since she'd gone running. More than that since she'd gone to the gym for a workout. She shouldn't have pushed herself so hard today. She'd undoubtedly be sore tomorrow.

But if her muscles ached, perhaps it would be for the best. It would serve as a reminder. She wasn't going to slide back into the old self-destructive pattern. It wasn't going to start again. It couldn't. Because she was no longer the same girl.

She used her forearm to wipe the sweat off her face and straightened up. No, she was no longer the same weak person she used to be. She might have had a lapse with the fried chicken and the brownies, but she was taking control of her life once more. She wouldn't let her love for Quinn—for anyone—make her vulnerable, she thought, reaching for the door-knob.

Before she could touch the knob, the door swung open. Quinn stood in the doorway, his face creased with worry. "Where have you been?"

Until yesterday, the protectiveness in his tone would have pleased her. But her emotions were too volatile, too close to that fine line between love and hate, for her to accept his concern. She bristled. "I told you I was going jogging."

"It's been two hours."

"I took a break for a while. And I didn't think I had to check in with you," she said, brushing past him to enter the apartment. "I stayed on the base so there was no need to worry..." Her words trailed off as she caught sight of the suitcase. "What's going on?" she asked.

"We have to move out."

She pushed back a strand of damp hair that had come loose from her ponytail and turned to face him. "Why?"

"I just came from Mikita's office."

Her heartbeat, still elevated from her run, slammed into a new rhythm. "What did he say?"

"The Feds moved in on the drug gang early this morning. They have the entire group in custody."

"They're in jail?"

"Yes."

"We're no longer in danger?"

"That's right."

"Then—" she looked back at the suitcase "—it's over."

"Yes."

She'd known it would happen. She just hadn't expected the announcement to come so quickly, without any fuss or fanfare. It seemed too easy, for something that was going to be so difficult. She inhaled unsteadily. "We can go home."

"I'll be meeting with my lawyer first to finalize the guardianship documents for Charli, but we'll be able to return to Maple Ridge in a few days."

"We?"

"I thought since Charli's so accustomed to you, it might be best if you came with us."

"For Charli."

"Yes."

"And that's all?"

He stepped closer, lifting his hand to stroke her cheek. "Things won't be the same once we get home. I don't want to say goodbye to you yet, Rachel."

Oh, damn. Damn! How much longer was he going to drag this out? How many more times would they extend their temporary association? She wasn't going to go on like this. She couldn't. Last night had shown her that. So despite the way she felt her body soften at his touch, despite the way she was already swaying toward him, she squared her shoulders and stepped back. "No, Quinn."

His hand dropped. "I don't want to say goodbye," he repeated. "We're good together, Rachel. When we get home—"

"What? What exactly do you think will happen?"

"I thought we could continue to see each other."

She shook her head. "It's a small town. We both know we can't continue what we're doing. No one's going to believe I'm simply your baby-sitter. It would be easier for both of us if we ended this affair now."

"I don't want it to end."

"That's the definition of temporary, isn't it? Eventually it has to end."

Quinn looked at her in silence for a minute. A muscle twitched in his cheek. "Then be my wife," he said finally.

"What?"

"I remember you said you didn't want a permanent relationship, but I'm not going to interfere with your career. And you don't have to lose your independence—"

"Quinn, are you saying you want to marry me?"

"It seems like the best solution. It would put a stop to any gossip that might have gotten started about us."

Rachel rubbed her face, getting rid of the remnants of sweat from her run. Her T-shirt stuck clammily to her back, her ponytail drooped against the back of her neck. And Quinn was asking her to marry him.

Fifteen years ago this would have been a dream come true. No, she hadn't gone so far as to even dream this could happen. Quinn Keelor wanted to marry her. Shock took her voice. She could only stare.

"I know you've grown attached to Charli," he went on. "This way you won't have to leave her, either. You'd be able to watch her grow up."

Oh, God. It was more than she'd ever dreamed, way more.

"Charli needs a mother," Quinn said, reaching for her hand to stop her from retreating further. "She probably already has bonded with you. I know you don't really want to leave her."

Her heart swelled with love and with a mad, irrepressible seed of hope. Could it be possible? Not only Quinn Keelor, but Charli, the abandoned cherub with the powder-soft baby scent and the wispy blond hair and the trusting blue eyes and the solid little body that felt so right in her arms…

Rachel inhaled unsteadily as the future she had wanted too strongly, too deeply, to dare to consider until now flitted through her mind. A child of her own. Her arms wouldn't need to feel empty ever again. On the parents' nights at school she would have her own child to take pictures of and to cheer for during the Christmas pageant, and she'd have Quinn by her side as they drank the watery punch and made small talk with the other families. And when she went home it wouldn't be to a lonely apartment, it would be to their daughter's goodnight kiss and Quinn's embrace and…

But a marriage only for the sake of a child never worked. That's how it had been for her parents—they'd married because Ann had been pregnant, and it had led to nothing but misery for all of them. She searched Quinn's gaze. "Is that the only reason you want to marry me? Because of Charli?"

"No, that's not the only reason." He smiled. "Like I said, we're good together."

She waited, but that was as far as he went. The hope wavered. "You mean we're good in bed."

"Among other places."

"So you want me to marry you so you can get free baby-sitting and plenty of regular sex."

His smile faded. "Rachel..."

"Those seem like rational, logical reasons, all right. What about love?"

He went suddenly, completely still. And just like last night, the words she wanted to say hung heavily in the air between them. Only this time she wasn't going to retreat. This time she would take the chance.

"I love you, Quinn," she said, proud of the way her voice was steady despite the shaking in her knees. "I don't care if you don't want to hear it. I'm through burying my feelings. I love you."

He tightened his grip on her fingers.

She could feel tears burn her eyes at his silence. She had known it would be like this. That's why she'd delayed for so long.

But why should she worry about losing him? It didn't look as if she'd really ever had him in the first place.

"I love you," she repeated. "But I won't be compared to some impossible ideal. I'm not willing to take whatever you deign to give me, while you keep your heart locked away for Louisa."

"This has nothing to do with Louisa."

"No? Did you love her?"

"Of course I loved her."

"Do you love me?"

The hesitation was no more than the blink of an eye, but it was long enough to cut Rachel to the bone. Snatching her hand from his, she spun around.

"Rachel, what I feel for you is completely different from

what I felt for Louisa, because you're different people. I like your warmth and your generosity. I admire your strength. I respect your intelligence.'' He came up behind her and lowered his head to the crook of her neck. ''And I can't get enough of your body.''

His breath teased over her damp skin, making her quiver with longing. ''But do you love me?'' she whispered.

He pressed his lips to the side of her throat, his tongue sending sparks of pleasure across her skin.

She felt something tear apart inside. Blinking hard, she pushed his head away. ''Quinn, no. We can't keep using sex to avoid our feelings.''

He caught her shoulders. ''You don't have to decide right away. You can take a few days to think it over.''

She pressed her knuckles to her eyes. But she wasn't going to back down now. And she wasn't going to run to the kitchen and hide her insecurities under a pan of chocolate brownies. ''No,'' she said. ''I'm not going to get caught in the pattern.''

''What?''

''I'm not unlovable,'' she said, turning around to face him. ''I'm not going to spend my life loving someone who won't love me.''

''I'm offering you marriage. And a child.''

A tear brimmed over her eyelid and trickled hotly down her cheek. ''But without love, our relationship wouldn't last. I know. I've seen it happen. We'd only end up hurting each other and Charli.''

''Our situation isn't the same as your parents'.''

''In all the ways that matter, it's the same pattern. There are just too damn many patterns.''

Quinn brushed her cheek with the tip of his thumb, feeling the heat of her tears burn through to his soul. He had never felt more helpless in his life. He wished he could lie. He wished he could promise her the love she wanted, but he respected her too much to pretend.

Did he love her? He didn't love her the way he had loved

his wife. He'd known that yesterday, when the idea of marriage to Rachel had first occurred to him.

And dammit, he didn't *want* to love her. Emotions made a man weak. They lowered his defenses. They led to mistakes and death and betrayal and disaster—

Yet the idea of giving her up, of watching her walk away, was absolutely unthinkable.

"Excuse me," Rachel said, pulling away. "I need to pack my things."

He acted without thinking, stepping in front of her and wrapping her in a hard embrace. "Not yet."

She trembled. "Quinn, let me go."

"Not yet," he repeated. "I want to hold you. I want to see you smile. I need to feel your heat surround me—"

"No!" She struck him hard in the chest with her fist. "No, Quinn. I'm not going to take any more."

"But I—"

"This has always been about you, hasn't it? Your nightmares, your problems, your needs." She hit him again, fresh tears flowing down her cheeks. "What about *me?* What about *my* needs?"

The pain in Rachel's voice was more than he could bear. "I've tried to take care of you."

"Take care of me? If you mean the sex, then yes, you've performed admirably."

"I mean I've always cared, Rachel. That's why we should get married. I don't want you to be the target of gossip again. I saw what it was like for you as a teenager."

"I survived just fine." She shoved away and headed for the bedroom. "You don't have to feel responsible for me."

He followed her through the doorway, standing to one side as she tossed her suitcase on the bed. "But I do feel responsible," he said. "I always have. Even when we were kids."

"Don't pretend, Quinn." She wrenched open a dresser drawer and scooped out handfuls of clothes to dump in the suitcase. "You never knew I existed. You didn't see anyone but Louisa."

"That's not true. I saw how you felt about me, but I was too caught up—"

"What do you mean?" she asked, her head snapping up. "How do you know how I felt?"

He gestured impatiently. "That crush you had on me. I didn't know how to handle it—"

"You knew?" she cried. "How? I never told anyone."

"Your eyes, Rachel. They've always shown what you're feeling."

Hot color flooded her face. "Oh, my God. You knew all along?"

"Yes, I knew. But—"

"My God," she repeated, the strength seeming to go out of her knees. She sat down heavily on the edge of the mattress. "All those years of watching your games. All those times I helped you study. You knew."

It had been the wrong thing to say, he realized belatedly. He hadn't stopped to think how she would react. It had been so obvious to him, he'd assumed she had been aware that her crush hadn't been a secret. "We were young, Rachel. And we—"

"Did Louisa know, too?" she asked. "Did you two have a good laugh about how the Blimp—"

"It wasn't like that," he said. In three strides he closed the distance between them. "Rachel, please don't do this to yourself."

She rolled away from him before he could touch her, scrambling to the other side of the bed. The same bed where they had slept in each other's arms. Now it was like a barrier between them. "God, I'm a fool. I loved you fifteen years ago. And you knew. And you didn't care then, either."

"I did care."

"Right. You pitied me. You felt responsible. Damn, I should have seen it. I just didn't want to."

"What do you mean?"

"I'm just another responsibility to you, aren't I? Like Charli. Like your team. You feel obligated to marry me because you think it's your duty to take care of me."

"You've got this all wrong."

She shook her head. "No, I think it's finally starting to make sense. Why are you keeping Charli?"

"You know why. You saw the paper Darlene signed."

"You look at that baby as a mission, don't you?" she went on. "You don't want to love her, either."

"I'm willing to make a lifetime commitment to her," he said. "That's more than most men would do."

"That's true. But you're not like most men." She wiped her eyes roughly with the back of her hand. "You're so determined to be strong by burying your emotions, you can't see that it takes more strength to set them free."

Quinn clenched his jaw. She was talking about strength, when he felt completely powerless. "Rachel, don't go yet. We can work this out somehow."

She snapped shut her suitcase. She didn't move away, but everything about her seemed to withdraw. Her back straightened and a veil of defensiveness descended over her gaze. "No, Quinn."

His pulse stuttered with a surge of panic. "Rachel!"

The smile she gave him was strained, and so full of sadness that he felt his eyes sting. She was retreating further and further with each second that went by. He could still touch her if he lifted his arm, but he knew she was already out of his reach.

"I love you, Quinn," she said finally. "But I won't go back to the way I used to be. I'm no longer going to settle for what you're willing to give. Yes, I want Charli, and I want the pleasure you and I can share with our bodies, but that's not enough. I want it all, Quinn. And if I can't have your love, then I'd be better off on my own."

He swallowed, his throat thick with words he wished he could say.

Picking up her suitcase, Rachel walked out the door.

Chapter 15

It was the kind of ideal day depicted on postcards. The sky was an inverted azure bowl, speckled with gracefully wheeling gulls. The sea was a gently undulating expanse of blue, lapping rhythmically at the glistening dark rocks. On the cliff top, the sun-warmed breeze caressed the ends of Quinn's hair and fluttered the ribbons that fastened Charli's bonnet beneath her chin. Stopping at the edge of the path, Quinn put the brake on the stroller and sank down to sit on the margin of grass.

Three days ago he'd come here with Rachel to watch the recruits, but apart from a lone sailboat to the west, the ocean was empty.

And he couldn't remember feeling so alone in his life.

He drew up his leg, leaning his forearm across his knee as he watched the waves roll in. Rachel had returned to Maple Ridge two days ago. She hadn't wanted to talk to him when he'd called yesterday. She'd thanked him for arranging to have her car returned from Buffalo, but her voice had held the same note of resigned sadness he remembered all too well from the day she'd left. She wanted to make a clean break. And he could understand that. She was a warm, loving woman, and she deserved a man who could love her in return....

Quinn closed his eyes and pinched the bridge of his nose. As much as he wanted Rachel to be happy, he didn't want to think of her with another man. The mere idea of Rachel sharing her heart with someone else made his muscles tighten with dark, primitive possessiveness. Was he jealous? Hell, yes. Did he have the right to be? Hell, no. Not if he wasn't willing to give her what she asked for.

The plastic beads that he'd strung across the front of the stroller clicked together. Opening his eyes, he turned to look at Charli.

Framed by the white lace bonnet, Charli's face was a circle of softness, her gaze as innocent as the blue water that sparkled on the horizon. Her eyes were the same color as her father's, and her mouth formed the same Cupid's bow that had characterized her mother's. Quinn studied her features, searching for other resemblances.

There were plenty of similarities. For Charli's sake, he hoped that the resemblance didn't extend past the surface. Had she inherited her mother's cowardice? Her father's duplicity? Would she grow up to betray her friends? Would she run away from her problems the way both her parents had?

He shook his head, a harsh sound coming from his throat. Who was he to condemn Darlene and John for running away? He'd been doing far too much of that himself.

"Well, kid?" he murmured. "Are you planning on giving me trouble when you grow up?"

Charli grinned and kicked her feet.

"Because if you are," Quinn said, "I'm warning you right now, I'm going to be running a tight ship."

The baby kicked her feet again and one of her white knit booties tumbled to the grass.

"I won't put up with any nonsense," Quinn continued, retrieving the bootie. He slipped it back on her foot, his blunt-tipped fingers awkward as he refastened the tiny bow over her instep. "You're going to grow up to be a responsible member of society. And if you ever get yourself in a situation when you need help, you'll come to me, right?"

Charli squirmed and waved her arms, arching against the back of the stroller.

Quinn reached for her, forgetting for a moment about the strap that held her in place. The stroller tipped forward precariously. Grimacing, Quinn unbuckled the strap across her waist and lifted her out. "Sorry, kid. You're going to have to bear with me for a while, until I get the hang of things."

The baby didn't seem to mind his ineptness. She settled happily onto his lap, her back supported by his broad palm as he positioned her to face him.

"We'll have to find a new place to stay, once Leona and her family come back," he went on, tilting his head from one side to the other to get her attention. "I guess you'll call her Aunt Leona. And you can call my father Gramps, just like her kids do. Do you remember him? He's the big guy with the red plaid shirt."

Charli crossed her eyes in her effort to focus on Quinn's face.

He stroked her cheek with the backs of his fingers. "I know you'd rather see Rachel than Aunt Leona and Gramps, but she probably won't come around when I'm there. It's not because she doesn't want to see you," he said, his voice roughening as he remembered Rachel's tearful face as she'd given Charli a goodbye kiss. "No, she likes you a lot. The truth is, I blew it."

Pursing her lips, Charli blew a stream of bubbles.

"She thinks I want to marry her out of a sense of duty," he said, wiping Charli's chin. "She thinks it's some kind of noble impulse left over from when we were kids and I felt sorry for her. But it's not like that. I want to marry her because that's the best solution for all of us. We were getting along fine. Why shouldn't we just continue?"

A gull screamed and dove toward the waves. Quinn looked

past Charli, his gaze going to the horizon. And a surge of loneliness, more powerful than before, made his breath catch in his throat.

He probably shouldn't have come here this morning. Their bags were packed, their flight was booked, and he'd checked out of the hotel. But the memories of this cliff top had drawn him back. Not because of that evening he'd spent standing here with Rachel. No, it was the time before that. When he'd stood here holding his wife.

He'd loved Louisa. Yes, he had. She had fit so perfectly into his life, he'd never considered living without her. But their love had been young and sweet. It had been based on affection and loyalty rather than passion. That's why they had been able to endure the long absences that had been such a large part of his profession. And then her illness had taken her away before—

Before what? Before their love could deepen? Before Louisa had had the chance to mature?

It had been raining the day of the funeral. It hadn't been a blustery, thundering storm but a resigned drizzle. There had been no wind to take the ashes, so the powdery flecks had drifted downward in a slowly widening arc until they had blended with the ocean. Moisture had clung to the sides of the empty urn like tears. But those had been the only tears shed as Quinn had said goodbye to Louisa. His eyes had been dry. He'd thought he was being strong.

You're so determined to be strong by burying your emotions, you can't see that it takes more strength to set them free.

Rachel's words swirled on the breeze, so warm and real that Quinn almost looked around to see if she had come back. But he knew she hadn't. She wouldn't, not after the way he had thrown away the chance she had offered him.

I love you, Quinn.

He clenched his jaw, feeling a sudden swelling at the back of his throat. Rachel's declaration hadn't been a surprise.

Some part of him had known how she'd felt all along. It hadn't been simply sex that they'd been sharing. For the past month she had stood by him through every difficulty, every revelation, every painful step of his slow climb back to life.

Yes, life. The difference between living and merely being alive. Emotions. Anger, joy, hate, desire, disappointment...the whole range of human feelings that he'd thought were buried with Louisa and his team.

He rubbed the silver band of the ring that had belonged to Charli's father. He still felt anger over John's betrayal, but mostly he felt sadness. His friends could never come back. Yet because of Rachel's patience and understanding, the memories of happier times, of how his friends had lived instead of how they had died, were beginning to surface more and more.

A wave, larger than the rest, broke on the rocky shore with a plume of spray. The salt-tanged air seemed to carry an echo of men's voices, the exultant "hoo-yah" of his team when they had done their first night landing at this very spot all those years ago.

The lump in his throat was getting too big to swallow past. Quinn parted his lips to breathe through his mouth. Yet he didn't try to shut the memories out. It took more strength than he'd thought he had, but he was determined to set his memories—and his emotions—free.

Gino had laughed at the catcalls from the instructors. He'd claimed the landing had been child's play, and if it hadn't been for Hoffman's quick thinking and the broad palm he'd slapped across Gino's mouth, they probably would have been sent out to do it again. Simms hadn't laughed—he'd have been asleep on his feet if it hadn't been for the boost of sugar he'd gotten from the candies that John had smuggled in.

Even then, John had gone outside the rules. But he'd never meant any harm. His uncanny ability to scrounge the best supplies wherever they'd been stationed had often proved invaluable to the team. How were any of them to know that his strength would turn out to be his weakness? And how could

Quinn continue to condemn Norlander when the same thing could be said about Quinn himself?

He'd thought that he had done his best to keep his mind on his last mission. But no amount of reason or logic could have predicted what John had been planning. And Quinn hadn't picked up on the signals or noticed that something was wrong with John because that would have meant trusting his emotions, wouldn't it? And he'd been too determined to ignore them.

Could the explosion have been avoided if Quinn *hadn't* tried to bury his heart with Louisa?

Maybe emotions didn't lead to disaster. Maybe ignoring them did.

Dammit, how much guilt was a man supposed to take?

Let it go, Quinn. You've been carrying this on your own long enough.

Rachel had made it sound simple. It hadn't been easy to let go, but the more he practiced, the less difficult it had become. And it was all because of Rachel and her love....

But Rachel was gone.

Because he hadn't had the courage to take another chance.

The sky blurred. With disbelief, Quinn felt something hot and wet carve a path down his cheek.

Charli wriggled on his lap and gave an impatient cry.

Quinn returned his gaze to the baby. "I told you you'd have to bear with me," he said, blinking against the moisture in his eyes. "It's going to take me a while to get the hang of this."

She waved a fist, then jammed it into her mouth and sucked on her knuckle.

"You hungry already, kid?"

She sucked harder, her tiny brows angling together.

"You ate half an hour ago," he murmured. He shifted the baby to his shoulder and rubbed her back. "What's wrong?"

Of course the baby couldn't answer him, but Quinn could make a guess. She was sensitive enough to pick up on his feelings. That's all he needed, right? An emotional barometer.

As if taking care of the kid on his own wasn't going to be challenging enough.

But he would manage somehow. She was his responsibility, his duty, his chance for redemption....

No, she was more than that. It was high time to admit that the feelings that had taken root in his heart for this baby had nothing to do with duty or with what she might represent. That was the real reason why he hadn't contested the guardianship document Darlene had signed. This little blond bundle of toothless grins and uninhibited wails meant more to him than simply an obligation. She was a child. *His* child. He couldn't imagine giving her up.

Holding the baby with one hand, he grasped the silver ring with his other hand and worked it over his knuckle. The band slid off his finger more easily than he had anticipated. He closed his fist around it, feeling the shape of the ring press into his palm.

This was how it had all started that night in the garage. The ring had been like a voice from the grave, a demand, a debt. Once he'd slid it on his finger, he hadn't intended to take it off. It had been a symbol of his duty and of the bond that would forever link him to his team.

Opening his hand, he focused on the gleaming silver. It was no longer a symbol or a voice from the grave. It was merely a piece of jewelry. It didn't belong to him, it belonged to Norlander's child. Quinn would keep it for her, and someday when she was older he would tell the kid about her father and remember the good times and forgive the bad—

"Charli," he whispered, pressing his cheek to the top of her head. "Your name is Charli, not kid."

She sighed against his neck, her breath puffing daintily over his skin.

Another tear followed the first and fell on the baby's wispy blond hair. Damn. Where were they coming from?

Let it go, Quinn.

Rachel's voice, softness covering a core of steel, whispered through his mind. Something crumbled inside him, like a wall that had been slowly wearing away and had finally reached the point where it had outlived its purpose.

His chest heaved with a sound that was too raw to be called a sob. Fresh sensations swept through him. Freedom... longing...love.

Love?

He inhaled unsteadily, catching the delicate scent of the baby and the salt of his tears. Love. The final emotion, the biggest, the hardest to free. Yes, he loved this child. That's why he wanted to keep her.

And he loved Rachel. That's why he wanted to marry her.

It was so simple.

And yet it was shattering the defenses he'd cowered behind for a year. He might have lost the people he'd loved, but that didn't mean he'd lost the ability to love again.

Yet the love he felt for Rachel wasn't like anything he'd known before. It wasn't familiar and comfortable. It was fierce and certain and so strong he was sure it must be glowing like the sunshine that surrounded him.

A gull screeched once more, its lonely cry echoing through Quinn's bones. He swallowed hard and looked around. All right, he was in love with Rachel, but the realization had come two days too late. She'd laid her heart bare for him, but he hadn't been ready to accept it. He'd hurt her. He'd driven her away. He'd lost her.

The last time he'd had to deal with loss, he'd reacted by running away, by walling up his emotions and denying their existence. But he was through running away.

He slipped John's ring into his pocket, tipped back his head and lifted the baby into the air above him. His mouth stretched into a smile that he didn't even think to control. "Charli!" he said.

She gurgled, delighted with her new position.

"Charli, I love you. I love Rachel. And we've got a plane to catch."

The baby didn't seem surprised by his statement. She had probably known all along.

Curls of fragrant smoke floated from the barbecue pits by the picnic tables, and snatches of music drifted from the newly repaired bandstand where the high school brass ensemble was warming up. It was a perfect day for the Maple Ridge Summer Festival, and the town had turned out in full force for the occasion.

"On your marks," Rachel called, holding the flag straight out from her shoulder. Pennants fluttered gaily in the breeze, marking out the course across the field. "Ready, set, go!" She brought the flag down with a sweep of her arm and jumped out of the way.

Fourteen pairs of shrieking children lurched away from the starting line. Two girls hit the ground immediately, their joined legs poking straight out behind them. Rachel took a step toward them, ready to intervene at the first sniffle, but they scrambled to their feet and hopped off in pursuit of the others.

Emily shouted from the sidelines. "Count, Brad, count! One-two, one-two! That's it, Brett! Match your steps, match your steps."

The competitors in the three-legged race, junior division, wobbled their way across the field. Several pairs drew ahead from the rest, their more-orderly gait obviously the result of prior practice. Emily's six-year-old twins were in third place and closing the gap fast.

Rachel called out encouragement to all the children by name. Most of them had been in her kindergarten class at one time or another. They were much bigger now, and fortunately more coordinated, but she still thought of them as her children.

Two yards from the finish line, the pair that had been in the lead stumbled and spun around, trying to regain their footing. They collided with the team behind them, knocking everyone off balance just long enough for the third-place Townsend twins to dart past. Amid hoots of glee, Brett and Brad crossed the finish line first.

"Yes, *yes!*" Emily cried.

Rob laughed and slipped his arm around his wife's shoulders. "Gee, I wonder where those boys get their competitive streak."

She rolled her eyes and jabbed him playfully in the ribs. "I can't help it, Rob. I'm living vicariously through my children, remembering the days when I too could run."

He patted her swollen abdomen. "Another month and you'll be running after Junior."

"Our soccer player," Emily said, covering his hand with hers and giving it a squeeze. "Come on, let's go congratulate our budding Olympic sprinters."

Rachel smiled and waved as her friends moved off to join the crowd at the finish line, then picked up the stack of folded burlap bags and went to distribute them to the children who were already gathering for the potato-sack race.

"Hi, Miss Healey."

She handed a sack to a freckled girl in a pair of bright red dungarees. "Hello, Lenore."

"Look, Miss Healey. I got my ears pierced," she said proudly, tipping her head to show off the tiny gold hoops in her earlobes.

"That's very nice, Lenore."

"It was my birthday present from my auntie Janet. I'm seven now."

"Yes, you're growing up fast," Rachel said. She remembered how Lenore had wanted to spend her first day of school standing in a corner with her thumb in her mouth. "Good luck in the race."

"Thanks!"

"Can I have the bag on the bottom?"

Rachel moved her gaze to the next child. "Of course, Jeremy. But all the bags are the same."

Twisting his baseball cap so that the brim faced backward,

Jeremy McInnes grinned a gap-toothed smile. "I want the one on the bottom."

Shrugging, Rachel shifted the stack in her arms and pulled out the bag that was on the bottom. Unlike Lenore, Jeremy had always been very sure of himself, just like his grandmother, Hazel. His family could trace their roots back to the town founders.

"I got a new puppy, Miss Healey," another child informed her. "His name's Bogie. He chewed up my dad's slippers."

"I'm gonna have a new sister."

"My shoes squeak. Want to hear?"

Rachel smiled at the chatter as she finished giving out the bags and started the process of lining the children up for their race. Little things were so important at that age. It was wonderful to still feel a part of these children's lives. How fortunate she was to have chosen teaching as a career. While she didn't have children of her own, being able to follow the progress of her former students was almost as good.

Yes, she'd made the right decision, she told herself, calling out more encouragement as the potato-sack race got underway. She had a full, rewarding life. She was happy. She was satisfied. Yes, she was. Indeed, she was.

A baby cried somewhere behind her. Stomach knotting, Rachel had already pivoted and taken a step toward the sound before she caught herself. It wasn't Charli. Quinn wasn't back yet. And even if he were, it wasn't any business of hers if Charli cried. He could deal with the baby on his own perfectly well. It wasn't her responsibility. All that was over.

The baby fell silent, and Rachel breathed a sigh of relief.

"There you are, darling!"

At the familiar voice, Rachel looked around in surprise. "Mom?"

Ann Healey, looking polished and sophisticated in a peach linen dress and a single strand of pearls, lifted her hand to wave at her daughter as she moved toward her through the crowd. "My goodness," she said, laughing breathlessly when she reached her. "The festival is getting bigger every year."

"I think everyone in the county came," Rachel said, giving her mother a warm hug. She hung on just a fraction longer than usual, pressing her cheek to Ann's for a moment before she smiled and stepped back. "I hadn't expected to see you here. Why didn't you tell me you were coming?"

"Oh, it was a last-minute impulse," Ann said, hooking her arm with Rachel's. Her hair, as dark and thick as Rachel's, was styled in a short bob that accentuated the elegant line of her jaw. Although she had just turned fifty, her face had the ageless quality that came from strong bones and diligent skin care. "The meeting in Chicago went more smoothly than I had anticipated, so I thought I'd take some time to visit my favorite daughter."

"It's good to see you, Mom. You look great."

"Thank you. So do you. Have you lost weight?"

Rachel kept her smile in place. "As a matter of fact, I've gained five pounds."

Ann hesitated, then shook her head. "Don't worry, darling. It'll come off."

Whether or not it did was immaterial to Rachel. As she'd told Quinn, it wasn't her appearance that mattered, it was what she felt about herself inside. And leaving Quinn had been the right decision. She'd taken control of her life. That's what was important.

"Are the races over now?" Ann asked.

"Uh-huh. The potato-sack race was the last. Would you like to get a hamburger?"

"Oh, why not?" she said, falling into step with Rachel as they walked toward the line at the barbecues. "If you can look that good with an extra five pounds, I'm willing to chance it, too."

Rachel relaxed. It was good to see her mother again. They really did have a wonderful relationship.

"I've heard several compliments already on how well you

organized the children's activities," Ann went on. "You're so good at this kind of thing. I admire you."

"Thank you."

"You have a special flair for dealing with young children. That's why you're such an excellent teacher. Is that Emily Townsend over there?" Ann asked, dipping her head toward the group at the other end of the field.

Rachel followed her gaze and smiled at the way the twins were dancing around with their first-place ribbons. "Yes, that's her."

"The poor thing. She's being so brave about her pregnancy. How long did you say her leave of absence would be?"

"At least a year." Rachel paused. "Having a child isn't all that much of a sacrifice."

"Not for a man, perhaps, but—"

"But you had me, Mom. Was it that bad?"

Ann halted, her eyes filling with distress. "Of course not, darling. My only regret is that the circumstances couldn't have been better for you."

"But your life would have been easier if not for me."

"Easier, certainly. Better?" Ann lifted her hand to Rachel's cheek and tucked a stray lock of hair behind her ear. "No, I love you, Rachel. I never regretted having you for an instant."

"And yet from the day I was old enough to wonder what I'd be when I grew up, you've done your best to talk me out of being a wife and mother."

"Have I?"

"With every word."

"I didn't want you to make the same mistake I did, darling," Ann said, reaching for Rachel's hand. "I didn't want you to get hurt by committing your love to the wrong man. I wanted you to be cautious."

Tension tightened Rachel's shoulders. A restless, vague dissatisfaction stirred at the back of her mind as she listened to the familiar refrain.

Why did this bother her? She agreed with her mother. She loved her. They never argued. They got along beautifully.

Pulling Rachel over to a nearby picnic table, Ann waited until they were both sitting down, then turned to face her. "This is about Quinn Keelor, isn't it?"

Rachel didn't bother to ask how her mother knew. Judging by the looks of veiled pity she'd noticed today, most of Maple Ridge knew about her affair with Quinn. And the fact that she'd returned home alone.

That was probably the real reason behind Ann's "last-minute impulse" to attend the Summer Festival. She'd heard the gossip and had wanted to make sure that her daughter hadn't done something foolish.

Foolish? That was putting it mildly. "I'm in love with him, Mom," Rachel said finally. "But he doesn't love me, and he probably never will. So I left him. And I left the baby he's going to be raising. I've decided to concentrate on my career and get on with my life instead of leaving myself vulnerable to the pain of loving the wrong man."

"Good for you," Ann said, squeezing her hands. "It sounds as if you did the right thing."

"Did I?"

"Of course you did. In the long run, you'll see that it was the best decision."

Rachel studied her mother's pale hands and well-manicured nails. And the tension that tightened her shoulders spread. A dull ache began to pound behind her eyes.

It had all seemed so clear three days ago. She had believed she was taking control of her life. She had thought she was being sensible by facing reality, by thinking of her needs instead of Quinn's. But all it took was her mother's wholehearted agreement to stir Rachel's doubts.

Leaning forward, Rachel brushed a kiss across Ann's cheek and rose to her feet. "I'm sorry, Mom, but I've got to go."

"We'll talk later, then."

"Sure."

"Love you."

Rachel swallowed hard. "Love you too, Mom."

The driveway was empty—Quinn's truck was probably still at the garage where he'd left it two weeks ago—but there was a light burning in an upstairs window of the Keelor house. So he was home after all. Taking her foot off the accelerator, Rachel let her car coast to a stop at the curb.

How many times had she ridden her bicycle past this red brick two-story as a teenager, hoping for a glimpse of the town's golden-haired football hero? How many times had she paused over there beside the oak tree with the tire swing and pressed her schoolbooks to her chest as she'd attempted to calm her breathing before she had mounted those steps to the porch and lifted her shaking hand to knock on that door?

And how many nights had she spent staring at her darkened bedroom ceiling, replaying in her head every word, every gesture, every look that Quinn had given her?

With a sigh Rachel shut off the engine and rested her forearms on the steering wheel. In fifteen years she hadn't gotten very far, had she? As a matter of fact, she had come full circle...because she was still lurking outside Quinn's house, still replaying every moment of their time together, still hopelessly in love.

But things were no longer the same. Quinn had changed, as had she, and her love for him was far different from her innocent, bittersweet teenage yearnings. It was a woman's love.

And she had been dead wrong to think that she would be able to control it.

The ultimatum she'd given Quinn had seemed like the only choice open to her. Everything or nothing. Her love only in exchange for his love. Her needs as well as his needs.

But if it had been the right choice, why was she so miserable? Why did seeing the children at the festival this afternoon bring back that aching emptiness in her arms? Why did her mother's approval ring hollow? Why had she spent the past four hours driving aimlessly while her heart kept drawing her back here?

Maybe she was just a slow learner. A glutton for punishment.

Or maybe she had made a mistake.

Don't go yet. We can work this out somehow.

She bit down on her lower lip as she remembered Quinn's plea. Had she acted too hastily? Had she let her old insecurities and her injured pride cloud her judgment? Had the conditioning—the brainwashing—of her childhood made her *expect* their relationship to fail?

It had been humiliating to learn that Quinn had known about her old crush. On top of her panic over slipping back into her self-destructive patterns, it had been the last straw. She hadn't wanted to listen to more. She hadn't wanted to give him any more chances.

A figure moved in front of the light upstairs. The window was in the master bedroom, the one that Rachel had used when she'd stayed here.

Why was Quinn in there? What was he thinking? Was he thinking about her? About them? Was he feeling as confused and regretful as she was?

Without taking time to analyze her actions, Rachel opened her door and walked toward the house. She didn't think about what she would say to Quinn when she saw him. She'd been doing far too much thinking and analyzing already.

The door was unlocked when she reached it. Not wanting to disturb Charli if the baby was asleep, Rachel stepped inside and called out softly. "Quinn?"

A floorboard creaked overhead. Pressing her palm over her stomach to quiet the butterflies, Rachel moved up the stairs. "Quinn?"

Only silence greeted her. She paused on the upstairs landing, her hand tightening on the post at the top of the banister. He must have heard her come in. His silence could only mean that he didn't want to see her.

Not that she could blame him. She'd been the one to leave him, hadn't she? She shouldn't be surprised if—

A male figure streaked toward her from the shadows. Before she could draw back, he was behind her, a rough hand covering her mouth.

"Not one sound, lady," a strange voice rumbled.

Her first thought was that it had to be Quinn. He'd been paranoid about security all along, and he could have mistaken her for an intruder.

But her body didn't recognize this man's touch. And one whiff of the man's stale, cigarette-scented fingers told her it wasn't Quinn. She reacted automatically, jamming her elbow backward into the man's ribs and stomping down hard on his toe. He loosened his hold on her mouth just enough for her to let out a scream.

But Rachel's cry for help ended abruptly when she felt the cold, hard point of a metal blade at her throat.

Chapter 16

An ordinary man wouldn't have heard the noise. Over the drone of the crickets and the low hum of the truck's engine, it was nothing but the suggestion of a cry, too distant and too muffled to identify with any certainty. But Quinn was no ordinary man. He was a man in love. And the sudden clenching in his heart told him that Rachel was in trouble.

He turned off the engine and opened the driver's door, every sense alert as he stepped outside to survey the area. Rachel's car was parked by the curb, its windows rolled down. The engine clicked once as it cooled—it hadn't been here long. His gaze swung to the house. There was a light upstairs. She must have gone inside....

No, she no longer had a key. She had given it back to him before she'd left. And why would she have come here? Not to see him. She hadn't wanted to talk to him for the past four days, so why would she want to see him?

He paused beside the truck and glanced around again. The neighborhood was uncharacteristically quiet. No dogs barking, no radios playing, no children fussing about going to bed.

Everyone was probably still at the festival. Rachel should have been there, too, but he'd searched that crowd for what had seemed like hours until Ann Healey had informed him her daughter had already left. He'd stopped by Rachel's apartment three times and had looked in every logical place to no avail until a feeling of uneasiness had made him decide to check the last place he would expect her to be.

He couldn't logically explain what had brought him here. He didn't try. He was listening to his heart.

Reaching back into the truck, he pushed aside the bouquet of roses that were already wilting and picked up his cane. The place where Charli usually sat was empty—his father had been only too happy to watch Charli for the evening when Quinn had explained what he wanted to do. It would have been too difficult to hold both his cane and the baby while he went down on his knees. But of all the scenarios he'd imagined when he'd anticipated his reunion with Rachel, this wasn't one of them.

Moving swiftly across the dew-slick lawn, he approached the house through the shadow of the oak. Flattening himself to the wall, he worked his way around to the side of the porch, ducked below the front window and crouched to one side of the door.

It was ajar. The hairs on the back of his neck prickled. From somewhere inside, he heard the sound of a brief scuffle, then a man's low voice. Judging by the echo, whoever it was must be upstairs.

If this had been a mission, Quinn would have waited until the rest of his team could position themselves before he moved in. As it was, he should probably consider taking the time out to call the police. But his ears still rang with that desperate, choked-off cry. And he only knew he had to find Rachel.

Swinging around, Quinn discarded his cane and grasped the corner post of the porch. He shinnied upward and pulled himself onto the porch roof. He ignored the sharp stab of pain from his leg and inched his way across the shingles to the dark window of the spare bedroom. Rising to his knees, he pried off the screen and set it down beside him, then braced the heels of his hands against the window frame and pushed upward. The lock gave with a quiet snap and Quinn slipped inside.

"I told you, there's nothing to find."

Every nerve in Quinn's body thrummed with alarm at the sound of Rachel's voice. It came from the hallway. Her words were sharp, her tone level, but he could feel her fear.

"Don't lie. The bitch must have left the book here."

At the gravelly voice, Quinn clenched his teeth and moved silently to the door.

"What book?" Rachel asked.

"Norlander kept a journal. It's gonna be my ticket out of this. That book's gonna buy me a suspended sentence, maybe even one of them witness programs."

Norlander's journal? Quinn's blood went cold. Mikita had assured him that the entire gang had been rounded up. He'd said there was no more danger.

But considering the bickering between the agencies involved, there was always the possibility that someone had slipped through the cracks. And whoever this was knew about the journal. He knew that Darlene had come to Quinn. So as long as this man believed...

"The Navy has the journal," Rachel said. "They know everything."

Damn, Quinn thought, there went their only bargaining chip.

"You're lying," the man snarled.

"It's over. You should give yourself up—"

"Don't you tell me what to do, lady. I'm the one who's giving orders around here."

His nerves screaming at the need for restraint, Quinn curled his fingers around the doorknob and slowly, slowly eased the door inward and peered through the slit.

They were standing directly in front of him. The man was

not much more than a boy, eighteen or nineteen, with a tall, wiry build and a pockmarked face. But his eyes betrayed an age far older than his years, as did the deadly, casual confidence with which he held a switchblade to the skin below Rachel's ear.

There was a sudden boom in the distance, followed quickly by another, then the sound of rapid-fire explosions.

And for an instant Quinn felt himself transported into the past, and he smelled the swamp and the smoke and the blood. He heard the screams, he felt the shock wave and the fire and—

He shook his head, wrenching himself away from the memory. That nightmare no longer had any power over him. His only concern was the present, and Rachel needed him.

"What the hell was that?" the boy muttered, glancing behind him.

This was his chance, Quinn decided. A split second later the bedroom door smashed against the wall and he burst through the doorway. The boy barely had time to bring his head back around before Quinn moved behind him, grabbed his wrist and twisted the knife away from Rachel's neck.

Gasping, she staggered forward and spun around. Her eyes widened. "Quinn!"

There was another series of booms. Quinn flinched, trying to stay on top of the memories. The tip of the knife nicked his forearm.

"Quinn!" Rachel cried, lunging back toward him.

With a quick sweep of his foot, Quinn knocked the boy's legs out from under him. He followed him down, pressing one knee to the center of his back. Tightening his grip on the boy's wrist, he jerked hard. The knife flew across the hall, struck the wall and clattered to the floor.

"Quinn, my God, you're bleeding!" Rachel said, falling to her knees at his side.

He spared a brief glance for the red line on his skin. "It's just a scratch. Are you all right?"

"Yes, I'm fine." Her hand shaking, she pressed her fingertips to his arm. "How did you get here? How did you know—"

"Hey, man! You're breaking my arm!"

Quinn twisted the boy's wrist another inch farther up his back. He knew exactly how much strain the bone could take without snapping, and he had a few more millimeters to go. "Shut up."

"Hey—"

Quinn increased the pressure of his knee just enough to knock the breath from the boy's lungs. He had no intention of harming him, but the image of Rachel standing helpless in this boy's grasp made it damn hard to maintain his control.

Rachel's hands fluttered up to Quinn's face, her fingers touching his jaw in a hesitant caress.

His pulse was still pounding, his muscles still tensed for combat. And Rachel's touch was channeling his need for action into another urge altogether. A more basic, more primitive urge.

He wanted to be alone with her. To love her.

Now.

Forever.

But things weren't going to be that way just because he wanted it. He had so much lost time to make up for, and a whole heart full of promises he still wanted to give her.

"I'd better call the police," Rachel said, drawing away and getting back to her feet.

"Good idea," Quinn said.

"And you need a doctor."

He didn't need a doctor. He needed Rachel.

Short, sharp explosions echoed from the distance. Quinn's nostrils flared at the sound, but this time the memory didn't jar him. He focused on the woman he loved, and he felt her strength flow into him. "Rachel, what the hell *is* that noise?"

"Fireworks," she said. She gave him a wobbly smile. "It's from the park. The Summer Festival."

* * *

Rachel brushed her fingers along the top of Charli's head, following the delicate curve around to the wispy curls at the nape of her neck. The baby snuggled her cheek against the sheet, her mouth pursing briefly as she made a few faint sucking sounds in her sleep. Smiling contentedly, Rachel rested her palm on Charli's back and felt the steady rise and fall of her breathing.

There was no point trying to fool herself any longer. While Rachel would always enjoy her job and have a special relationship with the children who passed through her classroom, she loved *this* child.

All right, there were risks when it came to loving anyone. And it was going to be hard for Rachel to overcome the conditioning of a lifetime. But there were good reasons why her heart had led her here tonight. From the moment Quinn's father had brought Charli back to the house, Rachel knew that whatever happened between her and Quinn, one way or another, she would do everything in her power to remain a part of the baby's life. It wouldn't be a sacrifice; it would be a privilege.

Through the open window came the sound of car doors slamming, then men's voices and the crackle of a radio. An engine revved, the gravel on the driveway crunched and the sounds faded as the patrol cars moved down the street.

The front door closed with a solid thud. Rachel's smile faded. She felt her pulse speed up with anticipation as she heard Quinn take the stairs two at a time and stride down the hall.

It seemed as if it had been hours since she'd seen him, but that was only her anxiety wreaking havoc on her perception of time. There were things she needed to say to him, but for the life of her, she didn't know what. Or how. Or if she even should.

Everything had seemed so clear to her four days ago, so

black-and-white. But now her feelings were a confused jumble of shades and colors.

"Is Charli asleep?" Quinn asked.

"Yes. She barely woke up when Doug brought her upstairs." Rachel turned around. She couldn't see Quinn's face. All she could see was his tall, broad-shouldered silhouette, filling the doorway. He crossed his arms, and she caught a flash of white gauze.

Her breath hitched as she remembered how he had seemed to come out of nowhere to rescue her, his well-honed body moving with such lethal purpose as he'd wrested that knife away from her attacker. Even though she'd been scared out of her wits, or maybe because she'd been so scared, seeing Quinn like that had set off a reaction deep down in some primitive part of herself.

That brief touch she'd given him hadn't been anywhere near enough. She wanted to kiss away the pain of the new wound in his arm…and the old scars on his body…and she wanted to hold him, to love him.

"Are you sure you're all right?" Quinn asked. "That punk didn't hurt you?"

She swallowed, pushing away the memory of the cold blade at her throat. "I'm fine."

"The guy's name was Silvestro. He was in jail in Buffalo on a drunk-and-disorderly when the Feds picked up the rest of the gang, so he was released before the word got out to the local cops."

"Why did he come here?"

"Seems that the Feds aren't the only ones who get their communications screwed up. Silvestro heard that Darlene was dead, but he hadn't heard that we had John's journal."

"Do you think anyone else might come here looking for it?"

"The CIA people I met on the base assure me he was the last one."

"God, I hope so."

Quinn lifted one shoulder. "We're in Maple Ridge. What could happen?"

Rachel released an unsteady laugh. "That's what I used to think. I used to believe that you were overreacting with your worries about security, but you were right. When I saw that knife slice into your arm—"

"It's over, Rachel," he said firmly. "My arm's cleaned and bandaged. That punk is on his way to jail. One of the cops even put the screen back on the window I used. It's over," he repeated.

It's over. She didn't want it to be over.

No, wait. She did.

Oh, God.

His expression still shadowed, he took a step toward her. "Why did you come here tonight, Rachel?"

She looked at him in silence for a moment, her pulse still racing, anticipation still humming through her veins, when out of her doubts and confusion a startlingly simple answer formed on her lips. "I missed you, Quinn."

A tremor went through his frame. Mutely he held out his hand.

Not giving herself time to think, she crossed the room and took his fingers.

This touch still wasn't enough. She felt the smooth pad of his palm, the strength of his knuckles, but she wanted so much more. She slid her fingers between his, the friction of skin to skin a teasing reminder of other ways their bodies had linked together. She loved what his hands could do to her, the way his caresses could be tender or passionate or urgent.

Wait. Something was different. Where was the familiar ridge of smooth metal? "The ring," she said. "The one from your team. You're not wearing it."

"No. I put it away."

"You...put it away?" she repeated, stunned. She knew how significant that ring was to him. He hadn't been without it for a month.

"I'll give it to Charli when she's older, when we tell her about her parents."

"That's going to be difficult—" The pronoun he used registered all at once. "When *we* tell her?"

Quinn drew her out into the hall and closed Charli's door. "Rachel, I need to talk to you," he said.

No, the last time they'd talked, she'd said far too much. She splayed her fingers over his shirt, feeling the firm contours of his chest, remembering the masculine textures and tastes. She moved closer, drawing in his unique scent, reveling in his solid warmth, feeling how perfectly matched their bodies were as she molded her curves to his planes and angles. "There you go again with the talking," she murmured, skimming her palm downward as she echoed the words he'd once said to her.

With a groan, he recaptured her hand and stepped back. "Please, Rachel."

She looked up into his face. In the light that shone over the staircase, she could see that the skin around his eyes was crinkling with a hint of a smile. And his gaze was so clear and steady and filled with purpose that it took her breath away.

"I'm going to buy the garage business from my father."

This wasn't what she'd expected. "Oh?"

"I want you to know I intend to stay in Maple Ridge for good. It's a great place to raise a family. I've told my lawyer to start the process of formally adopting Charli."

"That's wonderful."

"And I'm also planning on getting involved in the town again, maybe see if the high school needs a football coach."

"They'd love to have you."

"What about you?"

"What?"

He held her gaze, naked emotion shining from his eyes. "If I asked you again."

"What?"

"To marry me."

"But—"

"Please, hear me out. I can understand why you turned me down before. You were right about everything you said. I was an idiot."

"I didn't say that."

"You should have. The truth was staring me in the face for weeks, but I was too slow to accept it."

"What truth?"

"I'm making a mess of this again, aren't I?" he muttered. Raising her hand to his lips, he pressed a long, slow kiss to her knuckles. "I had the roses and the ring and was ready to crawl on my knees to beg you to forgive me, but I don't want to wait any longer." He lifted his head. The smile that had been playing around his eyes spread to his lips. "I love you, Rachel. With my heart, my body, my brain, and with every breath I take. I love you so completely, I feel it in every fiber of my being."

Her eyes filled with sudden, hot tears. "You love me?"

"I wake up thinking of you. I go to sleep dreaming of you. When we're apart, I feel as if my arms are empty. When we're together, I feel complete."

How she'd longed to hear the words from him. Yet never in her wildest imaginings had she guessed they would sound so beautiful. "Oh, Quinn. I love you, too."

"Even after the way I hurt you—"

"I've always loved you, Quinn. So much it frightened me. I shouldn't have put conditions on it. I just was afraid I wasn't strong enough."

"Not strong enough?" he said hoarsely. "Rachel, over this past month, you've shown me the true meaning of strength." He leaned down to kiss a tear from her cheek. When he straightened up once more, his own eyes were gleaming with moisture. "I want us to spend the rest of our lives together. And I want us to be a family. You, me and Charli."

No words could get past the lump in her throat. All she could do was stare. She didn't even want to blink. She didn't want to miss one second of the moment in her life when all of her dreams were coming true.

"And maybe, someday, we could make a baby of our own," he said, releasing her hand to cradle her face in his palms. "That's what I want. But this isn't about my wants and my needs. It's about you. What do you want, Rachel?"

What did she want? How could he ask? He'd just expressed her deepest desires in words that were so eloquent they were singing in her soul. She parted her lips. "I want it all."

"All?"

She grasped the front of his shirt and lifted herself up on her toes. "I want your child and your body and your love, Quinn. And I intend to stick around for a long, long time to make sure you deliver."

His smile widened. "Is that an order, ma'am?"

She laughed. "It's a promise."

Sweeping her into his arms, he headed toward the room with the largest bed. "Let's go watch the fireworks before Charli wakes up."

She clasped her hands behind his neck. "We wouldn't be able to see them from here through the trees. Besides, they ended more than an hour ago."

"Trust me, Rachel. They're just getting started."

* * * * *

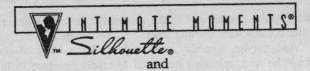

INTIMATE MOMENTS®

Silhouette®
and

DOREEN ROBERTS

invite you to the wonderful world of

RODEO MEN

A secret father, a passionate protector,
a make-believe groom—these cowboys are
husbands waiting to happen....

HOME IS WHERE THE COWBOY IS
IM #909, February 1999

A FOREVER KIND OF COWBOY
IM #927, May 1999

THE MAVERICK'S BRIDE
IM #945, August 1999

Don't miss a single one!

Available at your favorite retail outlet.

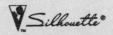

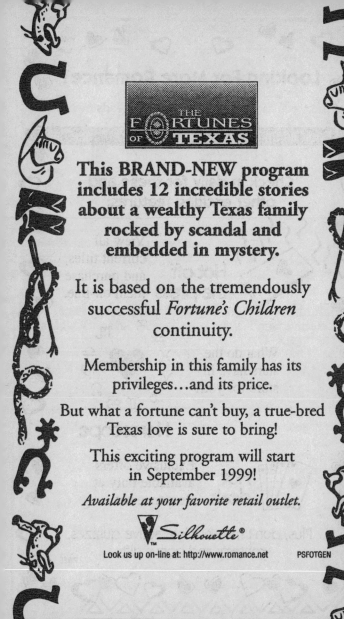

*This August 1999, the legend
continues in Jacobsville*

DIANA PALMER

LOVE WITH A
LONG, TALL TEXAN

A trio of brand-new short stories featuring
three irresistible Long, Tall Texans

GUY FENTON, LUKE CRAIG
and CHRISTOPHER DEVERELL...

This August 1999, Silhouette brings readers an
extra-special collection for Diana Palmer's legions
of fans. Diana spins three unforgettable stories of
love—Texas-style! Featuring the men you can't get
enough of from the wonderful town of Jacobsville,
this collection is a treasure for all fans!

*They grow 'em tall in the saddle in Jacobsville—and
they're the best-looking, sweetest-talking men to be
found in the entire Lone Star state. They are proud,
hardworking men of steel and it will take
the perfect woman to melt their hearts!*

**Don't miss this collection of original
Long, Tall Texans stories...available in
August 1999 at your favorite retail outlet.**

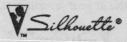